Summer of Love

by

Cynthia Breeding

Nostalgia Road: The Sixties

Summer of Love

Cover Art by *The Wild Rose Press, Inc.*

The Wild Rose Press, Inc.
PO Box 708
Adams Basin, NY 14410-0708
Visit us at www.thewildrosepress.com

Publishing History
First Edition, 2025
Trade Paperback ISBN 978-1-5092-6244-1
Digital ISBN 978-1-5092-6245-8

Nostalgia Road: The Sixties
Previously Published Highland Press 2016
Published in the United States of America

Books by Cynthia Breeding
published by The Wild Rose Press, Inc.

Historical Novels:
The Templar's Woman
Knight of Rosslyn (sequel to *The Templar's Woman*)
The Last Pirates
Knight of the Red Rose
The Viking's Yuletide Woman
Gunslinger

~

Ghosts of Culloden series:
Highlander Unleashed
Highlander Untamed
Highlander Unconquered

~

Nostalgia Road: The Sixties series:
Looking for Love
Summer of Love
The Love Beat Goes On

~

Contemporary Novels
Bedroom Blarney
Night Prey
Cruising along Nostalgia Lane
Christmas Dreams (a time travel)

Chapter One

September, 1966

Mary Anne Wade sidestepped two macho football players swaggering down the freshly waxed linoleum hallway of Middletown High School to their next class. Not that she expected them to notice her—she wasn't the cute, bouncy, cheerleader type—but it would be nice to get through the first day of her senior year without bruises from being bumped against the wall.

Nothing ever changed in Middletown, Minnesota, except the seasons. Cold, gray winter gave way to the green of spring to be followed by the heat of summer haze and autumn's splash of color. Then the cycle repeated itself with as much surety as the sun rising in the east and setting in the west. While the nation was embroiled with riots connected to the Civil Rights movement and antiwar protests and rallies were held elsewhere, the residents of Middletown went about their daily tasks in the same routine manner as they always had. The popular crowd still consisted of athletes and pom-pom girls, like it had since the Fifties.

Mary Anne tossed her long, dark hair past her shoulders and entered her English class as the tardy bell rang, bringing a stern look from the teacher. As she slipped into a seat beside Ruby Jones, her friend smiled and popped her bubble gum. Mrs. Howell narrowed her gaze on Ruby.

"No gum-chewing allowed. Get rid of it."

Ruby rose and sauntered to the wastebasket. "Whatever."

"And watch that tone of voice, young lady."

"Yes, ma'am," Ruby said as she returned to her seat, not looking the least bit contrite. As soon as Mrs. Howell busied herself with the roll call, Ruby stuck another piece of gum into her mouth.

"You're going to get detention the first day of school," Mary Anne whispered.

Ruby shrugged and brushed a strand of her short, bleached hair out of her eyes. "So I'll do a sit-in at the principal's office."

"No talking," the teacher said without looking up.

"I guess freedom of speech doesn't apply in English class," Ruby muttered. "How ironic."

Mary Anne didn't answer, but she agreed with her friend. School was like prison. Rules, rules, rules. No skirts above the knee. No heavy eye makeup…hadn't any of the teachers ever seen pictures of Twiggy? The boys had to keep their hair off their collars and their shirts tucked in like they were at boot camp or something.

Consequences for disobeying rules were prison-like too. Isolation in detention or in-school suspension, as though students were animals that needed to be caged. Heaven forbid that anyone should skip a class, like they did in the big city high schools. Nancy Sinatra's boots might have been made for walking, but not in Middletown, Minnesota. Here everyone was expected to follow meekly along like so many ants in a line, only wearing penny loafers or saddle shoes.

"Take out your notebooks, please," Mrs. Howell said. "I want you to write down the classroom expectations that I have."

Which was a different way of saying *more rules.* Just once, she'd like to let the rebel inside her out. Tell the teacher off, get up, and walk out. Show the world she didn't have to be part of the In crowd. Just to be who she was. Mary Anne sighed. Her mother would have a cow. She opened her black spiral, then gaped, her eyes widening, as she saw Ruby's notebook. Large flowers in neon blue, yellow, purple and red splayed across the cover, over a design of wavy black and white lines varying in width, giving the illusion of movement.

"Where did you get that? I don't think it's allowed."

Ruby gave her an innocent look. "What's wrong with flowers?"

"They're psychedelic," Mary Anne whispered. "You'll freak 'em out."

"They're *cool*."

"Still, you'll probably get busted—"

"*Girls*." Mrs. Howell was glaring at them over the rim of her eyeglasses. "If your discussion is more important than what I have to say, please share it with the class."

Several students turned to smirk at the call-down, and Mary Anne felt herself blushing with embarrassment. She doubted they would smirk at Janie Nelsen, the cheerleader who sat in the front row. But then, Mrs. Howell wouldn't be scolding Janie, who always obeyed the rules and was a real kiss-up.

"Well?" Mrs. Howell said.

"We were just talking about flower power," Ruby said. Two girls tittered and she raised her chin defiantly.

"The Rolling Stones have them on the cover of their new album."

"We are not discussing rock-n-roll or drugs in this class," Mrs. Howell said.

Mary Anne frowned. "We're not—"

"Are you defying me, Miss Wade?"

"No. I just wanted to say we aren't talking about drugs."

Mrs. Howell raised an eyebrow. "That is debatable."

A boy sitting nearby raised his hand. Mrs. Howell gave him a curt nod. "Yes, James. What is it?"

"With all due respect, ma'am," James said, "I researched the subject for an essay last spring on the counterculture taking place in America. Mary Anne is correct. Flower power isn't about drugs. It's symbolic of passive resistance and nonviolent ideology."

Mary Anne pressed her mouth closed before it could drop open. She wouldn't have thought someone as studious as James Lambart would have taken any interest in the free-lifestyle hippie movement, let alone respond to Mrs. Howell. But then, he was kind of an enigma.

He'd moved to Middletown last year from somewhere in Georgia. His dad was vice-president of the local bank and his mother a counselor at the middle school. Maybe that was why he seemed to always analyze everything. Mary Anne's younger sister Wendy had heard his strange accent and developed a crush on him immediately. Once she found out he owned a horse, she'd invited him to join the Hill Riders Club which went trail riding every Saturday. Although he showed up regularly at their place, he remained only polite, much to Wendy's disappointment. James was a decent sort, with a build more like a tennis player's than a football star's, which in Mary Anne's opinion was to his credit. Wendy said he ran track. He kind of reminded her of Clark Kent with his black-framed glasses and light brown hair cropped close.

"In that case," Mrs. Howell said, "perhaps you would like to further enhance your research and present the findings to the class. Miss Wade and Miss Jones can help you, since it seems to be a topic of mutual interest."

Ruby groaned and Mary Anne felt her face heat again, but James looked only slightly nonplussed. "Yes, ma'am," he said. "How long do you want it to be?"

Mary Anne shot him a quick glance, wondering if he was being sarcastic, but he was looking directly at the teacher with an impassive expression.

Mrs. Howell seemed a bit unsettled. "Make it a full class period." She turned to the rest of the class. "Now, if you will write this down…"

Mary Anne kept her eyes on her paper, although she only scribbled down about half of what Mrs. Howell said. Before class was over, she slipped a note to James, careful to wait until the teacher's back was turned. She didn't need to land in the principal's office on the first day of school. Her mother would have a conniption.

I'm sorry.

James wrote something down and passed it back.

Don't be.

Mary Anne glanced at him, wishing she could say more, but he only shook his head and smiled. Strange how that changed his looks. He didn't even seem irritated that he had more work because of speaking up.

He truly was an enigma.

****

"Hey, babe. You haven't stopped complaining about

school since you got here. Not that I blame you. I still remember what crap it was two years ago. " Bob Colby took a drag on his cigarette and offered Mary Anne one, then flopped back on the sofa in his uncle Bill's farmhouse living room.

She sat down on the sofa and took the cigarette, holding it a bit awkwardly and lighting it not nearly as deftly as Bob had done. She took a puff, trying not to inhale.

"You're missing the effects of the nicotine if you don't suck the smoke in." Bob began to grin. "But you are kinda cute to watch."

Mary Anne loved his smile. It always started out slow, with the left corner of his mouth lifting slightly as if he were issuing an invitation to share some private joke. Then his eyelids would drop, his gaze intensifying as if waiting to see if she caught the joke. When she mimicked the expression, his grin would widen, making her feel that there was an invisible bond between them. "You're kind of cute yourself. I've missed you."

Bob sobered. "I wrote you that I ran into a little trouble when I went to Chicago."

"I know." She probably shouldn't have brought it up. He didn't like talking about his past, especially since his other uncle, George, was in prison. But she'd started to worry when Bob, who'd gone to Chicago to clean out his uncle's apartment, ended up staying there for months. She knew he'd moved down from Chicago two years ago because of some kind of trouble, but she didn't know what it was. She wondered if that trouble had resurfaced while he was there, but decided this wasn't the time to ask. She didn't want to make him mad. "I'm glad you're back."

"Me, too." Bob's mood lightened and he reached over to take her hand, pulling her closer to him, then putting an arm around her shoulders. "So what's my high school sweetie been doing while I've been gone?"

Mary Anne didn't much care to be reminded she was still in high school while Bob had graduated and was working at the casino down the highway where there were lots of older girls. Still, he had called her "my sweetie" which made her feel special.

"Nothing much. You know how it is in Middletown. Wendy is still a pest and still trying to convince me to learn to ride a horse. My cousin Jo drives up to St. Cloud every weekend to see Luke since he's at college. That's about it."

"Hmmm." Bob put a hand under her chin and lifted it, planting a kiss on her lips. "You been saving yourself for me?"

A warm tingle slid down her spine. Did Bob want her to be his steady girl? Before he'd left, he'd tried to get past second base, but she hadn't let him. She secretly wondered if that was why he'd stayed so long in Chicago. "I haven't dated anyone."

"Good. You're my main squeeze." His fingers dropped down to brush across her collarbone. She caught his hand before it could slip lower, and he sighed. "Do you want a beer to loosen up?"

Mary Anne shook her head. She'd driven out to the farmhouse right after school. If she went home smelling of alcohol, her mother would suspect—and probably demand to know—where she'd been. Since her mother didn't approve of Bob in the first place, Mary Anne didn't want to stir things up so soon after he'd returned.

She sat up. "I'd better go before Mom starts

wondering where I am."

"You mother still hates me?"

"She doesn't hate you," Mary Anne said as she stood to leave. "Maybe it would help if you came to dinner."

"I wouldn't want to wear out my welcome," Bob said wryly.

He was probably being sarcastic, but she couldn't really blame him. Bob had been accused unjustly of aiding his uncle George when she'd been abducted a year ago, and it had taken a lot of coaxing on her part, as well as Luke's, to convince her mother to even meet Bob. He hadn't exactly fit in with her Mayberry RFD family, but then Mary Anne didn't feel like she fit in with them either. How many times had she listened to Wendy and Jo prattling on about horses, school socials, and church picnics as though they were the only things that mattered? Bob Dylan might write about times a-changing, but Mary Anne suspected her sister and cousin would be content to spend their lives in Middletown.

She felt restless and wanted adventure. So did Bob. That was why they were so right for each other.

Chapter Two

"How was the first day of school?" Mary Anne's mother Vivian asked as they gathered around the table for supper that evening.

"It was great," Wendy replied before anyone else could. "Tim and Tommy are in three of my classes. They might even make boring math class fun."

"You mean you'll have cohorts in crime?" Jo asked.

Wendy giggled. "Maybe."

"I thought the school was going to separate the twins," Vivian said, "so they wouldn't pull so many pranks."

"Our cousins would find a way to do that anyway," Mary Anne said. "They're both immature."

Wendy made a face at her. "Just because you're a senior and we're juniors doesn't mean we're little kids."

"Only when you act like it," Mary Anne replied, thinking about the stupid practical jokes the twins liked to play.

"You just don't get it when something is funny," Wendy retorted. "You are so weird."

"You're the one who's weird," Mary Anne flung back.

"That's enough," their mother said and gave Mary Anne a stern look. "It's immature to insult your sister."

"Yeah." Wendy smirked at her.

"That goes for you as well," Vivian said.

Mary Anne only half-listened as the conversation drifted to Jo's day. If her mother only knew how mature she really was. She was seeing a man, not some schoolboy, and Bob liked her, had called her his main squeeze. That made her practically a full-grown woman. Maybe she should have allowed him a little touch. Women did that, didn't they? She was *mature* enough not to let him go farther. Maybe if she could convince him to go steady…

"Mary Anne. Aren't you listening?" Her mother's tone was clipped, meaning she'd asked a question, probably more than once.

"I was just thinking. What did you say?"

"I asked how your day went. The start of your senior year is important and I want you off to a good start."

Probably better not to mention she and Ruby were already in trouble in English class. "Nothing out of the ordinary."

"Any new students?" her mother asked.

Mary Anne shook her head. "Only the ones I've known all my life."

"What about James?" Wendy asked. "Is he in your classes?"

"He's in my English class."

"Do you sit close to him? I think he's so cute," Wendy said.

Close enough that he'd gotten himself involved in a group project they'd have to do. Mary Anne didn't want to mention that either, so she asked Wendy, "Do you still have a crush on him?"

Instead of denying it, Wendy only blushed. "I like to listen to him talk, and I think he has really pretty eyes."

Mary Anne raised a brow. "He wears glasses."

"So? They make him look smart." A dreamy expression crossed Wendy's face. "When he takes them off, his eyes are like brown velvet."

"Luke's eyes change color depending on how he's feeling," Jo said.

"And James has a dimple in one cheek when he smiles," Wendy added.

Jo nodded. "So does Luke."

Mary Anne refrained from rolling her own eyes. Once Wendy and Jo started discussing boys, there was no stopping them. What silly conversation. No one would ever accuse her of talking about how *cute* Bob was. Only an immature girl would use such a term. She would describe Bob Colby as a handsome, good-looking man.

Not that anyone asked, which was probably a good thing since her family didn't know he was back. Yet.

****

"May I join ya'll?" James asked the next day as Mary Anne and Ruby set their trays down on a cafeteria table. A subtle scent of aftershave surrounded him. Bob wore a different brand, much more manly.

"I suppose so." Mary Anne glanced at the brown bag he held. No one in high school brought food from home, even though her mother had offered to pack lunches for her and Wendy. It was considered square, but maybe James didn't know that, coming from Georgia. Should she mention it?

Ruby was never one to be quiet. "You brought your lunch?"

James nodded as he pulled two chairs out for her and Mary Anne and then seated himself. "We had roast chicken last night, with my grandmother's homemade bread," he said as he took out a sandwich and unwrapped it.

Subtle herbal flavors wafted from the chicken and Mary Anne could smell the freshness of the bread too. She looked at her tray with the ever-abundant "Hot Dish"—a mixture of macaroni, hamburger, and tomato sauce that was usually tasteless, coming from the school's kitchen—and back to his sandwich. He'd taken out a small, plastic container of potato salad, which was probably homemade as well, considering she could see egg slices, celery, onions and pickles in it. Her mouth watered.

James hesitated, his hand—and the sandwich—halfway up to his mouth. "Do you want to trade?"

Mary Anne felt her cheeks warm. "No, of course not. Why would you ask?"

He smiled and Mary Anne saw the dimple Wendy had mentioned last night. Funny she'd never noticed it before.

"You're eyeing my sandwich like a cat about to pounce."

"You think I look like a cat?"

"No. I only meant—"

"Hey, guys! Can I join you?" Wendy didn't wait for anyone to say yes as she slipped into the one empty chair at the table, nearly letting her Hot Dish slide off the tray.

Most of the time, Mary Anne felt irritated when Wendy tried to crash her lunch, but today she almost welcomed the intrusion. James had just compared her to a cat, which she found disconcerting. But then, James was the reason Wendy had chosen to join her today.

"Don't you usually eat with Jo?" Ruby asked.

Wendy waved her hand. "Jo had to go to the library

to get a book for English class."

"I wanted to talk about our English project as well," James said.

Wendy looked from one to the other. "You guys are doing a project together? Can I help? What's it about?"

"Nothing," Ruby said.

"It's really not important," Mary Anne added.

"Counterculture," James stated. "How 'flower-power' is growing into a movement in San Francisco to protest Vietnam. Kids are beginning to question the violence, not just over there, but here as well."

"That's a weird subject for English class," Wendy said. "Did you choose it?"

"No," Ruby said. "The teacher assigned it."

Wendy looked puzzled. "I thought senior English was British Lit, not social studies."

"Well, we have had a second British invasion with the Beatles and all the other English rock groups," Mary Anne said quickly, hoping it would silence her sister. "Maybe Mrs. Howell wanted us to compare then and now."

"That is a good point," James agreed. "Maybe we can work that idea in. Just because Mrs. Howell assigned the project as punishment doesn't mean we can't have fun with it."

Wendy's eyes widened and she looked at Mary Anne. "You got into trouble the first day of school?"

Mary Anne groaned, wishing James hadn't mentioned the reason. Wendy would probably blab it to their mother tonight. "Ruby and I were just talking."

"After the teacher told you to be quiet, I bet," Wendy said. "You never like being told what to do."

"Who does?" Ruby asked. "I mean, we should have

the right to free speech. It's in the Constitution."

"The First Amendment, actually," James smiled, the dimple reappearing, "but the classroom is not a democracy."

"You got that right," Ruby answered. "They're dictatorships. Every teacher is a dictator."

Mary Anne nodded. "That—"

"So how did you get involved?" Wendy asked James, cutting off what Mary Anne was going to say. "I can understand Mary Anne getting into trouble. She's almost as bad as our twin cousins. But you? You never do anything wrong."

The tips of James' ears turned slightly pink. "I'm no Sir Galahad, believe me."

Wendy practically had stars in her eyes and for a moment Mary Anne wondered if her sister was going to blurt out something stupid like thinking James *was* a knight in shining armor, after all. Thankfully, such a remark was curtailed by the ringing of the bell, signaling lunch was over.

"Back to the salt mines," Ruby muttered.

"We didn't get a chance to discuss the project," James said. "Maybe we could meet after school today?"

"I can't," Ruby answered.

Mary Anne had planned to visit Bob after school. He'd be back to working afternoons and nights at the casino by the weekend, so she didn't want to miss a chance to see him. Not that she was going to mention that in front of Wendy. What excuse could be used?

"We don't have anything to do after school," Wendy said.

Mary Anne frowned. "We?"

"Yeah. I got assigned a paper to write on current

events in my history class." Wendy gave James a big smile. "I can use the same topic."

James gave her a faint smile and turned to Mary Anne. "This afternoon, then?"

Mary Anne wanted to throttle her sister for spoiling her plans. But until she could figure out a way to get her mother to agree to let her date Bob again, Mary Anne had no choice but to stay quiet. Instead, she nodded.

"See you this afternoon."

****

The afternoon dragged by like a turtle with only three legs crossing a freeway. James kept checking the wall clocks in each of his classes, sure that there must be some electrical short where they were plugged in that had caused them to slow down. He barely listened to the Trig teacher describing six different ratios that could express relations between a pair of sides in a right triangle. He set the Bunsen burner's flame too high in Chemistry, nearly igniting the lab, and was completely in the wrong century when asked a question in World History.

And all because of a meeting after school with Mary Anne Wade.

James had noticed her the first day he attended classes here last year. She'd been in American History. At the time, she had a white streak in her sleek, dark-brown hair. She'd worn red lipstick and had her nails painted the same color. Her eye makeup made her green eyes look tilted. He thought she was the most exotic-looking girl he'd ever seen, since the girls back home— and here in Minnesota—all teased their hair into beehives and wore white nail polish and pale lipstick that made their mouths disappear.

She had a nonchalant attitude that intrigued him as well and always took a seat at the back of the classroom with Ruby. They were often late and James made it a point to be early, so he could smile at Mary Anne when she passed by his desk. Usually she was engaged in conversation with her friend and didn't look his way. Still, he had wanted to take her to the prom, but when he'd asked around, he found out she was seeing some guy named Bob.

But Bob had gone back to Chicago and this was a new year.

James nearly sprinted from his seat when the last bell finally rang. He was halfway to the library when he heard the foreign exchange student, Kevin O'Keefe, who lived with his family, call to him. James slowed down and waited.

"Where would ye be gallopin' off to so fast?" Kevin asked as he caught up. "Did someone set your tail on fire?"

Almost, if James could count the Chemistry lab. "To the library."

"It must be a very interestin' book ye are after then." Kevin's dark blue eyes sparked with interest. "Or is it a girl ye are meetin'?"

Sometimes, James wondered if Kevin had the ability to read minds or maybe was part leprechaun. He was a year younger than James, but they'd become fast friends—James thought of him as a brother—since Kevin's arrival a month ago.

"Actually, I am."

Kevin grinned. "Ye might impress the lass a bit more if ye didn't go barrelin' through the door like a bairn lookin' desperately for his mother."

"Bairn?" James thought a moment. "Oh. You mean child." He had trouble sometimes getting used to Kevin's vocabulary. "I am not desperate."

Kevin shrugged, but his grin widened. "I'm just thinkin' the lasses prefer someone cool like Steve McQueen—a fine Irishman—more than Maxwell Smart."

James shook his head. "Maxwell Smart is a TV character."

"Ye know what I mean." Kevin ambled along beside him. "Who is the lass?"

"Just a girl I've been assigned to work on an English project with."

"A lass with no name? Is she related to Clint Eastwood, then?"

James frowned, trying to make the connection. Ah. The man-with-no-name from *The Good, The Bad, and The Ugly*. Kevin tended to omit transitions sometimes. He might be watching too many American movies.

"Well?" Kevin asked. "Don't be tellin' me ye don't remember her name, not at the speed ye were travelin'."

Tenaciousness was another trait James was learning that Kevin possessed. If he didn't tell him, Kevin would badger it out of him eventually anyway.

"Mary Anne Wade."

Kevin paused. "Is she sister to Wendy?"

"Yes." James slowed his steps as he remembered Wendy planning to meet with them as well. She was a nice girl, but he felt uncomfortable with the way she watched him sometimes. When they went riding on Saturdays, he was careful not to bring his horse alongside hers. Had she been trying to flirt at lunch today? He hoped not, because he didn't want to encourage her, but neither did he want to give up riding. He liked the group and, in particular, it gave him a chance to see Mary Anne, at least occasionally.

"If ye can keep a secret," Kevin said, "I rather fancy Wendy."

James stared at him. Could Kevin be the answer to the problem of Wendy? "Your secret is safe with me. Good luck." He began to smile. "By the way, she will be joining us in the library."

Kevin's eyes widened. "Why didn't ye say so?" Without waiting for an answer, he picked up his pace and hurried toward the library.

James' smile widened as he followed. Maybe he had the luck of the Irish with him and things would work out just like he hoped.

Chapter Three

Wendy was already seated at a table when Mary Anne walked into the library after school. A tall boy with dark auburn hair cut in Beatle fashion stood talking to her sister. Mary Anne hadn't seen him before, but his hair nearly brushed the back of his collar and she wondered how long it would be before Mr. Hund, the assistant principal, would be barking orders to have it cut.

As if she had conjured the man, he came through the doors opposite her. His name in German meant "dog" so most of the kids called him The Hound. He even kind of looked like one with his drooping jowls and rather large nose that practically twitched in anticipation of catching someone committing an infraction of school rules. Too bad he wasn't more like Shultz—or even Klinger—from *Hogan's Heroes*.

For some unexplainable reason, Mary Anne had the urge to protect the new student from a loud—The Hound had been a former coach used to yelling—reprimand. She hurried in the opposite direction from the table, knocking some books off a shelf where they had been left for re-stacking. They crashed onto the floor.

Mr. Hund's head jerked around at the commotion, his eyes narrowing on her as he stomped over. "We do not run in the library."

"Yes, sir." *We probably shouldn't be breathing air*

in the library, either. Mary Anne knelt to pick up the books, letting her hair swing forward to cover her face so he wouldn't see her expression. She really wanted to drop several of the books on one of Mr. Hund's sneakers as she stood, but managed to rein in the action. Ruby would probably have done it.

Frowning, he watched as she put the books back on the shelf. "Please remember to conduct yourself in a ladylike manner from now on and don't run."

"No, sir," Mary Anne said and watched as he walked away. The Hound was a great one to talk about ladylike manners. His own daughter, who should have graduated last year, had suddenly left school in April to visit a sick aunt in Minneapolis. Everyone knew she'd gone all the way with her boyfriend—he'd bragged about it—so her sudden departure didn't surprise anyone, except maybe Mr. Hund.

At least he was gone now. The auburn-haired boy's hair was safe for now.

Mary Anne made her way back to the table as James entered the library and joined her. He seemed to know the new student, and she looked at him quizzically.

"This is my foster brother, Kevin," James said by way of introduction.

"Hello." Mary Anne said and wondered what had happened to Kevin's parents that he'd been placed in foster care, when he spoke.

"Pleased to meet ye."

"You aren't from here?"

"He's from Ireland," Wendy said as if Mary Anne couldn't figure that out herself.

Kevin nodded. "I'm a foreign exchange student."

"I call him my foster brother because for a year he

will be…kind of," James added.

"Is that Southern hospitality like I've read about?" Wendy asked, smiling at James.

"I suppose ya'll could say that," James answered.

"I'd love to hear more about it," Wendy said.

Mary Anne refrained from rolling her eyes. Wendy had read *Gone With the Wind* twice since James had moved here. Before that, she probably didn't even know where the state of Georgia was.

"Well, I hope you won't be bored in Middletown," Mary Anne said to Kevin. "There's not much to do here."

He gave Wendy the briefest glance before he answered. "I don't think I'll be bored."

Mary Anne caught the slight look. A part of her wanted to tell Kevin if he were interested in Wendy, he might as well forget it.

But then, it wasn't her business.

****

James sat down at the library table and opened his binder. He had a ton of homework, beginning with the math assignment that he was probably going to have to call someone about since he hadn't been paying attention in class. He also had to write up the results of the chemistry experiment that he'd somehow managed to salvage, and he needed to study for the history test, but right now, all he wanted to do was talk to Mary Anne. It was a good thing the English project would prove to be a starting-off point.

"So what's this project about?" Wendy asked.

"Flower power," Mary Anne replied. "Ruby had a notebook with big, bright flowers."

Kevin drew his brows together. "Flowers? What's wrong with flowers?"

"Nothing. That's just the point," Mary Anne said.

"Well, more or less," James responded. "The hippie movement in San Francisco is using flowers as symbolic beauty in contrast to the carnage of war."

"The teachers just don't get it," Ruby said.

"In Ireland we heard the hippies were drug users," Kevin said.

James nodded. "There is definitely that element, but it really didn't start out that way. Last spring when I was doing my research, I read several articles that said the hippies' primary concern was peace, that they want to raise individual consciousness and find out who they really are inside, and explore different lifestyles without being concerned about what others think."

"That sounds good to me," Mary Anne said. "Too bad the teachers don't agree. We have way too many rules."

Wendy shook her head. "Mom says rules are made for a reason."

"Maybe *some* rules," Mary Anne said, "but look how hippies dress in bright colors, tie-dyes, beads, and sandals, to express individuality. We have to follow a dress code."

James smiled. "In a way, they follow a dress code, too. Can you imagine Janis Joplin showing up for a concert in a dress like you'd wear to church and with her hair neatly combed?"

Wendy giggled. "Isn't she the one who drinks whiskey on stage?"

"Bourbon," Mary Anne answered. "I read it in a magazine. The article said she felt like a misfit in high school and liked befriending outcasts." Mary Anne could understand that. "She isn't a bad person just because she drinks."

"But she uses drugs, too," Wendy said.

"It's sad. She's so talented," James replied.

"Why would anyone want to take stuff like LSD anyway? Tripping out doesn't sound like fun to me," Wendy said.

"It didn't start out that way," James answered. "Dr. Leary began his Harvard Project to find out if acid-LSD and psychotherapy combined would rehabilitate prisoners."

"You're kidding," Wendy said.

"Nope. Even the CIA sponsored trials with students at Stanford to see what the effects of mind-altering drugs were." James grimaced. "Things got out of hand after that."

"Either way, Mrs. Howell is not going to let us talk about getting spaced out or stoned," Mary Anne said and then shrugged. "Unless, of course, we want to get suspended. It might be a way to stage our own little protest."

Wendy looked shocked. "You wouldn't dare!"

"Ummm." Mary Anne seemed to give it some thought. "It might be interesting to shake things up."

"Mom would ground you for the whole year," Wendy said.

Mary Anne frowned as if weighing the consequences. Then she shrugged again. "I was kidding, stupid."

James let out the breath he didn't realize he'd been holding. He liked that Mary Anne was different from most of the rest of the girls. Independent-minded. Spirited. Maybe even a little quirky. But he didn't want any of them to get suspended.

"I think it's best if we stick to the thesis that flower power is about protesting war," he said.

Mary Anne sighed. "I suppose you're right." Then she grinned wickedly. "But I'm going to wear some flowers in my hair."

****

"We're sure getting loaded down with homework early this year," Jo said at the dinner table later that evening. "We have this huge, ten-thousand-word research paper to do that's going to count for both English and history credit."

"Eleventh grade is when they teach how to do research, isn't it?" her aunt Vivian asked. "I remember Mary Anne working on hers last year."

"It was a real bummer," Mary Anne said. "I don't think I learned anything from it, either."

Wendy snickered. "Maybe that's why you have to do another one."

Mary Anne glowered at her. "It's just an English project."

"But the other kids don't have to do one," Wendy replied.

"Why not?" their mother asked. "Is it something special?"

Mary Anne kicked Wendy under the table.

"Ouch!"

"Did you just stick yourself with your fork?" Vivian asked.

"I...no," Wendy answered, narrowing her eyes at Mary Anne. "My foot bumped against the chair."

"You should be more careful," Mary Anne said and changed the subject. "You'll have the same assignment as Jo. What are you doing your paper on?"

"Counterculture. Hippies in San Francisco," Wendy said promptly. "The same as your *project*."

Their mother frowned. "Goodness. Why would you ever pick such a topic, Mary Anne?"

Wendy snickered again and Mary Anne sent her a warning look and attempted another kick, but her sister had moved her legs. Evidently, her glare had been understood, because Wendy stopped smiling.

"Some of us were discussing what 'flower power' meant, and Mrs. Howell thought it would be a good subject to explore," Mary Anne said.

"So you offered to research it?" her mother asked. "That is very mature of you."

"Thanks," Mary Anne replied, still watching Wendy like a hawk. "I hope we'll get extra credit."

Wendy looked as though she were going to remark, but then she reached for her milk. Mary Anne smiled at her.

The extra credit idea had been James' idea. Before they left the library this afternoon, he'd suggested they broaden the topic and do a lot more research into it. He figured it would be a way to get into Mrs. Howell's good graces, although Mary Anne was pretty sure James would not fit into that category with Ruby when she heard they had more work.

Wendy, of course, had offered to help so she could be around James. The new boy, Kevin, had also said he'd help, since Ireland's youth were going through some turmoil as well. She suspected his interest might be more in Wendy than history. James had suggested meeting every afternoon, but Mary Anne had managed to persuade him that Ruby couldn't meet every afternoon since she had a part-time job at an auto parts store. And

Mary Anne had plans to visit Bob, although she kept that to herself.

"Well, just don't get any ideas of running off to join one of those communes," her mother said and then turned to Jo. "Have you decided on a topic yet?"

"I think something to do with the differences in lifestyle between New York City and rural Minnesota."

"That would be appropriate," Vivian said. "I hope you choose Minnesota."

"Oh, I already have, Aunt Viv," Jo said.

Mary Anne started to shake her head, then stopped. Jo had grown up in Brooklyn until her archeologist parents had been killed in a car crash two years ago. She'd moved to Minnesota because the Wades were her closest kin, but how did she not miss the excitement of a big city? Of course, she had met Luke, so maybe that accounted for it.

"I don't know how I'm going to find time to exercise Luke's horse and my own, with all this work," Jo said. "Flame's gentle enough, but Silver Chief needs to be ridden regularly. Luke will be disappointed in me if I let that go."

"Mary Anne could exercise Flame," Vivian said.

"I'm not fond of horses," Mary Anne replied.

"Maybe because you're scared of them," Wendy said.

"I am not."

"I bet you are."

"It really would help," Jo said, "but you have to decide."

Mary Anne hedged, not wanting to hurt her cousin's feelings. "I have a lot of things to do after school."

"Like what?" Wendy demanded and then gave Mary

Anne a contemplative look. "Are you going to see Bob Colby again?"

Their mother frowned. "Bob Colby! Is he back?"

Mary Anne could have throttled her sister. Not only had she nearly spilled the beans on the reason for the English project, but now she had to blurt out the news that Bob was back. Mary Anne had intended to ease her mother into that information.

"Well, yeah," Wendy answered before Mary Anne could. "Tim and Tommy saw him driving that souped-up Chevy of his last week."

"Did you know about this?" Vivian asked Mary Anne.

Last week was before even Mary Anne knew Bob was back. She was surprised Wendy had managed to keep quiet about it for days. However, the look on her mother's face demanded a definite answer. Mary Anne nodded. "He called me on Sunday."

"And you didn't think to tell me?"

"I was going to." Mary Anne prayed Wendy hadn't seen her driving out toward the farm yesterday.

"I really don't approve of your seeing him," her mother said.

"He's not a bad person."

"He has a wild streak. Wasn't he in some kind of trouble in Chicago?"

"That was in the past." At least, Mary Anne hoped it was. She didn't know why Bob had stayed in Chicago for so long. She glanced at Jo. "Luke said Bob deserved a second chance. He hasn't done anything wrong in Middletown."

Jo nodded. "Luke did have some classes with him."

"Which doesn't prove anything," Vivian answered.

"Are you going to forbid me to see Bob?" Mary Anne asked, trying to keep herself from sounding rebellious.

"And if I do? Will you go behind my back?"

Mary Anne felt her face set and looked down. Her mother sighed.

"I do not like to forbid you to do anything. I hope I have raised you to respect my wishes."

Now her mother was trying to make her feel guilty, drat it. "I do respect you, Mom, but I am almost eighteen. I should be able to make my own decisions."

"*Almost* is the operative word. You are not an adult yet." Vivian thought a moment. "However, I don't want you sneaking out like you did before—"

"I told you I wouldn't do that again," Mary Anne replied.

Vivian nodded. "If Bob wants to date you, then, he has to come here to pick you up, tell me where you're going, and you need to be home by ten o'clock."

Inwardly, Mary Anne seethed. Her mother was treating her like she was in middle school. Still, it was a small victory of sorts, although she was sure Bob would balk at the curfew, or maybe even laugh. She was almost an adult, after all. Outwardly, though, she nodded. "We can do that."

"Good." Her mother smiled at her. "In return, you can do something for me."

Wasn't she doing enough by being agreeable and not arguing? Mary Anne tried to tamp down her resentment. "Like what?"

"You can help Jo exercise the horses. It seems only fair, don't you think?"

Wendy smirked. Jo looked stricken, as though she

wished she'd not brought up the subject of horses at all. Mary Anne swallowed hard. Blast it, she *was* afraid of the big beasts, but she was not about to admit that.

Reluctantly, she nodded again. "You have a deal, Mother."

Chapter Four

"My mother knows you're back," Mary Anne said to Bob the next afternoon after she'd driven out to his uncle's farmhouse.

Bob raised an eyebrow as he sat down on the sofa beside her and popped a beer. "Was she thrilled?"

"Not exactly." Mary Anne often thought Bob's sense of humor was funny, but not today. She eyed his beer. "Can I have some of that?"

"Sure. You want your own can?"

"No. I'll just share yours." Mary Anne took a sip when he handed it to her. She didn't care for the taste of beer, but she didn't want him to think her a child once she told him of the restrictions her mother had put in place.

Bob took back the beer. "So I'm *persona non gratis*?"

Mary Anne loved it when he used foreign words. "Actually, you aren't. Mom didn't forbid me to date you."

"She didn't?"

"No." Mary Anne hesitated. "She has some rules, though."

"Why am I not surprised?" Bob took a long draught. "What are they?"

"You have to come pick me up and we have to tell her where we are going."

Bob shrugged. "Okay."

"And I have to be home by ten o'clock." Her voice was barely a whisper. Bob stared at her, but at least he didn't laugh.

"Does that curfew apply with your other friends too?" he asked.

"I don't know." Her mother had never mentioned it since Mary Anne didn't date anyone else. With the exception of James and the Irish student, she'd known all the boys in her class since kindergarten. They'd all gone to elementary school together and scrabbled on the playground, and then the boys had avoided the girls like the plague during most of middle school. The girls had paid them back by giggling at their gawky growth spurts and squeaking voice changes. By the time they all reached high school, many of them had decided on staying on the family farms, although a few were interested in college. Not one of the boys she'd grown up with sparked Mary Anne's interest.

And then there was Bob. He was different. He didn't dress in khakis and polos or wear pointy-toed shoes, just like she didn't wear A-line skirts, lacy blouses or Mary Janes. Bob wore Wellington boots, denim jeans and an old leather jacket over T-shirts that clung tightly to him and showed lots of muscles. His dark hair touched his collar, but he wore it slicked back instead of shaggy like the English rock groups. He'd tinkered with his car enough that, even though it was loud due to short muffler pipes, it was also fast. He'd told her of winning drag races on an impromptu—and probably illegal—road track near a town about twenty miles away. Mary Anne would have loved to see one of those races, not that her mother would ever let her go.

"Well, the curfew probably doesn't matter," Bob said and set his empty beer can down on the coffee table. "I have to start work at the casino on Friday night, so I won't be available very often for date night." He put an arm around Mary Anne's shoulders and pulled her closer, then gave her a slow kiss. "I can come by after work, though, if you can sneak out of the house like you used to do."

Mary Anne liked his kisses, but she sat up when his hands started to drift. "I promised my mother I wouldn't sneak out anymore."

Bob raised one eyebrow quizzically and let his finger trace the side of her cheek. "Not even for me?"

She shook her head. "After being kidnapped last year, I realized it was pretty stupid of me to sneak out."

"You know I didn't have anything to do with that."

"I know." If it hadn't been for Jo following her, and Luke following Jo, she didn't know what might have happened. All because she thought a note was from Bob, asking to meet her, when it wasn't from him at all. "I don't want to hide our relationship like we did. Now that you're back, I want people to know we're a couple. Don't you want that too?"

"You know I do." Bob cupped her chin and leaned forward to kiss her just as the front door slammed. "Darn it. My uncle is home."

Mary Anne stood quickly. "I have to be going anyway. Mom won't like it if she finds out I drove out here."

Bob's uncle Bill came into the living room. "Whose car..." he began and then stopped when he saw Mary Anne. His gaze turned to his nephew and then to the empty beer can before settling back on Mary Anne.

"What brings you out here this afternoon?"

Mary Anne didn't really know what to think about Bob's uncle. The man had moved to Middletown several years ago and kept to himself, not attending any church or involving himself in community affairs. He was basically a handyman who occasionally worked construction.

"I came out to invite Bob to dinner tomorrow night at my house."

Mr. Colby looked surprised, while Bob just stared at her. It wasn't a spur-of-the-moment invitation. She had planned to ask Bob to come over before her mother had a chance to change her mind, but the conversation had gotten sidetracked. She didn't want to give Bob a chance to say no, so she turned her attention to his uncle. "My mother heard Bob was back, so she thought it would be nice to invite him to dinner." It was only a small, white lie. Her mother *had* said Bob was supposed to pick her up for a date. The date was just at her place. "I'll just see myself out," she said and walked toward the door. Mr. Colby stepped aside silently and she turned to Bob. "About six thirty?"

His dark eyes glittered, whether in amusement or anger she couldn't tell. She just hoped he wouldn't say no.

He finally nodded. "Six thirty."

A sense of relief flooded through Mary Anne as she left. Bob was coming to dinner! She wouldn't have to hide how she felt about him any longer.

****

Mary Anne hoped dinner would go smoothly. When she'd told her mother yesterday afternoon that she'd invited Bob, Vivian's mouth had set in a tight line, although she didn't say anything. Wendy had made a face and said she didn't like Bob, and Jo had been strangely quiet. Jo's reticence probably bothered Mary Anne the most, since it had been Luke who had said Bob really wasn't a bad guy. Her whole family looked like they disapproved when they heard his car roaring up the yard road, but she ignored them.

"He's late," Wendy said.

"Only a few minutes," Mary Anne shot back and went to the door to meet him.

A faint tinge of cigarette smoke lingered about him and Mary Anne hoped no one would notice. Wendy wiggled her nose and Mary Anne glared at her. Luckily, Wendy got the message and remained quiet.

"Come sit by me," Mary Anne said to Bob, indicating a chair as far as possible from her mother, who always sat at the head of the table.

He slid into the seat. "Thanks,"

Mary Anne's mother frowned. "I'll be right back. I have to bring in a couple more dishes from the kitchen."

Jo gave him a casual glance and then hurried after her aunt. "I'll help."

Wendy gave Bob a more deliberate look, then followed Jo. "I'll help too, Mom,"

Since when had Wendy become so helpful? Usually all she did was make sure the water glasses were full. A few minutes later they all emerged, Jo carrying a bowl of mashed potatoes, Wendy a squash casserole, and her mother a platter of roasted chicken. Jo went back for hot rolls and a cruse of gravy. Once all the food was on the table and everyone had been seated, Vivian folded her hands to say grace just as Bob reached for a roll. He pulled his hand back.

The prayer over, Vivian said, "I try not to fry too much food, so I hope you like roasted chicken," as she passed the platter toward Bob.

"Yeah, it's okay," he replied and helped himself to a breast and a thigh before giving the platter to Mary Anne. "Hot food is always good."

"You'll love Mom's squash," Wendy said.

"I don't care much for squash," Bob answered.

"Potatoes then?" Mary Anne asked, before Wendy could make a comment.

"Yeah. Thanks," he said. "Gravy too."

She handed him the cruse and watched him ladle it over the potatoes and meat. "My father had a good appetite too."

"Yeah? I haven't met him."

"He passed away several years ago," Mary Anne replied. Strange how suddenly she could hear his laughter in her head and almost feel the way he'd brush her hair out of her eyes and tell her she was his precious girl. She hadn't thought about that in years.

"Oh. Sorry about that. I didn't know."

"How could you not know?" Wendy asked. "Middletown is a small town."

"Not everyone sticks their noses into other people's business," Mary Anne retorted. She noticed her mother's mouth tighten, but then she put on what Mary Anne called her Sunday church smile.

"Are you planning to stay in Minnesota?" Vivian asked, "or will you be going back to Chicago?"

"Planning to stay," Bob answered and reached for another roll. "I've got a job at the casino, dealing Black Jack."

Wendy's eyes rounded. "You gamble?"

"Not me," Bob replied. "I just deal the cards. The pay's good and the tips better."

"Do you deal from the bottom of the deck?"

Bob looked amused and Vivian looked shocked.

"Wendy, where did you hear about that?" her mother asked.

"Tim and Tommy," Wendy said. "They say the house always wins because they stack the cards." She turned back to Bob. "Is that true?"

Bob shook his head. "That would be illegal. Besides, if no one ever won, how would I get tipped?"

Wendy looked contemplative. "Do you give the players *good* cards then? *So* they'll win?"

"Don't accuse him of anything, Wendy." Mary Anne scowled at her sister and turned toward her mother. "Make her stop."

Their mother laid her fork down. "I think perhaps it would be better if we changed the subject."

Wendy appeared unconvinced, but Jo spoke up. "I got a letter from Luke today. Does anyone want to hear what's new with him?"

"Yes," Mary Anne said quickly. "What's does he say?" Jo's getting a letter from Luke wasn't new. She got them nearly every day. For once, though, Mary Anne was quite willing to listen to the mundane things happening at college. At least, the topic of conversation was no longer Bob.

Somehow, they managed to muddle their way through the rest of the dinner, although it seemed to drag on and on as far as Mary Anne was concerned. Finally, after everyone had apple pie for dessert, Bob said he had to leave.

Usually, it was Mary Anne who was expected to

clear the dishes, but Jo offered to do it, giving Mary Anne the opportunity to walk out to Bob's car with him. They hadn't gone halfway down the walk when the front light came on.

"I guess you mother is watching us?" Bob asked.

"It's probably my bratty sister," Mary Anne replied.

"Who will then go tell your mother if I kiss you?"

Mary Anne hesitated. She wanted Bob to kiss her, but he was right. If her mother weren't watching, Wendy certainly was and she would blab her version of it.

"Probably."

He laughed and punched her shoulder lightly. "Then we'll have to wait until we're alone," he said.

Then he got into his car and drove away, leaving Mary Anne to wonder when that would be.

****

The bright sports lights made the football field look like it was the middle of the day instead of Friday night. The band, seated behind the fifty-yard line, was warming up with a medley of All-American songs ranging from "76 Trombones" to "When The Saints Go Marching In." The pom-pom girls shook out their huge clusters of stringy crepe paper while the cheerleaders hopped up and down as though fire ants were biting the soles of their feet. The lively crowd jostled Mary Anne as she and Ruby pushed their way through and climbed up the bleachers.

"It looks like the whole town turned out," Ruby remarked as they squeezed in beside Wendy and Jo.

"They probably did," Wendy answered. "It's the first football game of the season! You can even feel a hint of fall in the air."

"I don't even know why Mary Anne and I are here,"

Ruby muttered. "We don't like football."

"What else is there to do on a Friday night?" Jo asked.

"Nothing," Mary Anne said, which was precisely why she was here. The whole population probably *had* turned out since the football game was as much a social event—for young and old—as it was a sport in a small town. Right now, she could see elementary school children playing tag in the area behind the goal posts. Middle school kids hovered in clusters in front of the stands, trying to look cool while juggling their popcorn and soda pop bottles. Parents and grandparents of the players sat behind the band, where they had the best viewing, while other folks filled in the gaps elsewhere. Everyone was laughing and talking and appearing to have a good time. To Mary Anne, it was just noise.

She would rather have been with Bob, but he was working tonight at the casino, so what else did she have to do? Stay home and listen to records? Her mother would just accuse her of pining away The dinner had not gone especially well and Mary Anne didn't want to give her mother any reason for not letting her continue to see Bob. So here she was.

Across the field, kids were pouring into the bleachers on that side, so the opposing team's school buses must have arrived. They lost no time in screaming their mascot's name, followed by *"We're Number One!"* which only increased the frenzy of Middletown's cheerleaders, who promptly screamed back, *"Victory, victory is our cry!"*

V-I-C-T-O-R-Y! Mary Anne could hear boos and jeers from both sides as each tried to put down the other. The racket continued for what seemed hours and then the bands began dueling, each blaring out their "Fight Song" as the players ran out onto the field.

And then, as if some invisible hand had pulled the plug out of a socket, quiet miraculously ensued as Middletown's band began "The Star-Spangled Banner." Everyone in the bleachers rose, hands over hearts. Players on both sides stood at attention. Even the spring-loaded cheerleaders were still.

A blissful moment of peace before the referee's whistle blew and the hollering started again.

"Did you hear the high note one trumpet made at 'the land of the free'?" Wendy asked excitedly. "That was James!"

Mary Anne glanced at her sister. "How could you tell? There are several trumpets in the band."

"I know, but only his is a Silvertone."

"How do you know that?"

"Because James told me. He said it has a clearer tone." Wendy gave her a smug look. "I could hear it."

"Well, good for you." Mary Anne turned her head to the field as the screaming reached a fever pitch on their side. She assumed one of Middletown's players must have done something good with the ball, but she didn't know what, since there were a bunch of guys all piled on top of one another close to the end zone. She never had understood football. Only halftime made sense, since the bands marched in precise order and didn't collide with each other, although she suspected tonight she would have to endure Wendy pointing out James the whole time.

Mary Anne was spared, though, since Wendy decided to go down to the sidelines at halftime so she could see the band better and, no doubt, get a chance to talk to James. She certainly looked excited when she got back.

"Are you planning to stay for the entire game?" Ruby asked as the fourth quarter started. "We're so far behind, we can't win. The cheerleaders will start crying, which means most of the other girls will too. I can live without that."

"Yeah, me too," Mary Anne said and turned to Wendy. "We're leaving so we can beat the crowd out."

Her sister just nodded, keeping her eyes on the game, or more likely, on James, seated below them with the band. "I'll catch up with you at the Dew Drop Inn," she said, referring to the place at the intersection of two highways, just outside of town, which served as the local hangout after games.

"I don't know if we're going there," Mary Anne answered.

"Okey-dokey," Wendy said, her eyes still glued on the game…or the band.

"I've got the car," Jo said, "so we have a ride home."

"Good. Ruby will drop me off," Mary Anne answered and proceeded down the steps to where Ruby waited for her on the ground.

"Too bad we can't go to the casino," Ruby said as they walked away.

"Yeah, but we need IDs for that."

Ruby glanced at her. "I could probably get some fake ones."

"You think so?" Mary Anne felt a twinge of excitement. She knew some kids had fake IDs so they could buy booze or cigarettes, not that she was interested in either of those. But if an ID could get her in to see Bob while he was working…

"I'll check into it," Ruby said.

"Okay."

As they walked to her car, the cheering began to fade and then, suddenly, it turned to total silence. Mary Anne halted. "I wonder what happened?"

"Who cares?" Ruby opened her car door. "Let's go."

Mary Anne got in. As they drove away, the only sound she could hear was their tires scrunching on the gravel. She frowned, wondering again what had happened to still the crowd.

Chapter Five

When Ruby dropped Mary Anne off at her place a couple of hours later, she noticed the lights were still on. Was her mother waiting up for her? It was not quite midnight and it was a weekend, after all. Wendy had probably squealed on her for leaving the game early.

Mary Anne slowed her steps, thinking what she could say. They'd gone down the road to the casino on the vague hope they wouldn't be carded at the entrance, but they were. She'd tried to catch a glimpse of Bob over the security guard's shoulder, but it was too dark to see much past the door. Then they'd gone back to Ruby's, where her friend had snuck a couple of beers out of her parents' fridge. Mary Anne had drunk only half of hers, but Ruby had finished it off.

Mary Anne stopped to fish a piece of peppermint gum out of her purse and popped the stick into her mouth before she opened the door and went inside. She heard hushed conversation coming from the living room. Were Wendy and Jo waiting up for her as well? She didn't owe anyone an explanation.

"Ah, there you are," her mother said when she walked into the living room. "Come join us."

Mary Anne looked around the room as she took a seat in an armchair. Tim and Tommy were there, and Janie Nelsen, the cheerleader who sat in the front row in English class and always had the right answers. Why was she here? They didn't hang out together. At the moment, though, Janie was crying. Geez. Was losing a game that important?

"What's up?" Mary Anne asked.

"Billy Hoffman's been hurt," Jo said.

"Billy Hoffman? The quarterback?" He was one of the few football players who would say hello to everyone. "Did he break a leg or something?"

"He hit his head when he was tackled," Jo replied as Janie wept louder.

Mary Anne tried to remember if Janie was dating Billy. He was the football captain, and Janie would most likely be the Homecoming Queen this year, so they probably were. "Billy got knocked out?"

"Yeah," Wendy replied. "The ambulance took him to the hospital."

That must have been what caused the stadium to get so quiet as she and Ruby were leaving. "How bad was it?"

"We're not sure," Tommy answered. "Tim and I took Janie to the ER, but they wouldn't let any of us see him. The doc said he had a concussion."

Janie dabbed at her eyes with a handkerchief that Mary Anne recognized as one of her mother's. The piece of linen looked soaked, so obviously Janie had been crying a lot, although she didn't look it. When Mary Anne cried—not that she did very often since it was silly—her eyes swelled nearly shut, her nose looked like Rudolph's, and her skin turned all splotchy. Except for the watery eyes, Janie looked fine, but maybe that was some kind of rule that cheerleaders always looked good.

"The doctors will take good care of him," Mary Anne said a bit awkwardly.

"I know." Janie sniffled, and even that didn't sound gross. "It's just that he asked to take me home later and I told him he couldn't since my parents are out of town. Now I feel bad."

"Don't worry," Tim said. "Billy will get over it."

"And you can spend the night here," Vivian said, "since your parents aren't home."

"I wouldn't want to impose—"

"You can sleep in my room," Wendy offered. "I'll bunk down with Jo."

Janie looked from Wendy to Jo. "Are you sure?"

"No problem," Jo answered. "I'll just push Wendy out of bed if she snores."

Wendy protested, "I don't snore!"

Tim and Tommy started to tease her and even Janie gave her a wobbly smile. "I think being around people tonight might be a good thing for me."

"Then it's settled," Vivian said.

"I need to call my parents, though, and let them know."

"The phone's in the kitchen," Wendy said. "Come on, I'll show you."

Mary Anne used the time while her mother followed them into the kitchen to make her way upstairs. At least no one had questioned her on where she had been.

****

"Is there any word on Billy?" Janie asked the next morning as Tim and Tommy rode their horses over after breakfast.

"We didn't go by the hospital," Tim said as they dismounted and tied their horses to the rail close to the porch. "Our mother tried to call his mother this morning, but there was no answer. We can go by after we ride, if

44

you want."

"I don't think I feel like riding this morning," Janie said.

"But this is the Saturday we were going to talk about the horse show," Wendy said and then got more subdued when her mother frowned at her. "I guess we can do that another time."

"The horse show isn't until spring," Jo said. "We've got lots of time to plan."

"I'd forgotten we decided to do that," Janie said. "It might help me keep from worrying about Billy. If I can ride double with someone over to my house, I'll join you."

"I think it would be a good idea if Mary Anne got involved with the horse show this year as well," Vivian said.

"But she can't even ride!" Wendy said.

"She can learn. There's plenty of time," Vivian replied.

Mary Anne stared at her mother. What in the world had gotten into her? Everyone knew she didn't ride. They might not know she was scared of the big animals because she used the excuse that they smelled, but it was understood that she didn't ride nor did she want to. 'I'm really not interested in a horse show."

"Flame needs exercise now that Jo is riding Luke's horse." Vivian leveled a look at Mary Anne. "Besides, you need to be involved with something besides spending time with Bob."

So that was what this was about. Did her mother suspect where Ruby and she had gone last night? Mary Anne narrowed her eyes and looked at Wendy. Her sister wouldn't have known where they had gone, but she might have guessed. Then again, maybe someone else from town had seen Mary Anne at the casino door. Everyone in a small town seemed to know everyone else's business, probably because there wasn't much else to do except gossip. There were two elderly sisters who liked to keep tabs on young people and report infractions to parents. Snoopy old maids. But Mary Anne could hardly picture Millicent and Minnie Gustafson being at a casino, of all places, let alone on a Friday night. They weren't exactly the little old ladies from Pasadena riding around in a sports car. They used canes and drove one of those cars that you couldn't tell which end was which.

"Aw, come on," Tommy said. "It's a blast."

"For you, maybe," Mary Anne answered, trying to squelch the anxiety that was spreading through her. "I've never been interested."

"We didn't ride either until we learned while we were in England as exchange students," Tim said. "Look at us now. We won red ribbons at the county fair last year."

"And Jo and I won blue," Wendy added. "So did Janie."

"I already know that," Mary Anne retorted. "It was all you could talk about for weeks."

"No one would expect you to win ribbons," Janie said. "But you might really like riding if you tried it."

"There, you see," Vivian said before Mary Anne could think of a reply. "Everyone agrees. You can begin this morning when the others go trail riding."

"But I have other plans."

"Like what?"

Mary Anne had planned to drive over to Bob's to see how his first night of work went, but she was not about to say that. "Just plans."

Her mother arched an eyebrow. "Are you forgetting the agreement we have?"

She remembered only too well. "You said I had to exercise Flame. You didn't say I had to join the riding club."

"It will be safer for you to ride with the group," her mother replied. "And better than riding with Bob in that hotrod he drives. That's more dangerous."

Mary Anne wasn't quite sure if her mother was referring to Bob or his car, but she decided it better not to pursue the subject. Better to return to the original subject. "I'll just slow the group down. They like to gallop."

"That's true," Wendy said.

For once, Mary Anne could have kissed her sister. "I don't want to make them all slow down because of me."

"They won't have to," Janie said. "I'll be glad to keep my horse at a walk until you're comfortable with moving faster."

It was just Mary Anne's luck to have the *nice* cheerleader as a house guest. The rest of the squad was stuck-up and wouldn't have offered. But then, most of those snobs wouldn't have spent the night, either.

"That is kind of you to offer, Janie," Vivian said.

Kind was not the word Mary Anne would have used, but she bit her tongue. What point was there in arguing? If she refused, her mother wouldn't let her see Bob. Maybe Janie would get bored with sidling along at a walk, after a couple of times, and Mary Anne could get out of riding with the club. She sighed.

"I'll go change into jeans."

****

"Sorry I'm late," James said a short time later when he arrived at the Wades' and dismounted to join the group on the porch, glad they hadn't left yet. "I stopped by the hospital first." He turned to Janie. "There's been no change. The nurse on duty said Billy is still in a coma. She also said he can't have any visitors."

Janie nodded, her eyes growing bright with tears again. "I can't go riding knowing Billy's still unconscious. I want to be with him. I need to go over and sit in the waiting room."

Vivian gave her a sympathetic look. "I'll drive you over, dear."

"I appreciate that, but if you'll just drop me off at home, I can take my parents' other car," Janie replied.

"Nonsense. You don't need to be sitting by yourself in the waiting room," Vivian said. "I'll stay with you. We'll leave just as soon as I finish the dishes."

"I'll help."

As they went inside, James turned his attention to Wendy, who was leading both Flame and her horse Jupiter from the barn. He smiled. "Are you going to try some trick riding today with two horses?"

Wendy giggled. "That's a thought. Maybe I could do a circus trick, one foot on each horse's back."

Tommy laughed. "We'd like to see you try!"

"Who do you think you are?" Tim asked, chuckling. "Annie Oakley?"

Wendy bristled. "You don't think I can do it?"

"No way," Tommy said.

Wendy thrust out her chin. "You just watch, then."

"I was just kidding," James said. "There's no sense in taking chances and getting hurt, Wendy."

She turned to him, eyes wide. "You care about my getting hurt?"

The way she was looking at him so intensely almost made him squirm. Wendy looked like she was waiting on an answer. Before he could respond, though, the screen door opened again and Mary Anne came out. James forgot what the question had been as he focused on Mary Anne. She rarely came out of the house on Saturday mornings when the club went for their ride, although he always hoped she would. And today she was wearing jeans, which she hardly ever did either.

Jo stepped down from the porch and took the sorrel's reins from Wendy. Then she gestured toward Mary Anne. "Come on. Get acquainted with Flame."

James felt his own eyes widen as he watched Mary Anne slowly take the steps down. He thought she didn't like horses. "Are you going to ride with us?"

"I have to," Mary Anne replied and then eyed the horse with what looked like trepidation.

Jo took Mary Anne's hand and laid a slice of apple in her palm. "Go ahead. Feed it to Flame. She likes apples."

"She's got big teeth," Mary Anne said, causing Tim and Tommy to hoot.

"I thought you said you weren't afraid of horses," Wendy taunted.

Mary Anne's face flushed in either anger or embarrassment. James couldn't tell for sure, but he wanted to tell everyone to stop teasing her. He took several steps closer.

Jo intervened. "Hold out your hand like this," she said to Mary Anne, demonstrating a flat hand with a piece of apple in the middle. "Flame will just lip it off."

Mary Anne paled as the horse's muzzle moved. James stared at her in amazement. She really was scared of the horse. It had never occurred to him that she might be. As he watched, Mary Anne took a deep breath and shoved her hand forward. She started to squeeze her eyes shut, but then forced them open. James silently admired her courage.

Flame nickered and then blew through her nose. Mary Anne jumped back, colliding with James. His hands went up to catch her waist so she wouldn't fall, and for just a moment, he had the pleasure of holding her before she stepped away.

"That was loud," Mary Anne said.

"Flame's just saying thank you," Jo replied and stroked the sorrel's satiny neck. "That's the first step in her getting to like you."

Mary Anne didn't look as if she cared whether the horse liked her or not. She was keeping her distance.

"If we're going to ride, let's ride," Tommy said, going to his horse.

"Mount up, everyone," Tim added as he pulled himself into the saddle.

Wendy did the same, then looked down at Mary Anne. "Come on."

Mary Anne's face had gone chalky again. If she was that afraid to ride, the horse would sense it. Even a calm horse with a good disposition would grow uneasy, not knowing what her rider wanted. That would be trouble. James stepped forward. "Have you ridden before?"

Mary Anne shook her head quickly.

"You don't look too happy about this. Why are you riding if you don't want to?"

She hesitated a moment. "I have to. Unless I agree

to exercise Flame, my mother won't let me see Bob."

James felt as though he'd been tackled by a linebacker. All the air suddenly seemed to leave his lungs. He'd seen Bob a few times last spring before he'd left for Chicago. James had thought he'd looked like a hood, with his greased-back hair, leather jacket, and loud car. The kind that would play loose and fast with a girl. James hadn't known Bob was back.

Apparently, Mary Anne was still bedazzled with the city boy. What did she see in him, anyway?

James sucked in a huge breath of air. He didn't believe in fighting, but neither was he a wimp. Bob presented a challenge. One that James was willing to meet.

Chapter Six

Mary Anne looked at Jo holding the reins to Flame, then at the horse, and swallowed hard. The mare looked huge standing this close. She'd always been able to avoid the great beasts by pretending indifference. Just because her sister and what seemed to be half the kids in Middletown had all been horse crazy since they were in middle school didn't mean she had to be.

Her mother had never pushed her to ride. Why now? Even as Mary Anne thought the question, she knew the answer. Her mother didn't want her dating Bob and she thought Mary Anne would not agree to the bargain. Well. Her mother didn't know how special Bob was. Mary Anne knew he didn't fit in with the wholesome, country lifestyle, but neither did she. That was one of the things she liked about him…and he came from Chicago, which made him act more sophisticated than the boys at Middletown. He never spoke of his background and Mary Anne thought maybe something tragic had happened to him, which also lent a bit of mystery.

So. If she got on the horse, her mother would have to keep her end of the bargain and let Mary Anne see Bob. She swallowed again and stepped forward.

"Wait."

Mary Anne halted at the sound of James' voice as if it had been Gabriel blowing his trumpet.

"What?" Wendy asked.

"If Mary Anne has never ridden before, she should really have a lesson or two in the paddock before getting out on the road," he said.

Jo nodded. "I remember Aunt Viv teaching me in the paddock first."

"I agree," Mary Anne added quickly, thankful for the reprieve. "Of course, Mom's taking Janie to the hospital this morning, but we can wait until she has time."

"No need to wait," James said. "I can teach you the basics."

Mary Anne's stomach felt like lead had just settled in it. So much for her reprieve.

"But James is supposed to ride with us today," Wendy complained.

The feeling of lead lightened. Maybe there would be a reprieve after all. "Wendy is right," Mary Anne said, hoping her sister wouldn't topple off her horse in surprise that they agreed on anything. "I wouldn't want to keep you from enjoying the ride."

"I can ride anytime," James replied. "You need to be able to control your horse so you don't have an accident."

Wendy looked as though she wanted to give Mary Anne a good kick and she took a prudent step back. Little did James know she had no interest in controlling the big animal. Mary Anne was tempted to say she had a peace treaty with horses…she didn't get on their backs and they kept their hooves and teeth away from her. No doubt that would make her the laughingstock of the riding club, but she didn't really care. She didn't fit into their mold any more than she did with the cheerleaders and athletes. "Really. It's okay. Why don't you all just enjoy your ride?"

Her mother chose that ill-fated moment to come out of the house with Janie. She looked at the group. Everyone was mounted except James and Mary Anne. Vivian raised an eyebrow. "Do you need help mounting, Mary Anne? I'm sure James can help you."

Mary Anne recognized the deceptively soft tone her mother used with the question. The softer and seemingly irresolute her mother sounded, the more of an iron-clad will lay behind it. In this case, Mary Anne was quite sure it meant "no riding, no seeing Bob."

"Mrs. Wade, I'd like to suggest Mary Anne have a lesson or two in the paddock for safety's sake before she rides with the group," James said. "I'll be glad to teach her the basics this morning since you're leaving."

Wendy glowered at Mary Anne like it was her fault. Her sister should be blaming their mother instead. Vivian, however, was ignoring both her daughters. She smiled brightly at James.

"I think that's a wonderful idea, James, and so mature of you to think of safety."

Mary Anne bit back a groan. There would be no reprieve after all.

****

James could hardly believe his luck. What an opportune moment for Mary Anne's mother to appear. *And* for her to approve his giving Mary Anne lessons. He was aware of the irony that getting Mary Anne on a horse would also allow her to see that guy from Chicago, but first things first. James would be spending time with Mary Anne and she couldn't refuse his company.

"I can stay and help," Wendy said.

"You just said you wanted to ride today," Tim said.

"I can ride another time," Wendy answered.

Tommy snickered and leaned over to sotto-whisper. "Does someone have a crush on James?"

Wendy turned red. "I do not!"

James felt his own face heat, although he pretended not to have heard the interchange as he bent to adjust a stirrup on Flame. Wendy reminded him of one of his younger cousins. He certainly didn't want to encourage her.

Her mother gave her a sharp glance. "The way you and Mary Anne argue, nothing will be achieved. Now go and enjoy your ride."

Wendy's lower lip stuck out as she wheeled Jupiter and spurred him to a canter, tossing up gravel in their wake. The rest followed at a slower pace.

Janie watched them leave and then gave Mary Anne an encouraging smile. "Soon you'll be able to ride like that too."

"I'm not sure I want to," Mary Anne replied. "I only agreed to exercise Flame."

"Horses are social animals," James said, "so you'll be doing Flame a favor by allowing her to be part of the group."

Vivian nodded. "Well spoken, James. Wendy said you understood horses."

"Thank you, Mrs. Wade," James replied with mixed emotions. He liked having Mary Anne's mother's approval, but he wasn't sure he liked Wendy talking about him. Since Kevin said he'd taken a fancy to her, it might be a good idea to encourage that.

Vivian had walked to her car, but she paused as she opened the door and looked at Mary Anne. "I'll expect to see some progress when I get home."

Mary Anne's expression turned dour, but she didn't say anything, only nodded.

James waited until her mother and Janie had gone. Then he turned to Mary Anne. "Why are you afraid of horses?"

She frowned. "I'm not."

James hooked his thumbs in his belt loops and waited.

Her frown deepened and Mary Anne shuffled her feet. She looked up at him and then away. "Maybe I am, just a little." She lifted her chin and looked back at him. "Go ahead. Make fun of me."

"Why would I want to do that?"

"Everybody else does."

"Well, I'm not everybody else," James replied, "and I don't think feeling scared of something is funny."

She searched his face. "Tim and Tommy do. Tommy used to drop spiders into Wendy's lap to make her scream."

"That's mature."

Mary Anne shrugged. "Well, we *were* kids. Tim brought a snake into the house once. I nearly stepped on it. Mom thought I was being attacked, with how much I screeched. The twins teased me about it for days."

"And you think they'd tease you now?"

"They would if I fell off the horse," Mary Anne said.

"You are not going to fall off."

"How do you know that?"

"Because, first of all, you aren't going to ride today."

Mary Anne's eyes grew wide. "I'm not? You're going to help me fool my mom?"

James shook his head. "No. I'll exercise Flame and

take her over some of the practice jumps in the pasture. I want you to spend your time today getting to know her. I'll show you how to unsaddle Flame and brush her down. Then you can lead her around with her halter and give her hay and fresh water. I'll not let you get in the saddle until you're comfortable handling her."

"What if that doesn't happen?"

James smiled. "It will. Trust me."

****

"So you didn't ride today?" Wendy asked Mary Anne at supper that night.

"Who told you I didn't?"

"James," Wendy replied. "I asked him how it went. I guess you won't be seeing Bob anytime soon."

Mary Anne sighed. She should have known her sister couldn't keep her nose out of anything that concerned James. Mary Anne had actually been rather proud of herself that by the end of the afternoon she could stand beside Flame and feel relaxed. The mare had actually nuzzled her hand for a second apple slice, and Mary Anne hadn't dropped it.

But that probably wasn't going to count toward her agreement. She glanced sideways toward her mother, who smiled at her.

"I think you did fine today," Vivian said.

Mary Anne resisted smirking at Wendy, but couldn't help feeling a bit smug that her sister had her mouth hanging open in surprise. "I think I made progress."

"You did," her mother said. "I talked with James before he left, and I agreed that it's better to take things slowly. I certainly don't want you endangering yourself. He said once you gain confidence, you should be fine."

"What confidence?" Wendy asked. "It's not like Flame is a bucking bronco, for Pete's sake."

"Remember when I first came here?" Jo asked. "I'd only ridden at a Brooklyn stable and didn't know that much about taking care of a horse. I had to learn."

"But you weren't scared," Wendy said. "Not like fraidy-cat Mary Anne."

"That's enough, Wendy," her mother said. "Apologize for insulting your sister."

Wendy pouted and then mumbled, "Sorry."

Like she meant it. Mary Anne knew it was an automatic response to their mother. She'd done the same thing many times, so she let it go.

"Flame is the perfect horse to learn on," Jo said. "She's calm and gentle."

"I sort of noticed that today," Mary Anne replied. "I just hope she stays that way once I'm in the saddle."

"She will. Trust me," Jo answered.

Mary Anne nodded. "That's kind of what James said."

"And he promised me he wouldn't let you in the saddle until you felt you were ready," her mother said.

"So he's going to be coming here to give Mary Anne lessons?" Wendy asked.

"Yes, on Saturdays," Vivian replied. "He said for as long as it takes."

Wendy frowned. "But that means James won't ride with us!"

"You have a whole group to ride with," Vivian said. "It's important that Mary Anne feels confident about handling a horse. James has offered to help and I find that admirable."

"I don't know why she needs to ride at all," Wendy

grumbled. "We did fine without her."

"I'm right here," Mary Anne said. "Stop acting like I'm not."

"Your sister is right," Vivian said. "I'm surprised at you, Wendy."

Mary Anne wasn't surprised at all. If James spent his Saturdays teaching her to ride, that meant Wendy couldn't gawk at him and try to flirt.

A mischievous thought lodged itself in Mary Anne's brain, but she couldn't seem to get it out. The more she tried, the more the idea intensified, causing her to smile.

Maybe she'd prolong her "learning" just to keep James away from Wendy. She *had* called Mary Anne afraid, after all.

Besides, her sister shouldn't be throwing herself at a boy anyhow.

Chapter Seven

"Where's the Bug?" Mary Anne asked Ruby the next afternoon as her friend picked her up driving her parents' big Pontiac.

"Battery is dead," Ruby answered, "and I don't have the money to buy a new one until I get my paycheck, so I'm having to drive this clunker."

"Well, at least the speakers are good," Mary Anne said as she turned up the radio to listen to "Like A Rolling Stone." "I like this one."

Ruby grinned. "You like anyone named Bob."

Mary Anne felt herself blush. "No, really. Dylan is good, although his songs are kinda weird."

"You think?"

"Well, yeah. Take this one…someone who's riding on a high horse and then loses it all to have nothing. Sad."

"Maybe it's deserved," Ruby answered. "Maybe that's what will happen to the high-and-mighty popular kids who rule high school."

"That reminds me. Did you hear that Billy Hoffman is in a coma at the hospital?"

"I heard he had a concussion," Ruby said. "How do you know he's still in the hospital?"

"My mom called his mom this morning. Tim and Tommy brought Janie over to our house Friday night after the game."

Ruby glanced over at her. "Are you hanging out with cheerleaders now?"

Mary Anne looked out the car window as they neared the main street of Middletown. "Please. Like I fit in with that crowd."

"They think they're so cool in this little hick town," Ruby said. "So why did the twins bring Janie to your place?"

"She felt bad because she had told Billy he couldn't take her home since her parents weren't there. When she started crying, Tim felt sorry for her."

Ruby snorted. "Janie's such a Pollyanna. Geez, I'd take a guy up on an offer if my parents ever left home."

"Would you? Really?"

"Sure. Why not?" Ruby pulled the car into an empty space near the corner drugstore and shut off the motor. "You go over to Bob's place, don't you?"

"Yes, but his uncle is around."

"Does he keep an eye on you?"

"Well, he doesn't sit in the same room," Mary Anne replied, "but he's around. You know. Around."

"Okay. So no hanky-panky at the house." Ruby laughed. "You still have the car, though. You can steam up the windows at the passion pit."

"I wish. Mom won't let me go to the drive-in movies with a guy."

"Maybe you should negotiate that," Ruby said. "After all, she's making you learn to ride a horse. You should be able to call the shots about where you go on a date."

"I wish I could." Mary Anne had a feeling her mother would probably ground her for weeks if she tried. "Anyway, Bob's working weekend nights at the casino."

Ruby grimaced. "Yeah, that's tough. I'm not going to be able to get fake IDs for a while, either, since I have to buy a new battery for the Bug."

"It's probably just as well," Mary Anne said. "If someone saw me out there, they'd tell my mother for sure."

"Who'd see you? It's so dark, you practically need a flashlight. Besides, how many folks in Middletown like to gamble? Everyone is so straight-laced around here."

"I don't think it's just folks from Minneapolis who drive out," Mary Anne replied. "It's a long way."

"Well, gambling is only legal on Indian reservations, and one of them is here," Ruby said. "Since there's a hotel, they probably have way more people from out of town than locals."

"Bob's uncle goes there."

"Which one? The one Bob lives with or the one who went to prison?"

Mary Anne didn't want to think about the horrid uncle who'd tried to arrange for her kidnapping and blame it on Bob. "The one who's here."

"I thought he kept to himself."

"He does, mostly." Mary Anne shrugged. "I suppose it gives him something to do."

"Too bad Minnesota won't lower the legal age to eighteen. Then we could have some real fun," Ruby said as she got out of the car. "And you wouldn't have to ask your mother's permission, either."

"Yeah," Mary Anne replied as she too got out of the car. She doubted turning eighteen was going to change anything at her house, even if it were the legal age. "For now, though, we'll just have to settle for cherry cokes at the drugstore."

Rudy laughed. "You're funny. Did anyone ever tell you?"

Mary Anne shook her head, not quite sure what Ruby meant.

When they entered, the soda fountain area was empty except for a couple of giggling freshmen girls sitting at one end of the counter. They had a movie magazine in front of them and didn't even look up.

"Wonder who the latest heartthrob for those kids is," Ruby said as she perched on a bar stool at the other end. "Probably Batman or Little Joe Cartwright."

"The cover has *Star Trek* on it, so maybe it's Captain Kirk," Mary Anne replied as she took a seat. "Actually, I think Mr. Spock is kinda cute."

Ruby rolled her eyes. "He is major weird."

"Different."

"Don't tell me you believe in that 'live long and prosper' stuff."

Mary Anne smiled. "Don't you think it would be kinda neat to go where no one else has gone before?"

"Not that far out," Ruby replied and added as an afterthought, "Maybe San Francisco, though. The TV says lots of kids are flocking out there to do their own thing. No parents. No curfews. No rules. Just hang out."

"They still have to have money to eat and a place to stay, though."

"Not really." Ruby shrugged. "They live in communes and work together. Nobody is better than anyone else. Everyone just accepts everyone. Pretty cool."

"They still have to eat."

Ruby gave her a wide-eyed stare. "Haven't you read anything about the Diggers in that flower-power research we're all doing?"

Mary Anne shook her head. "I'm supposed to be researching the anti-war aspect. So who are the Diggers?"

"They're actors and artists who don't believe in mega-rich capitalists," Ruby said. "Every afternoon, they provide free lunch at Golden Gate Park with donations they've gotten. They've set up free stores, too, where you can get—or give away—clothes and whatever else you need. Geez. I can't believe you haven't even heard of them."

Mary Anne felt her face grow warm. Ruby had lived in the Twin Cities and was so worldly compared to her. "Like I said, James asked me to check out the peace movement."

"Peace and love. It all ties in," Ruby said. "The Diggers are even working on a free clinic in Haight-Ashbury. Everything is taken care of out there."

Mary Anne frowned. "You make it sound like heaven or something."

"Maybe it is," Ruby said. "Hey, you said you liked Bob Dylan, right?"

"Yeah. Why?"

Ruby grinned. "Well, lady, he sang "The Times They Are A-Changin'." I think the movement has begun."

****

"What do you think about the hippie movement?" Mary Anne asked James Monday afternoon when they met in the library. No one had joined them yet and she wanted his opinion before Ruby got there.

"Which part?"

"All of it, I guess," Mary Anne said. "Ruby thinks

Haight-Ashbury is heaven on earth because everything is free."

James shook his head. "Nothing's ever free. Somebody pays."

"What do you mean? They rely mostly on donations for food and clothes."

"What about a place to stay? The cops aren't going to let them live in the parks."

Mary Anne knitted her brows. "Ruby says a lot of them live together in the old Victorian townhomes in Ashbury Heights."

"They don't get them for free. Who pays the rent?"

"I guess they pool their money, since they share everything."

James studied her. "Does that idea appeal to you?"

"Sharing?"

"Not so much sharing things," he answered. "Sharing values. Living with a bunch of people you don't know."

Mary Anne smiled. "Well, I guess you'd get to know them if you lived with them."

"That's not what I mean," James replied. "Kids are flocking to San Francisco for lots of reasons. Some are runaways. Some are dodging the draft. Others are just rebellious and don't want to work—"

"Who doesn't want to work?" Ruby asked as she joined them and plopped her psychedelic binder down on an empty chair.

"We were talking about the hippies," Mary Anne told her, "and what kind of people are going out there."

"Maybe kids who want to find out where their head is at," Ruby said. "Chill out and do their own thing. Smoke a little pot and get high."

"Shhhh!" Mary Anne said, dropping her voice to a whisper. "You want to get busted?"

Ruby rolled her eyes. "Don't worry. It's not like I have any."

"Now that you bring it up," James said, "that's another problem with what's happening in San Francisco. Kids are using drugs."

"Maybe to get more into their own heads," Ruby replied, "instead of how parents and schools and the rest of the Establishment wants kids to think. Is that so bad? You know. *Turn on. Tune in. Drop out.*"

James frowned. "That's Dr. Leary's motto about using LSD. It's dangerous."

"How do you know if you haven't tried it?" Ruby asked.

"I don't have to walk into oncoming traffic to know I'll get hurt or killed," James answered. "Stuff that alters your ability to think can't be good."

"Maybe it can," Ruby retorted and pulled a sheaf of papers from her neon flower-covered notebook. "As my contribution to this stupid project Mrs. Howell is making us do, I researched Timothy Leary."

Mary Anne looked around. "I don't think we should be talking about him—or drugs—at school."

James nodded. "I don't either."

"Relax, will you?" Ruby said. "Did you know Timothy Leary served in World War II? He worked with deaf patients in a hospital. He even earned a bunch of medals." Ruby looked at her notes. "That's weird. His wife's name was Marianne."

Mary Anne fidgeted. "Really?"

"Yeah, well. She killed herself."

James frowned. "Did we need to know that?"

"Dunno. I'm not a shrink," Ruby said. "Anyhow, Dr. Leary is one, and he got involved with hallucinogens. LSD *is* legal, you know."

"Probably not for long," James replied. "The FBI has been raiding parties at Leary's place in New York."

Mary Anne glanced at him. "It sounds like you've been researching this too."

"Only because I don't think anything that alters a person's state of consciousness can be good."

"Not even if it's a higher level of consciousness?" Ruby asked. "That's the whole idea of turning on."

"I prefer to be in control of my thoughts," James replied.

"The *idea*," Ruby said, "is to take your thoughts to a higher level. Instead of reading dull stories in Lit or listening to boring history—or worse, doing stupid math problems that make no sense—you can take a trip in your own mind." She raised her hands and put her palms together to assume a meditation pose. "Transcend time, space, speech and not even know who you are—where you begin or end. Just kind of floating in nothingness." Ruby lowered her hands. "Cool, huh?"

"Floating in nothingness doesn't seem to be a higher level of thinking, to me," James replied. "What's cool about that?"

Ruby shook her head and turned to Mary Anne. "What do you think?"

Mary Anne said a quick, silent prayer for divine intervention. She didn't want to answer the question since it didn't sound at all cool to her either. "I…" she began and then saw Wendy coming toward them, sparing her from an answer.

Mary Anne had never thought of Wendy as an angel

before, but at the moment she wouldn't have been surprised if her sister sprouted wings and a halo. Her prayer had been heard…and she wouldn't have to provide an answer.

****

When Mary Anne knocked on Bob's door the next afternoon, his uncle Bill answered it.

"He's getting ready for work," Bill said. "You can wait in the living room."

"Thanks." Since she knew where it was, Mary Anne didn't wait for him to walk her there. Bob's uncle wasn't the talkative type anyway. As she'd told Ruby, he kept pretty much to himself, hiring out as a jack-of-all-trades but not taking part in much else. Not that she blamed him. Middletown was practically a replica of *The Andy Griffith Show*'s Mayberry, centering its social activities on high school sports or church-organized events. Bob's uncle didn't have kids and he didn't attend any of the three churches in town. Maybe that's why he spent time at the casino. For someone who hailed from Chicago, he must be bored to tears with country life.

Mary Anne walked into the living room and sat down on the worn sofa and looked around as if seeing the room for the first time. The varied upholstery on the two armchairs had seen better days. The coffee and end tables were mix-matched pieces of different types of wood with different styles of lamps. A threadbare throw carpet covered scuffed, uneven oak floors, and a lone picture of a cabin in the mountains hung on one paint-faded wall.

Her mother would probably have a fit if she saw the haphazard condition of this farmhouse, since things matched in their house, the floors had thick carpets, and the walls were adorned with lots of pictures of family. But how important were material things? The hippies in the San Francisco communes probably lived with even less than this. What did it matter if Bob's uncle wasn't rich? Bob was all that mattered.

She heard him coming down the steps and got up to greet him. He looked a little surprised when he saw her in the doorway, but then he put his arm around her waist and drew her close for a kiss.

"I didn't know you were coming today," he said.

"The pay phone in the cafeteria wasn't working," Mary Anne answered, "so I couldn't call."

"Well, I've got a few minutes before I have to leave for work," he said and went into the living room and sat down on the sofa. "Come here."

Mary Anne snuggled against him, loving the feel of his arm around her and his fingers trailing down her arm. She'd just raised her face for another kiss when she heard his uncle clearing his throat in the hallway. Reluctantly, Bob released her.

"How was your day?' he asked.

"Boring as mud," Mary Anne replied. "You would think at least one of the teachers could make a class interesting, but no. We're reading Dante in English, studying the Bronze Age in history class, doing page-long calculations in math, and in chemistry—"

"You don't have to give me the list," Bob said. "I've been there, remember? And I'm glad I'm out."

"Yeah, I'll be glad when I graduate too."

He gave her a contemplative look. "Are you planning on sticking around after graduation?"

Did he want her to? Mary Anne's heart beat a little faster. She wasn't sure how to answer. All Bob had to do was ask her to be his steady girl and she'd stick by his side. She knew her mother wanted her to go to college. The money from her father's life insurance policy would cover both her and Wendy, but Mary Anne had no clue what she wanted to do. "I don't know," she said cautiously. "I think maybe I'd like to go to Minneapolis."

Bob grinned. "The big city and bright lights are calling you?"

Mary Anne didn't want to sound too definite. "Maybe. You're from Chicago. Do you like big cities?"

He sobered. "They're okay."

She wanted to ask more, but he didn't look like he wanted to talk about it. She wondered again if something bad had happened to him. "I thought maybe you were going to stay in Chicago when you went back."

"Nope."

His answer was quick and Mary Anne hoped it might have something to do with her, but she couldn't very well ask outright. "So you like it here in Middletown?"

Bob shrugged. "Right now, I'm making good money at the casino."

"I guess that's a good reason to stay."

He glanced over his shoulder, probably to see if his uncle was in sight, and then leaned closer and whispered, "Well, there is you, babe. I'd kinda like to see where that road leads."

Mary Anne's heart raced and little tingles shimmied down her neck from where his breath had tickled her ear. She wanted him to hold her again, but he'd already sat back. "I'd like that too."

Bob studied her. "Would you?"

She felt her face warm under his scrutiny. "Yeah. I

want to go on a real date."

His eyes half-closed. "Me, too," he said and then sighed. "It won't be soon, though. The casino's got me working seven nights a week."

"You can't get a night off?"

"Not right now. I'm new and they're short-staffed. Besides, I get paid overtime, so I can start stashing cash away. Maybe in about a month things will ease up."

"That's a long time."

"Well, you can still drive out here after school."

"Mom doesn't really like it when I do," Mary Anne said.

"Yeah, I heard."

Mary Anne frowned. "You heard?"

"Yeah." Bob got up and walked into the hallway to take his jacket off the coat rack. "I gotta get to work."

"Wait a minute." Mary Anne rose, grabbed her purse, and followed him. "What do you mean, you *heard*?"

Bob opened the front door and paused. "Why do you think my uncle hangs around?"

"He lives here. He probably doesn't want to leave you alone either."

Bob laughed. "Believe me, that's the last thing that concerns him. Besides, I'm twenty. I don't need a chaperone."

"Does your uncle think *I* need a chaperone, then?"

"Probably not." Bob stopped smiling. "But your mother does."

"My mother?"

"Yep." He hesitated. "She talked to my uncle once she found out I was back."

"She *what*?"

"Your mother told Bill we were not be left alone in this house. So you might say he's babysitting."

Mary Anne's face felt like it was on fire. Her hands, though, felt like ice when she clapped them to her cheeks. "I can't believe she did that!"

"Don't worry about it. I'll figure a way to get us alone together."

She couldn't answer. She needed to get away before the tears stinging her eyes began to fall. Mary Anne raced past Bob and down the steps to her car. Never in her life had she felt so completely humiliated and mortified.

Or so angry.

Chapter Eight

"You weren't in English class," James said to Mary Anne Wednesday afternoon when they'd all gathered in the library to do more research. He'd been worried she wouldn't come to the meeting today. "Were you sick?"

Ruby answered for Mary Anne. "Yes, she was."

James looked at Ruby. "You weren't there either."

"I was helping Mary Anne in the restroom."

Wendy narrowed her eyes at her sister. "You weren't sick this morning. Did you skip class?"

"Just shut up," Mary Anne muttered.

Wendy's eyes went wide. "You did skip!"

"Ye can decide just not to go to class in the U.S.?" Kevin asked.

"No, you can't," Wendy said. "We get into big trouble if we're caught."

Mary Anne glared at Wendy. "I suppose you're going to go tattle on me to our mother about that too."

Wendy looked hurt. "Too? What are you talking about?"

James gave Mary Anne a sideways glance and wished he hadn't brought the subject up. He should have known better, with Wendy sitting there.

"You told her I left the game early last Friday night, didn't you?" Mary Anne asked.

"No," Wendy said. "I got home about the same time Tim and Tommy brought Janie over. Don't you remember Billy Hoffman got hurt?"

"Of course I remember. How could I forget? The Hound reminds us every morning on the P.A. that Billy is still in a coma."

"I think it's a medically induced coma," James offered, hoping to change the subject. "My mom said it keeps the brain from swelling more."

"Why did you skip class?" Wendy asked Mary Anne.

She was as determined as a terrier cornering a rabbit and wasn't going to drop the topic. James frowned at Kevin, hoping he'd take the hint and divert the conversation, but Kevin just sat there smiling at Wendy.

"Maybe you shouldn't ask so many questions," Ruby said.

Wendy ignored her and continued the conversation. "Now that I think about it, you were mad this morning, too. You didn't eat and you hardly said a word to Mom."

"Maybe Mary Anne had a reason," Ruby said.

Wendy frowned. "Like what?"

"Just leave it be," Mary Anne said.

"No, I want to know."

"It's not your business," Ruby snapped.

Kevin came to Wendy's defense. "Hey. They're sisters. She cares."

Mary Anne made a noise that sounded suspiciously like a derisive snort. "Yeah, she and my mother really care about my happiness."

James hoped they weren't going to get into an argument in the library. They'd draw Mr. Hund's attention for sure and, since he was in charge of attendance, he'd remember Mary Anne had been absent from all her classes today. Then she really would be in trouble.

"Let's get started on our research, okay?" he asked.

"In a minute," Wendy said, not to be deterred. "Is this about Mom? Why are you mad at her? She's letting you see Bob."

James *really* wished he had not brought up the subject. He didn't want to hear any more about Bob.

Mary Anne stood, sliding her chair back so fast it crashed to the floor. The librarian frowned at them. "I told you to leave it alone! So leave *me* alone!" And Mary Anne turned and fled.

Ruby rose, giving Wendy a dirty look, and followed Mary Anne.

"What was that about?" Kevin asked.

"Who knows?" Wendy replied. "Mary Anne's always been moody."

James didn't think Mary Anne was moody at all. He wished he knew why—or what—had upset her, but talking about it evidently wasn't going to be an option.

Neither was research. James sighed and closed the binder he'd opened. Ruby was only available after school on Mondays and Wednesdays, and Mary Anne had said they should all be present to do the research. James couldn't find fault with that, but he had looked forward to working with Mary Anne this afternoon. Now that would have to wait.

He wished he knew why she was angry with her mother. Did it have something to do with Bob? He wished he knew.

****

"Hey, wait up!" Ruby called as Mary Anne hurried across the parking lot toward her car.

Actually, it was her mother's car, an old, straight-stick Chevy Impala that right now Mary Anne didn't even want to touch. She'd rather not have anything to with her mother or her things right now. But then, Mary Anne didn't have a job, so she couldn't afford her own car. She paused and waited for Ruby to catch up.

"Get in," she said.

"Sure," Ruby replied as she hopped in the front seat. "Where are we going? Back to the lake?"

"We spent most of the day there." Mary Anne shook her head. "I don't know. Anywhere. Maybe down to the river."

"It looks like it's going to rain." Ruby glanced over to her friend. "Besides, isn't that cave there, where you were held for ransom?"

"Yeah, but we'll go farther down, by the old bridge."

"You mean the one that's ready to fall down?"

"I'm not planning to drive across it," Mary Anne replied as she drove off the school lot. "I'm not stupid in spite of what everyone thinks."

"I never said you were stupid," Ruby said.

"Well, my mother thinks I am."

"She didn't say that, did she?"

"No, but why else would she go and talk to Bob's uncle and tell him to babysit us—me—like I'm some kind of child?"

Ruby hesitated. "She doesn't want you getting pregnant."

"She doesn't trust me."

"My parents are always harping about guys taking advantage," Ruby said. "Maybe it's Bob your mother doesn't trust."

"She's never liked him," Mary Anne replied as big

drops of rain began to splatter the windshield. "Blast it. We can't go to the river if it's going to storm."

"Let's just go to the drive-in cafe," Ruby suggested. "We can have root beer and burgers. I'm hungry anyhow."

"Jeepers, creepers." Mary Anne made a sudden U-turn on the highway and the car's rear wheels slid as she headed in the other direction.

"Careful!" Ruby laughed a little too shrilly. "This old jalopy isn't a 'Vette."

Mary Anne slowed down. "My mother's never given Bob a chance."

Ruby hesitated again. "She is letting you see him, though."

"Yeah! As long as I have a babysitter. Do you have any idea how embarrassing that is? And Bob *knew*. I can't believe his uncle told him. All I wanted to do yesterday was have the earth open up and swallow me. How am I going to face Bob? I really hate my mother."

"You're just mad."

Mary Anne frowned as she stopped outside their destination. "Whose side are you on?"

"Yours," Ruby replied. "I get how you feel. Before we moved here from Minneapolis, I was dating an older guy—Tony—that my parents didn't like either. I wrote him a letter. When he wrote back, my father tore the letter up before I could read it. I didn't speak to my father for weeks."

"But you got over it?"

"Kind of." Ruby shrugged. "I thought about running away, going back to the Twin Cities and staying with Tony, but I didn't even have bus fare."

Mary Anne pulled into the drive-in and stopped the

car. "Is that why you're working? To save money so you can go back to Tony?"

"I don't know if Tony will still be around," Ruby replied, "since I haven't heard from him. I know this, though. I don't like living in a small town. Too many people like Minnie and Millicent Gustafson keep their noses in everyone's business. Mainly, though, I want to get away from my parents and be my own boss."

"I'd love to be my own boss and make my own decisions," Mary Anne said as the carhop came to take their order. "Maybe I should get a job too."

Ruby nodded and looked at Mary Anne thoughtfully. "Maybe you should."

****

The more Mary Anne thought about getting a job, the better she liked the idea. Having her own money—that her mother couldn't tell her how to spend—sounded wonderful. She could even open up a checking account in her name and be independent. If Bob didn't want to stay in Middletown, she could move to the Twin Cities with him or Ruby after graduation.

"I filled out an application at the grocery store this afternoon," she told Ruby Friday evening as they settled in the bleachers for the football game. "They said they could use someone part-time."

"You gonna be a stocker or a carry-out?" Ruby asked.

Mary Anne shook her head. "Cashier."

"Groovy. They make more money." Ruby gave her a sideways glance. "Have you told your mother yet?"

"Not yet. I want to be sure they offer me the job first."

"What if your mom says no?"

"I'm seventeen. That's old enough to work part-time. I don't need her permission."

"Well, you know how it is in small towns," Ruby said. "If your mom says no…"

Mary Anne didn't need her friend to remind her. She was still angry with her mother for interfering with her visits to Bob. She hadn't said anything until dopey Wendy asked their mother at dinner last night why Mary Anne was mad at her. Their mother had raised both brows and said she'd like to know too. Mary Anne retorted she didn't like being treated like a child. Her mother had studied her for so long that Mary Anne didn't think she was going to answer. But she did. She had said if Mary Anne didn't like being treated as a child, she shouldn't act like one. The words stung.

Now Mary Anne smiled. "She can hardly refuse to let me work. Having a job is a mature, responsible thing to do."

Ruby nodded. "Good point."

"Don't say anything in front of Wendy," Mary Anne said as she saw her sister climbing up the bleachers toward them with Kevin following her. "I don't need her big mouth upsetting my plans."

"You got it," Ruby said and looked over to them. "I think Kevin likes Wendy."

"Well, I wish him luck," Mary Anne replied. "All she can think about is James."

Ruby glanced back at her. "And I think James likes you."

"Don't be silly."

"I'm not. How many people do you know that want to work on extra projects?"

Mary Anne grimaced. "Only because Mrs. Howell

assigned it as punishment."

Ruby grinned. "James doesn't seem to mind."

"Yeah, well. He's the smart type. They like to study."

"Maybe because—"

"Why are you sitting way up here?" Wendy interrupted as she and Kevin joined them. "We can hear the band better when we sit lower."

The only reason Wendy wanted to sit closer to the band was because she'd have a better view of James. Mary Anne exchanged a meaningful look with Ruby, who hid another smile. "We can see the game better from up here."

Wendy stared at her. "When did you decide you liked football?"

She hadn't, but the screaming cheerleaders and yelling parents weren't quite as loud higher in the bleachers. "You can go sit wherever you want."

"Mom said to…" Wendy stopped and closed her mouth abruptly.

Mary Anne narrowed her eyes. "What did Mom say?"

"Uh…nothing."

"Look!" Kevin said as the band began the fight song. "The team is comin' onto the field."

Wendy whipped her head around so fast that Mary Anne knew she did it to avoid answering the question and not because she was that interested in football either. When Wendy started questioning Kevin about whether they had football in Ireland, Mary Anne was sure her sister was avoiding the subject of their mother.

Mary Anne sat out the game, trying not to look bored. Since she didn't know what her mother had told

Wendy to do—probably watch her like a hawk and tattle—Mary Anne didn't dare leave the game early again. The stands on both sides of the field sounded like rolling thunder—the score was tight. A final field goal gave the victory to Middletown, and the crowd went so wild the bleachers shook.

She watched the cheerleaders do cartwheels and flips and hop up and down like their legs were coiled springs, and she wondered how they could be so excited over a game. She watched as The Hound walked toward them. Was the assistant principal actually going to tell them to calm down? It seemed a little harsh, even if their actions were silly. The Hound said something to Janie and Mary Anne saw her start to fall, only to be caught by the other girls. Then she noticed the coaches had stopped the football team from leaving the field. Instead they were gathered at the goal posts.

The big floodlights blinked off, leaving the field in darkness for a moment before coming back on. The crowd, which had been exiting the bleachers, stopped and grew silent. The P.A. system crackled, and then the principal, Mr. Robertson, came on. He cleared his throat.

"It is with great sorrow and a heavy heart that I have to announce that our star quarterback, Billy Hoffman, passed away this evening."

Chapter Nine

The halls of Middletown High School were eerily still on Monday morning. Subdued students walked silently through the corridors and entered classrooms to sit quietly at their desks. There were no shrill sounds of loud talk and laughter. Here and there, muted conversation took place, clipped and short as if the speakers said only what was necessary. It was as though the shock of the principal's announcement Friday night had not sunk in.

Or maybe it had and the message wouldn't leave their brains.

Mary Anne looked around her Physical Science class and wished Ruby were there, but Ruby wasn't inclined to take any science course she didn't have to take. Even James' presence would have been good, but he took Chemistry instead. Janie Nelsen's chair in the front row was conspicuously empty. Several girls sniffled into tissue and dabbed at watering eyes, the tears flowing more freely when they looked at Janie's empty desk. Mr. Harper, the teacher, tried to ignore them, while the boys shifted uneasily in their desks, not sure what to do.

Although neither Janie nor Billy had been personal friends of hers, Mary Anne couldn't deny being affected as well. It felt like a big plastic dome had settled over the school, silencing everything, in contrast to the buzzing talk that had taken place over the weekend.

Prior to the game, one of the football captains had announced the team would be playing this one for Billy. Afterwards, it didn't take long before the players started saying it felt as though Billy were on the field with them. The winning victory confirmed it. Hastily made posters appeared in shop windows announcing the football season would be dedicated to Billy and the goal was to win State. Even the pastor at church had said Billy would be looking down, expecting the team to carry on.

The girls were a different matter. Even before Mary Anne and Ruby left on Friday night, not only the cheerleaders but girlfriends of other team members had gathered around Janie, crying and hugging and surrounding her like a shield. Word quickly went around that Billy had given Janie his class ring the week before he got injured. The only record in the jukebox at the Dew Drop Inn café that played almost continuously was "Tell Laura I Love Her" as stunned students gathered at their favorite meeting place.

Wendy and Jo wanted to be part of that crowd and, since Mary Anne was the only one who had her driver's license, her mother had told her to take them. She hadn't argued, since she didn't want to stay home with her mother, and Ruby was at work, but once at the café, Mary Anne found herself listening to the lyrics more carefully.

She thought about those lyrics now as Mr. Harper began to drone on about some chemical experiment they were getting ready to do. The boy in the song had wanted to buy his girl an engagement ring so he entered a drag race to win the thousand-dollar prize. Mary Anne had immediately thought of Bob and how he liked to drag race, even when there was no prize involved. What would she do if he got hurt? Or killed? She knew the guys raced on dark country roads at night. Maybe it was a blessing in disguise that Bob had started working nights at the casino.

Even though Janie was not there, talk at the café on Saturday quickly spread the rumor that Billy and Janie had intended to marry after graduation. Mary Anne rather doubted that, since Janie wanted to be an elementary teacher and that meant college, but talk of marriage led Mary Anne's thoughts in that direction.

What would it be like to be married to Bob? He *had* written her when he was in Chicago, and when he came back, he *had* asked if she'd saved herself for him. Last week, he'd even *asked* if she planned to stay in Middletown and he had *said* he wanted to see where the road led with her. Didn't that mean he cared? Mary Anne knew he hadn't bought a class ring, so he didn't have one to give her. He was working at the casino, though, and he said he was saving his money. She'd be happy with even a tiny diamond ring.

"Miss Wade. Have you heard a single word I've said?" the teacher asked.

Mary Anne started. Mr. Harper never called on her. "I'm sorry. I guess I wasn't listening very well."

"I see." His voice softened a little. "I suppose it's to be expected with what's gone on. But please pay attention so you don't have an accident when we build our exploding volcano."

"Yes, sir," Mary Anne answered, her thoughts focusing on the word "accident." She really, really wouldn't be able to bear it if Bob had an accident. Even though she couldn't go out on regular dates because of his schedule, that schedule also meant he would not be endangering himself by drag racing like that boy in the song.

It was a fair trade if it meant being together in the future.

****

"Have you seen Mary Anne?" James asked Kevin as he looked around the crowd that had congregated in the basement of the church after Billy Hoffman's funeral on Wednesday.

"Nae since the cemetery," Kevin answered. "Maybe she went home."

"I see Ruby, but not Mary Anne," James replied.

Other than English class, he hadn't had a chance to talk to her. Given the circumstances, the riding club hadn't met Saturday, and doing research on Monday hadn't seemed appropriate either. Today should have been research day, but school had been let out early for everyone to attend the funeral.

James scanned the room again. It looked like the entire town was packed into the basement, which served as a social meeting hall and had a kitchen at one end. There were a number of people he hadn't seen before, including guys wearing letterman jackets from the neighboring towns that competed with Middletown. The Ladies' Aid Society was serving a lunch of ham sandwiches, potato salad, baked beans, and lime Jell-O mixed with fruit. Another table held an assortment of cakes and pies, but James wasn't hungry.

The whole week had been surreal, but this afternoon especially so. The organist had chosen traditional hymns like "Nearer My God to Thee" and "I Am But a Stranger Here" which seemed to sooth the older folks. Someone had arranged for a bagpiper to do "Amazing Grace" and Kevin wanted to ask the man to add "Danny Boy." Billy's parents had asked for a contingent of the school band to play the fight song, which had the athletes roaring to belt out the words and left most of the girls crying, including the cheerleaders, who'd worn their uniforms. Even Mr. Hund had looked suspiciously bright-eyed and Coach Gibbs had choked up on the eulogy.

Janie Nelsen had sat stoically beside Billy's parents, wearing a white dress that contrasted sharply with the dark navy and black most of the adults wore and made Kevin want to add "In The Arms Of An Angel" to his requests for the piper.

James had only attended a handful of funerals back in Atlanta, and those were for elderly relatives of his parents, people who had been either frail or ill. Most of the comments were things like, "She can finally rest in peace," and "He's no longer in pain," or something about a formerly deceased husband or wife waiting on "the other side." James had never dealt with someone his own age dying. Probably most of his classmates hadn't either, since they were milling around silently, looking like lost sheep in need of a shepherd.

"I wish the piper had not left," Kevin said, surveying the room. "'Tis nothin' like the pipes to make a person feel sad and happy at the same time."

"I don't think too many people care about feeling happy right now."

"I can see that," Kevin replied. "Too bad they didna have a good Irish wake."

"Isn't that like a party?"

"Nae. Well, aye." Kevin shrugged. "In a way I

suppose ye could say so. Way back in Celtic lore it was believed that grievin' held a dead person's spirit to the earth and cryin' kept it from leavin'."

"These are modern times."

"Wakes these days are to remember the good times. 'Tis why we have the laughin' and drinkin'." Kevin winked. "And, the Irish bein' a wee bit superstitious, just in case the spirit lingers, we want it to have a good time rememberin' life."

James found himself smiling at his foster brother. "That's an interesting outlook."

"Ye might say a wake restores the souls of the livin'." Kevin turned contemplative. "It's kind of like the song "Turn, Turn, Turn." For everything there is a season. American customs are different. For the folks here, right now is nae the time to laugh."

"You're right." Movement at the entrance to the stairs caught James' eye and he turned to see Mary Anne coming in. He started to smile. A smile that turned to a frown. He glanced at Kevin, wondering again if his Irish friend was part leprechaun after all. Kevin could not have been more accurate when he said it was not the time to laugh.

Bob Colby was walking in behind Mary Anne.

****

Mary Anne had been surprised when Bob called her before school this morning saying he wanted to see her this afternoon before he went to work. She'd been even more pleasantly surprised when he agreed to attend the funeral, knowing it was something her mother would approve, which in turn meant more lenience for Mary Anne.

Bob had been late and hadn't actually gone into the

church, but he was waiting outside when the service was over.

"How come you didn't just come in?" Mary Anne asked as they went down the stairs to the church basement. "There were lots of people standing in the back."

"I'm not much for funerals," Bob replied. "All that crying gets me down."

"It bothers me too," Mary Anne said. "I guess we're both just sensitive to emotions."

"Some emotions," Bob said, "but not all that gushy stuff about "being called home" and there "being a master plan" for each of us, like we don't make our own decisions. Who believes in that stuff?"

Mary Anne bit her lip and looked around, hoping her mother—or Wendy—wasn't anywhere close. When their father had died, the pastor had been a great comfort to her mother, even if Mary Anne felt there was only a big, empty hole left. Wendy had been just nine and, for months, their mother kept saying their dad was sleeping in heaven and would wake up. It sounded silly now, but at the time, every time her mother said it, Wendy had stopped crying. Bob would probably just think it was silly.

"I've never asked," Mary Anne said, "but are your parents alive?"

A closed expression crossed Bob's face. "I guess my father is. I never knew him. I found out my mother moved to Houston after she sent me here."

"So she wasn't there when you went back to Chicago?"

"Nope."

How awful. Even though Bob had been eighteen

when he came to Minnesota, that still sort of made him an orphan. "How did you find out?"

Bob grimaced. "When I went back. Someone else was living in the apartment."

Mary Anne's heart went out to him. "I—"

"Look, I really don't want to talk about it, okay?"

"Of course." How horrible to find out that way. No wonder he didn't talk about his family much. She just wished she could get her own mother to understand how much Bob needed her. It probably hurt him to think her mother rejected him too. The thought made Mary Anne angry again. She put her hand on Bob's arm. "I just want you to know that I will be here for you."

"Music to my ears, babe." Bob gave her an intent look. "Do you mean it?"

"Yes. Very much."

"You'd really wait around if I…had to leave again?"

Mary Anne felt confused. "Do you have to go back to Chicago?"

He shook his head. "The U.S. Army."

"*What*?"

"The Army," he repeated. "Vietnam isn't going away."

Mary Anne's hand flew to her mouth to cover her gasp and to keep a sob from erupting. She listened to the news on TV sometimes and knew the war—or whatever they were calling it—was escalating, but Vietnam had always seemed so far away. She knew about the Selective Service and the draft, but it had never really affected Middletown, since most of the kids went on to some kind of vocational school if not college. Even the boys who remained on their family farms could apply for a deferment.

"Can't you get out of it?"

Bob shrugged. "Not unless I run off to Canada."

"But you have a job!"

"Not one that counts when it comes to recruits," Bob answered. "I got the letter yesterday. That's why I called this morning. I leave in two weeks."

Two weeks! That wasn't much time at all! Bob was going to have to go overseas and fight an enemy that wasn't even important. She'd been worried about his drag racing earlier. Now that seemed laughable, except that tears were welling up in her eyes. Her tears began to flow as Mary Anne turned and ran back up the stairs, away from the awful news.

Billy Hoffman had died because of a stupid ball game. Vietnam wasn't a game. What if Bob got hurt? Or killed?

Chapter Ten

From across the room in the church basement, James watched Mary Anne's expression change from smiles to something that looked like shock and then tears. When she turned and ran from the room, with Bob Colby following her, James started after them.

A restraining hand on his arm stopped him. He frowned and shook Kevin's hand off. "I need—"

"To leave it be," Kevin finished for him. "Nae good will come from pokin' your nose in business that is nae yours."

"I will make it mine."

One of Kevin's dark brows rose. "Ye are nae a fighter."

"I didn't say I was going to fight. I just want to know why that…that…jerk made Mary Anne cry."

"And ye will find out if she has a mind to tell ye," Kevin answered.

"But—"

"I've brought you some food." Wendy's arrival with a full plate stopped their conversation.

"I'm not hungry, thanks," James said. He knew after having seen that…that *idiot* upset Mary Anne that he wouldn't be able to swallow a bite.

"I'll take some, if ye doona mind," Kevin said.

Wendy looked disappointed, but she offered the plate to him. Kevin made some remark on how good the ham was, but James tuned the conversation out. What could Bob have said that made Mary Anne cry? In the South, boys, rich or poor, were raised to be gentlemen. Only the worst kind of cur made a girl cry. James had noticed the guys in Middletown had good manners too—most of them, anyway—but Bob Colby didn't look like he was from here. While a few of the boys in high school sported the Mod English look of mop haircuts and lapel jackets without lapels, and wore pointy-toed boots like the Beatles did, most of them still wore khakis and polos with wingtip shoes and kept their hair short. Bob had been wearing jeans and his leather jacket and had his hair slicked back, like James Dean in that old movie *Rebel Without a Cause*. James wondered what Mary Anne saw in the guy. Wendy interrupted his thoughts.

"Are you sure you don't want something to eat?" she asked. "The Ladies Aid Society takes offense if people don't finish off what they've made."

James understood the expectations of hospitality. He'd grown up ingrained with protocol. Food was offered as both a comfort and a friendly gesture. Refusal was considered rude. He glanced over to the tables where the buffet had been set out. A couple of elderly ladies who looked like they might be sisters were eyeing them with interest. He tilted his head toward them. "Like those two?"

Wendy followed his gesture and started to giggle, then quickly stopped as though she remembered where she was and for what reason. "Not them. They're Millicent and Minnie Gustafson. They never bring anything. Mainly, they're just nosy."

"Oh." James didn't want to be the cause of any gossip from old ladies, especially if it concerned Wendy.

He reached for the last sandwich—Kevin had devoured the rest—and bit into it, even though his mouth felt as dry as a plowed-under wheat field that hadn't seen rain in weeks. "Whom should I thank, then?"

Wendy pointed. "The ones over there by my mom. They're the ones who are the best cooks, too."

"And what is your mother's specialty?" Kevin asked.

"Pie. Especially apple," Wendy replied.

Kevin smiled. "Will ye show me which one is your mother's? I'd love a slice."

Wendy looked at James. "Would you like some of her pie too?"

"Yes, I would," James answered.

Wendy smiled and turned to lead the way. Kevin stayed right beside her, while James lingered behind. Since he'd already discovered Kevin had a sweet tooth, James suspected his friend was almost as eager to sample the pie as he was to keep Wendy company.

James wanted to taste the pie for another reason. His own mom always said every Southern woman loves having her cooking complimented. He suspected that was true of Northern women as well. He'd soon find out. Right now, he needed every advantage he could get.

****

"Wait up, babe!"

Mary Anne slowed down and wiped her tears with the back of her hand as Bob caught her arm and turned her around.

"Are you crying for me?" he asked as he pulled her into an embrace.

She nodded, nestling her head onto his shoulder. "I don't want you to go."

"I don't think Uncle Sam is giving me a choice, babe." He stepped back. "Let's go. People are leaving the church."

"Okay. Where's your car?"

"In the shop. That's why I was late," Bob answered. "Where's yours?"

"Mom has the keys."

"Guess we'll walk, then." Bob turned in the opposite direction from the town square.

"Where are we going?" Mary Anne asked.

"The park. It's got benches and more privacy than a café."

She followed him the few blocks to the town park. She hadn't been here in at least two years, although she used to love it. To one end were tennis courts where she would pretend to be Billie Jean King, which wasn't hard to do since Wendy was a lousy tennis player. To the other end was a municipal swimming pool. Mostly the "In" crowd hung out there in the summer, but it was closed for the season now. The park itself consisted of a fairly large green space, with gravel pathways winding through various flowerbeds. Only the marigolds and chrysanthemums were blooming this late in the fall, their oranges and yellows matching the leaves of the maple trees planted throughout the park. Tulips would blossom in the spring and roses in the summer. Mary Anne fought against more tears. Would Bob be around next summer?

"Come on, babe. Don't cry again," Bob said as he reached a bench and sat, tugging her down beside him. "I hate tears."

She sniffled and wiped at her eyes. "I can't help it. What if something happens to you?"

"Nothing's going to happen."

"How can you be sure? I don't want to lose you. Every day we hear on the news about soldiers being killed over in Vietnam."

"Not everyone gets sent to Nam," Bob said. "Besides, I'm just leaving for boot camp. Maybe, if I'm lucky, they'll kick me out of the Army."

Mary Anne blinked. "Are you going to try and get kicked out?"

He shrugged. "Don't know yet. I'll have to wait and see how I like it."

She drew her brows together. "You think you might *like* it? Nobody likes the Army. Well, maybe if you're a general or something. But not kids."

"I'm not a kid." He grinned and flexed a bicep. "Haven't you noticed?"

"That's not what I meant." Mary Anne attempted a smile. "Maybe you could apply for vocational school. That would get you a deferment."

"I was just glad to get out of high school," Bob replied. "I sure don't want to go back to a classroom."

"But it would be a way to keep you out of the Army and…" Mary Anne hesitated. "You could be here with me."

Bob studied her for a moment before answering. "Is that an invitation?"

"Yes. I want to be with you, spend more time with you."

He paused. "I'm not sure you really know what I'm asking."

Mary Anne frowned and then felt her face heat. "Oh. You mean…*that*."

Bob smiled. "*That* is what guys and girls do who care about each other."

Her face felt as though it was going to explode into flames. They'd come close to having this conversation before Bob had gone to Chicago. But that was over a year ago. Bob had come back and she was older now. "You want…to go all the way?"

His gaze intensified. "Do you?"

She didn't know. Mary Anne had been careful not to let him go too far before. But Bob wanted her for his girl. Hadn't he just said so? If they cared about each other, it would be all right. Wouldn't it? Slowly, she nodded. "I think so."

"You have to be sure. I don't want to be accused of rape." Bob's voice changed. "Tell you what. Boot camp is ten weeks. When I come back, you give me your answer." He stood and pulled her up with him. "I'll walk you back to your mother's car."

"Are you mad at me?"

He didn't answer for a moment as they walked and then he shook his head. "No. You're just not quite as grown up as you think you are."

Did Bob think she was a child? What if she lost him because he thought she was too young for him? "I'm almost eighteen!"

He smiled. "I'll keep that in mind, babe."

****

"Where'd you go earlier?" Wendy asked Mary Anne at supper that night. "We all saw you run off with Bob."

"I didn't *run off* with Bob," Mary Anne replied. "We went for a walk in the park, that's all." Geez. She had hoped her mother wouldn't notice. Now her mother was frowning. Mary Anne should have known her tattletale sister wouldn't keep still.

"I didn't see Bob at the funeral," Vivian said.

"He had to take his car into the shop and got there late."

"Why didn't he stay, then?" her mother asked.

"He followed me outside," Mary Anne said.

"Why did you leave?"

Mary Anne really didn't want to talk about it right now. She was still too close to tears. She glared at Wendy, who returned her look with open curiosity. Jo's expression was more sympathetic, although she didn't say anything. "It's personal. Okay?"

Her mother's eyebrows rose. "No, it's not 'okay.' For you to leave so abruptly without expressing proper condolences to the Hoffmans was rude. I had hoped I raised you better than that. I don't think Bob is a good influence."

If her mother were to find out what the subject of their conversation had been, she'd really think Bob was a bad influence. Thankfully, no one had overheard that. "I just wanted to get away."

"You're always running after Bob," Wendy said. "Every time—"

"Will you just shut up?"

"I—"

"Girls. Enough. Both of you are old enough not to argue at the table."

"Then can I be excused?" Mary Anne asked.

"In a minute." Vivian laid down her napkin and gave Mary Anne a thoughtful look. "I want to know what is going on, first. I may have to rethink our agreement about your seeing Bob."

"You won't have to worry about that for long," Mary Anne retorted.

"Watch your tone of voice, young lady." Vivian

frowned. "And, what do you mean by that?"

Mary Anne pushed back her chair and stood. "I'll tell you, then, since everyone wants to poke their noses into my business. Bob got a letter from Selective Service. He leaves for the Army in two weeks. Now is everyone happy?"

Without waiting for a reply, she turned and ran from the room. Nobody understood her. Nobody.

Chapter Eleven

As Mary Anne put on a pair of jeans Saturday morning, she considered refusing to take a riding lesson today, but she didn't want to jeopardize the ten days before Bob left by having her mother refuse to let her see him. Her mother was still upset with her for leaving the funeral reception. Mary Anne knew she'd been moody the past few days, although her mother had let her bad attitude slide, probably thinking it was an aftermath of Billy's death.

To some degree, that was true. The entire student body—or at least the seniors—had wild swings in mood and behavior the past week. One minute there would be animated conversation, maybe even a giggle, as though someone had forgotten the tragedy. The laughter was sharply curtailed by dark looks from other students. Then an eerie silence would fall over the class, slowly becoming a restive stirring until someone would begin to talk.

Janie had been absent from school all week and she didn't show up for the riding club this morning, either, not that Mary Anne had expected her to. If something like that had happened to Bob… Mary Anne shut the thought down. She'd replayed the possibility already too often.

Jo poked her head inside Mary Anne's bedroom. "Are you ready?"

99

"I'm dressed. I don't think I'll ever be ready to ride," Mary Anne answered as she walked toward the door.

"Sure you will," Jo said. "You may not be crazy about horses like Wendy and I are, but you've got to admit Flame has taken a liking to you."

"Monstrous beast that she is," Mary Anne replied, except she meant it only half-heartedly. Since two Saturdays ago when James had gotten her acquainted with the mare, she had been feeding her every day and even doing some grooming, although she was still scared of the horse's powerful hooves. It was meant as a compromise to pacify her mother since Mary Anne had not actually ridden Flame yet. Oddly enough, when she walked Flame in the paddock using the halter rope, the horse followed her placidly. A couple of times the mare had even pushed Mary Anne's shoulder gently with her muzzle, although Mary Anne's initial fear was that those big teeth were going to sink into her. When that didn't happen, she found herself gradually beginning to relax around the animal.

Jo smiled. "She won't seem so big once you get in the saddle."

Mary Anne sighed. "I guess I can't put that off any longer, can I?"

"The longer you put it off, the more time you'll have to worry about it," Jo answered. "Sometimes, it's just better to do it."

Mary Anne's heart skipped a beat. Jo couldn't possibly know about the conversation with Bob, but maybe she was right. Would it be better just to go ahead with what Bob wanted? Her mother had had a long talk with her and with Wendy when they each turned thirteen. They'd both been told—in no uncertain terms—that intimate relations had to wait until marriage. Their mother had also told them if they felt strongly attracted to a boy it was because of their changing hormones and they were too young to know what real love was. Mary Anne frowned and paused on the stairs. She knew how she felt and she was sure Bob cared for her. Didn't that make a difference?

"Are you really that scared?" Jo asked. "Flame will know if you are."

Mary Anne started. She hadn't even been thinking about the horse. "Uh…I'll be fine…I think."

"I think you'll be fine too," Jo said as they went down the steps. "James has already told your mom that he wants your first riding lesson to be inside the paddock, so you don't have to worry about being out on the trail."

Mary Anne grimaced. "Wendy probably wasn't happy hearing James won't be joining them."

"She's not." Jo glanced at Mary Anne sideways as they reached the hallway. "Maybe the guy a girl thinks she wants isn't the right one."

Mary Anne followed her into the kitchen, not sure if Jo was talking about Wendy or about her.

****

James let out a breath he didn't realize he'd been holding when he saw Mary Anne come out onto the porch. He'd been waiting with Kevin and the other riders in the yard and hadn't been sure she'd really decide to continue working with Flame. From what Wendy had told him, Mary Anne had only agreed to learn to ride because her mother wouldn't let her see Bob Colby if she didn't—and Bob would be leaving in two weeks.

Even though James could sympathize with anyone whose service number had been called up, he couldn't deny he was glad Bob would be leaving. With this being Mary Anne's senior year, Bob's absence would give James the perfect opportunity to escort her to special events. Or at least, he hoped so.

"I don't see why you can't ride with us," Wendy grumbled as she rode Jupiter over to where James stood. "It's not like Flame is going to start bucking or take off at a gallop, even with Mary Anne in the saddle."

"Horses can be unpredictable," James replied. "Besides, I promised your mom I'd make sure Mary Anne was safe. It'll be better to stay in the paddock."

"James is lettin' me ride his horse since he'll be workin' with Mary Anne," Kevin said. "I've been lookin' forward to this mornin'."

Wendy glanced at him. "Do you know how to ride?"

"Ye are woundin' me pride," Kevin said with a grin. "The Irish have a way with horses." He took the reins of James' chestnut and vaulted into the saddle. "Ye see?"

James refrained from laughing. Kevin had been practicing that vault for over a week. The first time he'd tried, the gelding had shied and Kevin had landed on the ground with a rather hard thump. That hadn't deterred him, though, since he was determined to impress Wendy.

It seemed he'd impressed Tim and Tommy's girlfriends, too, since they were nearly gaping at him with awe. The twins weren't looking amused.

"Okay. It's a cool trick," Wendy said, "but can you *ride*?" Without waiting for an answer she spun Jupiter around and set him to a gallop.

Kevin's grin widened as he tapped the chestnut's flanks and took off in pursuit with the rest of the group following more slowly. James shook his head.

"Wendy's such a show-off." Mary Anne still stood

on the porch.

James turned back to her. "Let's hope she doesn't try that vaulting trick, then. Kevin got a lot of bruises learning that."

Mary Anne walked down the steps. "He seems to know how to ride, though."

James nodded. "His dad trains Thoroughbreds in Ireland. Kevin played polo over there."

"Polo?"

"You know…it's a little like croquet on horseback."

"I know what it is," Mary Anne replied and then smiled a little. "I don't think Prince Charles would like that description, though."

James smiled back. "Probably not. The game's actually pretty dangerous."

"Let's hope Kevin doesn't introduce it to the riding group then. Wendy is such a dope, she'd want to play."

"And you're afraid she'd get hurt?"

"Well, yeah." Mary Anne shrugged. "Most of the time, Wendy is a real pest, but she *is* my sister."

"I wish I had a sister. Or a brother."

"You're an only child?"

"Yes."

"That sounds like heaven to me," Mary Anne said. "No one borrowing my clothes without permission or sneaking into my room to read my diary—"

"You keep a diary?"

She blushed a little. "Not really a diary. More like a journal. It's not like I do daily entries or anything. I just sometimes write things in a binder."

"Kind of like when you're down or depressed?" James asked.

Mary Anne looked surprised. "Yeah. How did you

know?"

"I do the same thing."

"You? You always seem so upbeat…and polite."

"It's how I was taught to be," James replied. "In the South, hospitality is a way of life. So are big families."

"But you don't have brothers or sisters."

"No. My mother nearly died giving birth to me. My father didn't want to take any more chances."

"I'm sorry," Mary Anne said. "I shouldn't have asked. My mother keeps saying I talk before I think."

"It's okay. I've got a bunch of cousins in Georgia," James answered.

"But they're hundreds of miles away."

James nodded. "My mom really misses family. It's one of the reasons we applied for an exchange student. We're glad Kevin came to stay with us."

"But he'll be leaving at the end of the year," Mary Anne said. "Won't your mother miss him?"

"Kevin really wants to stay and go to college in the States. He's got an eye on Notre Dame. The Fighting Irish and all that. His chances of getting in are better if he finishes the last two years of high school here rather than going back to Ireland."

"I suppose that makes sense," Mary Anne replied.

"Do you plan to go to college next year?" James asked.

"I…I'm not sure. I was thinking of going to the Twin Cities maybe."

"The University of Minnesota is there, isn't it?"

"Yes," Mary Anne said, "but my grades aren't good enough to get in. I'm not even sure what I want to do."

"Well, college is a good way to find out," James answered. "The first two years are pretty much basic classes that will fit any degree."

"But four more years of school doesn't sound appealing at all." Mary Anne tilted her head as she looked at him. "I suppose it does to you, though. You're the intellectual type."

James wasn't sure if that was a compliment or an insult. He knew girls weren't overly impressed with a guy making the honor roll. Good grades were important to him, but he wasn't all *that* bookish. He played on the tennis team and ran track. Before he could decide how to respond, she asked another question.

"Do you know what you want to do after high school?"

He didn't have to think about the answer to that. "Yes. I am going to be a veterinarian."

Mary Anne's eyes widened. "But that takes *years* of school!"

"I know, but I really like animals, so it's worth the time."

Mary Anne looked thoughtful. "I suppose another benefit would be that you don't have to worry about getting drafted."

Was she referring to Bob? Probably. James didn't want to talk about him. "Hopefully, the conflict in Vietnam will end soon and no one will have to worry about the draft."

"It's already too late for some guys, though," Mary Anne said. "I suppose you heard my boyfriend got his notice?"

James steeled himself not to flinch at Mary Anne's use of the word *boyfriend*. He hoped he could change her mind once Bob was gone. For now, he would have to be patient. Thankfully, it was a trait his father had ingrained in him. "I heard."

"Well, I can tell you this dumb project Mrs. Howell has us working on has taken on new meaning," Mary Anne said. "I'm going to research all the anti-war protests and demonstrations taking place across the country. It's just not fair Bob has to go."

James kept his face impassive. "I don't know if that is the direction Mrs. Howell wants us to take."

"She didn't say we couldn't, did she? I'm entitled to my opinion, aren't I?"

"You are." Mary Anne was getting a stubborn look on her face, and since James didn't want to get into an argument about Vietnam—or Bob—he decided to change the subject. "We'd better get on with your riding lesson."

Mary Anne looked reluctantly toward the barn and then snapped her head around at the sound of tires coming up the gravel yard road. James turned to look and groaned at the sight of the souped-up Chevy.

"It's Bob!" Mary Anne squealed and rushed to the car as it skidded to a stop. She leaned down to the open window. "I didn't know you were coming over."

"I don't have to go to work until this afternoon." Bob leaned across the seat and opened the door. "Hop in, babe. We'll go for a ride."

James took a few steps forward. "What about your riding lesson, Mary Anne?"

"That'll have to wait," she said and slid into the car. "You can take Flame and probably catch up to the others if you hurry."

Before James could answer, Bob sped away, spraying bits of gravel from the wheels. Mary Anne waved a hand out the window. James didn't wave back.

He suspected she wouldn't be looking anyway. Slowly, he walked toward the barn, trying not to be angry. For the first time, Mary Anne had opened up a little and had a personal conversation with him. He should give himself points for that. It was a start.

But James had never wanted to punch someone out as much as he did Bob Colby.

Chapter Twelve

"Dear lord. Not again." Vivian's voice could be heard from the living room. "Girls! Come here and listen to this!"

Wendy dropped her spoon into her ice cream bowl and raced out of the kitchen. Jo followed her. Mary Anne finished her mouthful first. "What is it?" she asked as she entered the parlor.

"Riots have broken out in San Francisco Bay area," Wendy replied and rose to turn up the volume on the television. "Sit down and listen."

Mary Anne flopped into an easy chair and draped a leg over the upholstered arm. From what she could tell, a white police officer had shot a black teenager running from a stolen car the day before. Pictures of angry young blacks throwing rocks at police flashed across the screen, followed by other officers in masks firing tear gas into the crowd, forcing them back. Mary Anne sat up straighter when a newsman sounded close to losing his cool as he reported the mayor of Bayview had just declared a state of emergency and a thousand National Guard troops were being sent in to subdue the crowd.

The National Guard was part of the U.S. Army. What if Bob ended up being one of those soldiers who had to fight against this mob that sounded crazed?

"I guess it's not surprising," Vivian said when the news program went to a commercial. "Things have really reached a boiling point. Riots have already broken out in Cleveland and Chicago—and now this."

Chicago. Bob had only recently returned. He hadn't mentioned anything, but then, he hadn't really ever said what he had gone back for or what the "trouble" was that had caused him to stay. Had he gotten caught in the riots?

Mary Anne hadn't paid a whole lot of attention to the Civil Rights Movement the last couple of years, since Middletown's population was mostly German and Scandinavian. With the exception of the Sioux Indian reservation where the casino was built, none of the other small towns around had minorities either, so they weren't affected.

"Are they rioting because it was a white police officer that shot that boy?" Wendy asked. "He was running away from a car he stole."

"*Allegedly* stole," Vivian replied. "Part of the problem is we are too quick to jump to conclusions sometimes."

Mary Anne raised an eyebrow. Hadn't her mother done that with Bob? Her mother must have noticed the gesture because she frowned.

"A lot of blacks think they are being targeted by white officers," Vivian said.

"Because they look different?" Mary Anne asked. "Like they don't fit in?"

Her mother gave her a level look. "Perhaps."

"It's a shame," Jo said. "Even singers like Joan Baez can't help."

"Joan Baez?"

"She walked a hundred black children to an all-white elementary school and got turned away," Jo replied. "It was on the news."

Wendy smirked. "Mary Anne doesn't watch the news. Anyhow, I thought President Johnson made a law about integrating schools."

"The president *signed* a law, " Mary Anne said. "*Congress* makes the laws, which you would know if you paid attention in class."

"Like you do," Wendy retorted.

"Girls." Their mother frowned at both of them. "Stop arguing. There's enough unrest in the world without you two fighting with each other constantly."

They glared at each other for a moment and then Wendy lapsed into sullen silence. Mary Anne turned her attention back to the television, where the talk had turned to statistics on Vietnam casualties, making her forget the clash with her sister.

Mary Anne hoped and prayed Bob would not become one of those statistics.

****

Mary Anne walked into the library after school the following Wednesday to find her group already assembled at the round table where they did their research. Kevin must have told a joke, because James was laughing and Wendy was too, although Mary Anne was pretty sure her sister was just mimicking whatever James felt. Ruby looked bored, but then she usually did.

"Sorry I'm late," Mary Anne said as she took the chair James had pushed out for her. "I had to go pick up my uniform."

"So you got the job at the grocery store?" James asked.

"Yeah. That's why I couldn't be here Monday. I had a second interview."

"Congrats," Ruby said. "You'll love having your

own money."

Mary Anne nodded. "I'm looking forward to some independence, for sure."

"Mom said if you got a job, you had to save half the money for college," Wendy said.

Ruby snorted. "What if she doesn't want to go to college?"

"Mom says she has to," Wendy retorted.

"Well, maybe I'll make my own decision on that," Mary Anne said.

Wendy gave her a wide-eyed look. "But Mom wants us both to go to college."

"Maybe I don't *want* to."

"But—"

"If I have my own money," Mary Anne interrupted, "I can do whatever I want."

James cleared his throat. "What hours are you going to be working?"

Thank goodness someone was changing the subject. Wendy could be as persistent as a fly. "To begin, Saturday mornings."

"Oh, good!" Wendy practically squealed. "That means James can come riding with us again."

Mary Anne tried not to smile. That same thought had crossed her mind and, best of all, her mother couldn't argue with her over it. Her smug thought left as she heard James' response.

"We'll just move the lesson to the afternoon, then."

"I'll probably be really tired," Mary Anne replied.

"There's something about bein' on a horse and out in nature that will boost your energy right back up," Kevin said. "Ye'll see."

Mary Anne decided to ignore that remark. "I have to

work Mondays and Thursdays after school, too."

"But that means we can't meet on Mondays after school," James said.

"Nope," Ruby smiled, looking quite pleased. "And I work Tuesdays and Thursdays, so we can only meet one day a week."

James looked disappointed. "This research is important. I'd like to spend more than just one afternoon a week on it."

Ruby stared at him like he was an alien who'd just sprouted antennae. "Good grief. You talked Mrs. Howell into making this whole stupid thing a term project for extra credit. It's not due until December. Of course," she added, "you're free to do as much research as you want to. Just count Mary Anne and me out."

"All three of us were assigned to it," James replied. "We agreed we'd work together."

"Yeah," Wendy said. "Besides, Mom will *really* be mad if Mary Anne drops out of this."

Ruby gave Wendy a cool-eyed look. "And why, precisely, are *you* here? This isn't your assignment."

Wendy blushed and looked down at the table.

Kevin spoke up. "She's just tryin' to help."

Mary Anne knew the only reason Wendy attended was because of James, but her sister looked mortified enough without pointing that out. "Our mother is a real stickler for learning. Wendy can probably use this information for her American History class."

Wendy looked up, surprise briefly flitting across her face. "Yeah. Our teacher did say we'd have to write a paper."

"That sounds like a good idea," Kevin said. "Junior year is when you learn how to do research for a term paper, isn't it?"

"Yeah," Wendy answered.

He smiled at her. "Then I'll be needin' to learn as well. We can work together."

"I think that's an excellent idea," James said. "Maybe we can divide some of the work up."

"I have a better idea. Let's have Wendy and Kevin do all the research, then. It will be good experience for them." Ruby laughed and then shook her head when everyone stared at her. "Geez. I was only kidding."

Mary Anne hid another smile. Kevin didn't look like he thought Ruby was kidding at all. Even more important, he looked as though he *liked* the idea…and liked Wendy.

Her sister was really stupid if she couldn't see that.

****

James frowned at the group sitting around the library table and wondered what caused Mary Anne to smile. So far this afternoon, none of the news had been good. Mary Anne was going to be working on one of the two days they'd agreed to meet, and Saturday mornings as well. She hadn't actually agreed to riding lessons on Saturday afternoons, and James didn't know if her mother would make her learn to ride now that Bob Colby was leaving.

Somehow James would have to convince Mary Anne that Kevin was right. There was a sense of fulfillment in being in the saddle and riding the countryside.

"Let's get started on our research," Mary Anne said. "I'd like to drive out to Bob's place before I go home to supper."

Not exactly the words James wanted to hear.

"I'll go with you," Wendy said, "since I don't have a ride home."

"James and I can— Ouch!" Kevin bent down to rub his leg and give James a rueful look.

He hadn't meant to kick Kevin very hard, but the idea of Wendy being a chaperone for any meeting Mary Anne might have with Bob definitely appealed to James. "Yes, let's get started."

"I find this whole peace-and-love concept interestin'," Kevin said, apparently having decided not to comment on the kick right now. "I like the slogan 'Make love, not war.' A nice ring to it, it has."

James wasn't sure if Kevin meant that for Wendy or not since he was looking directly at her when he said it. "That sort of only applies to the hippies out in San Francisco."

"Don't kid yourself," Ruby said. "Not everything is all groovy there either. The hippies may be wearing flowers in their hair and spouting off about peace, but we've got plenty of folks still hating each other because their skin is a different color."

"That's true," James said. "Just this summer one of the leaders of the March Against Fear was shot on the second day of the walk. Another Civil Rights leader was killed in Mississippi when his home was fire-bombed."

"Yeah, and now there's talk about blacks uniting and fighting back instead of trying to integrate in a nonviolent way," Wendy said. "Our mother was talking about reading it in the paper."

Kevin nodded. "In Ireland, things are really heatin' up between us and Ulster in the north."

"Why?" Wendy asked.

"'Tis a bit of a long story," Kevin said, "but it goes

back to the 1600s when King William confiscated Irish lands and sent English nobles to live on them. It didn't take long before Irish Catholics were thought a threat to the English lords. They started implementin' laws to take away our rights to own guns, to go to school, or even to vote."

"But that's all changed, hasn't it?" Mary Anne asked. "I mean, this is the Sixties."

"Aye. Ireland won her independence in this century, but Northern Ireland—Ulster—remained British and the people stayed Protestant."

"And you can't get along." Ruby didn't make it sound like a question.

Kevin shrugged. "There's those who still want the whole isle to be independent from England. They formed the Irish Republican Army. Just last spring they bombed Admiral Nelson's pillar in Dublin."

James frowned. "I thought the I.R.A. was outlawed."

"That doesn't stop it from operatin'," Kevin answered. "In Belfast this summer, someone dropped a concrete block from a roof and barely missed the Queen as she passed by. The I.R.A. claimed credit."

"But why?" Wendy asked again. "Is it about religion?"

"Not exactly," Kevin replied. "A lot of young Catholics in Northern Ireland are educated but feel they're discriminated against in gettin' jobs and housing."

"Kind of like what Dr. King has been saying about blacks here," James said.

Kevin nodded. "In Ireland, Reverend Paisley leads the young people. They don't trust the Royal Ulster

Constabulary to protect their rights, so they protest."

"Our black people don't trust the cops either," James said. "Especially after what happened in the San Francisco Bay area."

Ruby smirked. "So not everything in San Fran is all peace and love, is it?"

"I guess not," James replied.

"But it's a place to start," Mary Anne said. "Whether blacks and whites are fighting each other or we're fighting Asians in Vietnam, the violence needs to stop. Too many people are getting killed."

James wondered if she was worrying about Bob, but he wasn't about to ask.

"It's a start," Mary Anne said again, a determined look settling on her face. "Peace has to start somewhere."

****

Mary Anne toyed with her scrambled eggs, pushing them back and forth on her plate. Although she had fervently prayed for a thunderstorm—or at least rain—Saturday morning dawned crisp, cool, and sunny. There wasn't any way she was going to get out of a riding lesson today. Her job training didn't start until Monday...the day Bob would be leaving. Mary Anne had hoped her mother would just let this whole riding thing go. But no. Vivian had reminded her they'd had an agreement and Mary Anne hadn't held up her part. If she didn't ride today, she would not be able to go out with Bob tomorrow night. His last night home. Mary Anne couldn't believe her mother could be so mean.

Jo looked at her. "How come you aren't eating?"

"I'm not hungry."

"You aren't on one of those stupid diets again, are you?" Wendy asked as she helped herself to a second slice of thick ham and some more toast.

"I'm not on a diet."

"Well, you better eat up," Wendy replied. "The riding club will be here soon."

As if she needed reminding. She had seriously thought about claiming to be sick—her stomach was queasy—but her mother was already eyeing her with a "don't even think of it" look that meant she'd brook no excuses. Mary Anne heaved a long sigh when horses could be heard coming up the yard road a few minutes later.

"Come on," Jo said. "I'll help you saddle Flame."

Mary Anne rose reluctantly and followed her cousin out toward the barn. "I don't know if I can do this."

"Sure you can," Jo said. "You know Flame likes you. Just relax and trust her."

Jo had just finished saddling the mare when James walked into the barn. Something about him seemed different, but Mary Anne wasn't sure what it was in the dim light. He was dressed in denim jeans and a chambray blue shirt that was almost standard uniform for the riders. His hair looked like it always did, not long, not short, combed to one side and falling slightly over his forehead.

"Where are your glasses?" Jo asked.

His glasses. Geez. She hadn't noticed he wasn't wearing glasses. That just showed how nervous she was.

"I cracked a lens," James replied. "Mom's going to drop them off at the optometrist's office this morning."

Maybe this was her reprieve, after all. "If you can't see well, we can put off the riding lesson."

James smiled at her. "I can see well enough to ride."

So much for that thought, then. Flame nickered near Mary Anne's shoulder and she jumped, causing the mare to toss her head.

"Easy there," James said.

Mary Anne wasn't sure if he was talking to her or the horse. She felt almost as skittish as Luke's horse, Silver, that Jo rode. Mary Anne remembered what Jo had said about trusting Flame. Tentatively, she put out a hand and stroked Flame's neck. Flame blew softly through her nose.

"Let's get you up and mounted," James said.

"Here? In the barn? I thought—"

"Better here than outside with everyone watching," Jo said. "You know how the twins can be."

Mary Anne definitely didn't want to be the subject of their taunts and jeers. She looked up at Flame. Her back suddenly seemed really high. "I need something to step up on."

"Allow me." James intertwined his fingers and bent over, forming a step. "I'll give you a leg up."

"Go ahead," Jo said, moving to take hold of the bridle. "I'll hold her still."

Mary Anne wasn't at all sure how stable any of this would be, but she grabbed hold of the saddle horn and placed her sneakered foot in James' hands. Surprisingly, she felt herself practically flying through the air. Even so, she only got her other leg partially over Flame's back.

"Hang on," James said as he put his hands around Mary Anne's waist and raised her over the saddle so she had room to swing her leg over. Although she wasn't heavy, she wasn't a lightweight either, but he'd lifted her as though she weighed no more than a feather pillow. How could anyone be that strong?

Mary Anne didn't have much time to ponder on it because Jo had looped the reins over Flame's neck and handed them to her. "I don't remember what you said to do with—"

"Neck rein," Jo answered. "If you want to turn right, press the left rein against Flame's neck. Do the opposite if you want to go left."

"Don't worry. I'll lead you to the paddock," James said.

Jo nodded. "I'll go and open the gate."

James placed a hand on one rein and began to move forward. Flame followed docilely. Mary Anne felt herself shift forward, then sway across the saddle, go slightly backwards and across again much like a slow version of using a hula hoop.

As they moved outside, Mary Anne saw the others standing by the porch. She tried to look nonchalant. Tim and Tommy hooted and clapped, which caused Flame to sidestep. Mary Anne grabbed the saddle horn to hang on, even though James had already steadied the horse.

"Geez. You don't grab the horn…" Wendy started and then stopped and stared at James as though starstruck.

Mary Anne looked down at him from her perch, wondering what had caused her sister to suddenly stop talking. At the same time, James looked up and the sun caught the gold streaks in his hair and deepened the color of his eyes. Mary Anne remembered Wendy had said they reminded her of brown velvet, although there wasn't anything soft about his gaze right now. His brows came together in a straight line as he glared at the twins. He looked like the guy from *Gunsmoke* about to take care of the bad guys.

Wendy was still gaping, but Tim and Tommy had stopped their laughing. Mary Anne almost giggled herself, thinking James had intimidated the twins. Which, the more Mary Anne reflected on it, was *really* hard to do.

And James had not said one word.

Wendy apparently had found her tongue. "I think I'll stay and help with the lesson," she said as she hurried toward them.

"No need for that," Kevin called out. "James can handle it."

"But I can help," Wendy said. "I'll give some pointers."

Her sister was no more interested in *helping* her than Mary Anne was in being given advice. Her sister was acting about as silly as those girls who fainted over the Beatles. "I don't want you to miss your ride, Wendy."

"But—"

"All the horses need exercise," Jo said. "We've not been riding much since what happened to Billy. Besides, too many people around will just make Mary Anne nervous and that will affect the horse. Let's go."

"Jo's right," James said. "An audience is not the best thing for a first lesson."

Wendy looked as though she were going to argue the point, but Jo took her arm and tugged her away. Wendy looked over her shoulder, giving Mary Anne a dirty look that said "later."

Mary Anne sighed, then clutched the saddle horn again as James led Flame into the paddock. Audience or not, she hoped she wouldn't fall off.

As if James sensed her fear, he glanced up. "You'll be fine, Mary Anne. I'll make sure of it."

Chapter Thirteen

Sunday night had finally come. Mary Anne had counted the hours until her date with Bob yet wished time would stand still so he wouldn't have to leave. She parted the parlor curtain to check the yard road, but there was no sign of him yet. She sat down on the edge of the sofa, careful to keep her black linen jacket closed over the red, spaghetti-strapped straight dress with a low neckline that she'd ordered from Sears. Her mother had only seen the bottom half of it.

She wanted to look sophisticated tonight and not like a high school kid. Bob was taking her to dinner at a hilltop dinner club known for its darkly lit interior and intimate atmosphere. Mary Anne had never been there, since it was mainly a place for the over-twenty-one crowd, but she'd heard about how romantic it was. She hadn't told her mother where they were going, simply that Bob wanted to take her someplace nice for his last night home.

His last night. Mary Anne felt unshed tears stinging her eyes and blinked rapidly. The last thing she needed was to look splotchy and red-eyed when Bob arrived. She heard Jo and Wendy coming down the hall and wasn't sure if she was relieved at the distraction or not.

"You look nice," Jo said when they entered the parlor.

Wendy squinted. "Is that a new dress?"

Mary Anne fingered the buttons on the jacket to make sure it was closed. "I ordered it a while ago. I just haven't worn it."

"It's kinda bright. Looks tight, too."

Trust Wendy to point that out. Mary Anne had managed to stand behind a kitchen chair earlier when she'd talked to her mother. "The material's pulling because I didn't straighten it before I sat down."

Wendy continued her scrutiny. "Heels, too."

"They're not that high." Mary Anne hadn't had enough money saved to order both the dress and a pair of spike heels, so she'd had to make do with the two-inch ones she had.

Wendy narrowed her eyes. "Where are you going all dressed up?"

Mary Anne shrugged. "Someplace nice."

"You'll stick out like a neon sign anywhere around here," Wendy said. "You'd have to go to Mankato to get to a fancy restaurant."

"There are some nice places not that far away."

"Like where?"

Mary Anne was spared an answer by the sound of Bob's car coming up the drive. She started to get up when her mother appeared in the doorway.

"You don't need to run out to meet him," she said.

Mary Anne started to protest, then stopped. She wasn't going to do anything that might make her mother change her mind at the last minute. With a sigh, she settled back on the sofa. Bob honked the horn and she started to fidget.

Her mother gave her a firm look. "Bob can come to the door."

It seemed an agonizingly long time before Mary

Anne heard footsteps and a knock. Mary Anne nearly flew off the couch and hurried to answer it.

Bob whistled when she opened the door. "Wow. You look really…" He paused and looked over her shoulder. "…nice."

Mary Anne didn't have to turn around to know her mother was behind her. Jo and Wendy probably were too.

"Thanks. I'm starved. Let's go," she said as stepped outside before her mother could start an interrogation. She turned slightly. "See you guys later."

Vivian's face looked pinched. "Remember to be home by ten. It's a school night."

Gosh, did her mother need to say that? Mary Anne didn't want Bob being reminded of high school. And ten o'clock! That was an early curfew, even if it was Sunday. Mary Anne wanted Bob to see her as an adult tonight. To remember her as an adult when he left for basic training tomorrow.

"Did you hear me?" Vivian asked. "I don't want to worry about you being out late."

Mary Anne felt heat sweep across her face. Her mother was treating her like a child. She might as well fold dimes in a hanky for Mary Anne to use in a coin phone in case of an emergency, like she used to do when they were kids.

"Don't worry, Mrs. Wade. I'll have her home by ten," Bob said.

Vivian nodded and closed the door.

Bob grimaced as he and Mary Anne walked to his car. "Your mother still doesn't like me."

Mary Anne didn't bother to deny it. "I don't know why. You're leaving for the Army. That practically makes you a hero."

He smiled. "Let's hope I don't ever have to be a hero."

"You're still leaving."

"Let's not talk about that either," he said and opened the car door for her.

Bob was acting like a real gentleman. Mary Anne almost looked back to see if her mother was watching from the window before she got into the car.

"I got a couple of new eight-tracks," Bob said as he put the car into gear and drove down the driveway. "Choose one."

Mary Anne picked them up. One was Simon and Garfunkel's *Sounds of Silence* which included "I Am A Rock." Mary Anne wasn't feeling that stoic. The other was the Beatles' *Yesterday and Today*, which seemed more appropriate. She slid it into the slot of the player Bob had installed under his dashboard and listened to Paul sing.

"I feel like he's really singing to me," Mary Anne said after several songs had been played. "Yesterday— or before you got your draft notice—my troubles really did seem to be far away."

"Yeah, well. There's another song coming up. 'We Can Work It Out.' "

Mary Anne shook her head. "I think those lyrics are about a girl who doesn't want to see things his way."

"Well, that's not you." Bob grinned at her. "Just concentrate on the title."

Mary Anne smiled back. "I would love to have things work out for us."

"Me too," Bob replied as he pulled the car into the parking lot of the Rendezvous. "Looks like a full house tonight."

"I wouldn't think it would be so packed for a Sunday," Mary Anne said as they walked to the front door and entered.

"The Rendezvous operates under a private club license which means they can sell booze on a Sunday," Bob said, "which is why there are so many people here."

She wrinkled her brow. "Are you a member?"

"Nah. The management gives out one-night guest memberships to get around it."

A door hostess wearing heavy eyeliner smiled brightly at Bob as she seated them and handed him a registry card. Her hand lingered over his as he signed and handed it back. Mary Anne tried to suppress a surge of jealousy. Instead, she looked around.

In one corner a woman in a midnight-blue satin gown played on a baby grand piano, illuminated by a candelabra on a stand beside her. Something from *Cabaret*, Mary Anne thought. The rest of the room where they were seated had dark wood wainscoting with red velvet wallpaper flocked with gold fleur-de-lis above that. Wall sconces that looked like old-fashioned oil lamps provided a dim, enticing atmosphere. White linen covered the small tables, each of which had a small chimney lamp placed in the middle. The effects of the flickering wick both highlighted and shadowed Bob's features, and he looked a little like Lee Van Cleef from *The Good, The Bad, and The Ugly*…dangerous, but intriguing. The atmosphere of the whole place seemed like something right out of a movie.

Bob gave a low whistle as Mary Anne slipped out of her jacket and he eyed her bodice. "Wow, babe. I wanted to tell you how great you looked when I picked you up, only your mother was there. I had no idea of how hot you really looked."

Mary Anne felt herself blush. The dress suddenly felt much more revealing under Bob's sharpened gaze than it had when she put it on earlier. She resisted the urge to tug at the thin straps to make sure the neckline wasn't too low.

"I've got a fake ID," Bob said, slowly turning his eyes toward her face. "Can I get you something from the bar?"

"Won't they want to card me too?"

"Probably not. Like I said, it's legally a private club. As long as the bartender doesn't directly serve you, he won't ask any questions." Bob pushed his chair back. "What'll it be?"

Mary Anne tried to remember which drinks were supposed to be good. She didn't care that much for beer. She'd sipped wine at home on special occasions like Christmas, but that seemed a little dull for such a glamorous place. Maybe she'd have a martini like James Bond. Shaken, not stirred. She smiled. "A vodka martini, please."

Bob hesitated. "Have you had a martini before?"

She didn't want him to think she was a naïve schoolgirl, but she didn't want to lie either. "Not really. It sounds good, though."

"They're pretty strong. I don't want you getting too tipsy. How about if I get you a Seven-Seven instead?"

"What's that?"

"Whiskey with soda pop," Bob replied, "so it won't go to your head so quickly."

She liked the fact that Bob didn't want her to get drunk. If her mother would only try and understand that he cared… Mary Anne nodded. "That sounds okay."

"Be right back."

Mary Anne watched him disappear into a side room where the bar was located and sighed contentedly. She felt very much the grownup, seated in a swanky restaurant that felt like a nightclub and having a cocktail before dinner. When Bob returned, she was happy to note that he'd chosen the same drink, which just proved he was responsible and didn't want to get drunk either.

She took a sip, the fizz from the carbonation tickling her nose. "Ummm. This is really good. I can't even taste the whiskey."

"It's a smooth drink. Lots of customers at the casino order it."

"Can we finish these before we order?" Mary Anne asked as a waiter started to approach.

"Sure," Bob said and motioned the waiter away. "Take your time."

The drink really tasted mostly of the soda pop. Mary Anne took a few more swallows. "I really like this place."

"Then let's do it right," Bob said.

"What do you mean?"

"We'll do a grand dinner. Finish the cocktails, then order what we want to eat. A glass of wine comes with the meal. Afterwards, we'll have a cognac with dessert."

"Isn't that a lot of alcohol?"

"Not that much. The food will absorb most of it."

"Okay." Mary Anne didn't want Bob to think she was totally unsophisticated. This drink wasn't that strong, and she'd had wine before.

By the time they'd finished dinner, a warm glow filled Mary Anne. The red and gold of the wallpaper seemed to flow together like the colors of sunset. "This place is so cozy and intimate, isn't it?"

Bob gave her a strange look. "I like that word…intimate. It makes me want to kiss you."

Mary Anne giggled. "Go ahead."

"Not here. Come on." Bob laid some bills on the table. "The Bluff isn't far from here. We can go park. It'll just be the two of us."

Mary Anne giggled again. "Okay. Sounds good."

"That's my girl," Bob said and rose to pull her chair out. "We've got a good hour before I have to get you home."

Mary Anne wobbled a bit and Bob steadied her, tucking her hand in the crook of his arm. "Just hang on to me, babe."

She nodded, then lifted her chin as they walked past the slinky door hostess, who gave her a cool-eyed look. Well, let her look. *She* wasn't leaving with Bob, Mary Anne was. And she had a whole hour before she had to be home.

As they walked outside, the evening air felt almost balmy for this time of year. Perfect for the romantic mood she was in. From the squeeze of Bob's hand on hers, he felt the mood too.

They had just about reached his car when a flashlight shone in their faces. Mary Anne put her hands up to avoid the glare. When the light shifted, she lowered her hands to see a police officer standing beside them.

"I'm going to have to see some IDs," he said.

Chapter Fourteen

"You are so busted!" Wendy said as she burst in to Mary Anne's bedroom the next morning.

Her sister's voice sounded like a kettle drum that served to increase the throbbing in Mary Anne's head. She didn't bother to open her eyes. She didn't need Wendy to remind her what had happened last night. The look of irritation on her mother's face when Mary Anne got home almost an hour past her curfew had changed to concern when she saw a police officer escorting Mary Anne. That concern turned quickly to anger when her mother found out *why* an officer had brought Mary Anne home.

The only good thing was she hadn't been arrested.

A sudden glare of sunlight as Wendy opened the curtains caused Mary Anne to wince and made the pounding in her head worse. She put a hand over her eyes to shield them. "Shut the blasted curtains."

"It's past seven," Wendy said. "Time to get up for school."

Mary Anne rolled onto her side and pulled the covers over her head. "No. Leave me alone."

"Mom's already mad. Do you want to make it worse?"

Mary Anne groaned and pushed the covers back. After the officer left, all her mother had said was that they would talk in the morning.

Unfortunately, it was morning.

Maybe there wouldn't be time to "talk" before school if she tarried. But then, putting it off until this afternoon would only give her mother more time to think.

Mary Anne swung her legs over the side of the bed and slowly sat up, hoping the hammering in her head would stop. The headache was making her feel nauseous.

"You look like crap," Wendy said.

"Thanks."

"Your face is puffy and your eyes are red," Wendy added.

"Will you just shut up?"

"I can't believe you got drunk," Wendy continued as though Mary Anne hadn't spoken. "That was really stupid."

Mary Anne wished she had something to throw at her sister, but the only thing handy was a pillow and even that seemed like too much effort. "I didn't mean to."

"Bob shouldn't have let you drink at all," Wendy said. "You aren't old enough."

So the officer had told her last night. And told Bob. They'd both endured a lengthy lecture by the cop, which was part of the reason she'd gotten home late. Thank goodness the officer hadn't questioned Bob's fake ID. Only the fact that Bob was leaving for the Army Monday had prevented him from going to jail.

Monday was *today*. Bob was leaving today. Ignoring her aching head, Mary Anne reached for her clothes and started dressing. "I've got to go say goodbye to Bob."

Wendy looked at her incredulously. "Do you think Mom is going to let you do that? After what happened?"

"If you don't snitch on me, I can drive over there before school."

Wendy shook her head. "Mom's driving us to school."

"What? I always drive."

"Not anymore," Wendy said.

"But Bob's leaving this morning. I won't be able to say goodbye."

Wendy hesitated, looking almost sympathetic. "I think that's the point."

Mary Anne sank back onto her bed, fighting tears as they welled up. She wasn't going to get to see Bob before he left, and he would be gone for at least ten weeks. Almost three months. She squeezed her eyes shut.

Her mother definitely had made her point.

And Mary Anne hated her for it.

****

Mrs. Howell, in Mary Anne's last-period English class, was prattling on about Dante's *Inferno* as if any of the nine circles of Hell were any worse than the day Mary Anne had just been through.

Not only had she felt sick until sometime after lunch, but Ruby was absent today. Mary Anne had hoped to borrow her car and skip a couple of morning classes to go see Bob. So what if she got caught? What did she have to lose? Her mother had told her this morning she was grounded until further notice. Not that it mattered a lot, since Bob would be gone.

But Mary Anne had wanted to say goodbye. She'd also wanted to reassure him—and get reassurance back—that she was his girl, that nothing had changed because of what happened last night. Now it was too late. Bob would have left on the noon bus for Minneapolis and the airport. She squeezed her eyes shut to keep tears from spilling.

"Are you okay?" James whispered.

Mary Anne took a deep breath and nodded. "My eyes are burning, that's all."

'Do you think you need glasses?"

"No talking," Mrs. Howell said.

For once, Mary Anne was glad to oblige. It kept James from asking too many questions. Since their riding lessons had begun and he'd not insisted she ride until she felt comfortable, and then the way he had eased her tensions when she finally did get in saddle, Mary Anne realized James had an uncanny ability to pick up on her emotions. She certainly didn't want him finding out how she was feeling right now. Anger at her mother, bitterness that Bob had been drafted, and resentment that she was still stuck in school all warred inside her head. James would probably try to make her feel better—which, right now, would have the opposite effect.

At least, he didn't know about last night's disaster. No one at school did. The police officer had brought her straight home, and her mother had forbidden big-mouth Wendy from speaking about it. Jo had assured them all she would keep quiet too.

James passed her a note. *Can we talk after school?*

Mary Anne stared at the note. Drat it. James knew something was wrong. Maybe she should just tell him she was sad because Bob left for the Army. That was an understatement, but maybe James would say he understood and let it go. Or maybe not. James was too honest to offer sympathy when he didn't mean it. She sensed he didn't like Bob. He probably thought Bob wasn't a "southern gentleman" like he was. Anyway, she didn't want sympathy. Mary Anne scribbled back. *Sorry. I have to go to work*.

James looked like he wanted to reply, but Mrs. Howell was peering at them over her glasses. He shoved the note under his book. He probably didn't want an additional assignment added to the project they already had. Mary Anne turned her attention to the teacher, although she didn't listen.

Having a job had never sounded so good. Not only was she going to avoid a prying conversation with James, but she was about to start earning money she could call her own.

And do with it whatever she wanted.

****

"Holy moly," Ruby said at lunch the next day. "Are you sure no one saw you?"

They'd grabbed sandwiches from the express line and gone outside before Wendy or anyone else could find them. Several students were sitting on benches in the small courtyard, but Mary Anne and Ruby walked toward a large oak tree near the cafeteria exit. If they positioned themselves just right, its trunk was large enough to shield them from searching eyes.

"I'm sure," Mary Anne said. "There weren't any kids at the Rendezvous."

"Was it as nice as they say? I've never been."

"Better. I felt so special." For a moment, Mary Anne let her thoughts drift back to how wonderful the evening had been. "We were going to the Bluff, too."

"The place overlooking the river valley?"

"Yeah. I've always wanted to go there on a date. Last night was a full moon. It would have been so romantic."

Ruby raised both brows. "You *do* know what kids do there, right?"

"Well, of course. They make out."

"They do more than that," Ruby said. "Since the drive-in movies have cracked down on kids steaming up the car windows from the back seats, the Bluff is where they go."

Mary Anne frowned. "Have you been there?"

"Once," Ruby replied, "but the cops got there just as we did and my date turned around fast."

"The cops?"

"Yeah. They raid the place all the time." Ruby paused. "Maybe it's a good thing you got caught when you did. Your mom would have really lost it if you'd been caught out there."

"My mother already went ballistic," Mary Anne said. "I'm grounded like forever."

"That's not really a big deal," Ruby answered. "I mean, with Bob gone. What's there to do in Middletown anyway?"

"I suppose you're right about that, but she also told me she's confiscating any letters Bob sends. Our mail comes right after noon, before I get home." Mary Anne crushed the cellophane from her sandwich into a tight ball. "It's so unfair."

"That's a bummer all right." Ruby looked thoughtful. "How about if Bob sends the letters to me? Then I can give them to you without your mother finding out."

Mary Anne stared at her. "You'd do that?"

"Well, sure. What are friends for? You know what base he's going to?"

"Yes. Fort Benning, in Columbus, Georgia."

Ruby smiled. "Good. Write Bob a letter and tell him to send the reply to me."

Mary Anne smiled back, finally feeling a slim shimmer of hope. "I'll do it."

****

By Wednesday afternoon when the group met in the library after school, Mary Anne felt marginally better. At least now she had a plan. She'd written Bob and given the letter to Ruby yesterday to send, since she didn't want to explain to Wendy—or anyone else—why otherwise she would stop at the Main Street post office. Being a cashier at the grocery store hadn't proved difficult either, and she planned on asking for more hours once her probationary period was over. The more money she could save, the better.

James was the only one seated at the table when she walked in. She put down her books. "Are we the only ones today?"

"Don't know," James replied. "I saw Ruby stomping down the hall a little while ago. She looked angry."

Mary Anne wondered if Ruby's mother was acting up again. Ruby hadn't been in English class, so Mary Anne had thought she'd gone home after lunch. Ruby's father was gone a lot and her mother tended to drink, sometimes too much, when he was gone. After the hangover Mary Anne had on Monday, she didn't understand why anyone would *want* to get drunk, but Ruby just shrugged it off whenever her mother did.

"I'm surprised Wendy isn't here…or Kevin." Mary Anne said.

"Kevin is probably with Wendy, wherever she is." James smiled. "He has a crush on her."

Mary Anne almost told James that Wendy had a

crush on *him,* but she bit her tongue. If James was that oblivious to Wendy's obvious attention, it would do no good to point it out. Besides, why burst her sister's bubble? Mary Anne's bubble had been burst. Let the kid enjoy her fantasy while she could.

Just as they were opening their binders to start taking notes, Wendy burst through the door at the far end of the library, followed by a disheveled-looking Kevin. Wendy ran toward them, ignoring the librarian's admonishment to walk. As she got closer, Mary Anne could see she was crying.

"What's the matter?" Mary Anne asked, getting up.

James pushed back his chair as well and glowered at Kevin. "What did you do to make her cry?"

"Nothin'. I was tryin' to stop a fight."

James frowned. "A fight?"

"Aye." Kevin tucked in the part of his polo shirt that was hanging out and raked a hand through his hair, wincing at a red spot on his temple. "Girls fight dirty."

"*Girls?*" James looked stunned. "You fought with girls?"

Kevin scowled at him. "Nae. I was tryin' to protect Wendy from gettin' hit."

"Wendy?" Mary Anne turned to her sister. "You were fighting?"

"It wasn't my idea. It was Ruby's."

"Ruby's?" Mary Anne studied her sister. Had Wendy somehow found out about the letter to Bob? "Why were you and Ruby fighting?"

"We' weren't." Wendy sniffled and took the linen handkerchief Kevin had produced from his pocket. "Not each other, anyway,"

"I don't understand," Mary Anne said. "Was Ruby

fighting someone?"

"She did look angry earlier," James said. "Maybe you'd better explain."

"Wait." Mary Anne held up her hand. "Where is Ruby?"

"In The Hound's office, I think," Wendy replied. "He came running down the street to break up the fight."

"Down the… Okay. Everyone sit down," James said. "Let's start from the beginning. What happened?"

"It wasn't my fault," Wendy said as Kevin held a chair for her. "I didn't say anything. I swear!" She started crying again, louder this time, drawing the librarian's ire once more. "You've got to believe me. I didn't say anything!"

"About what?" Mary Anne asked, beginning to feel uneasy.

James looked at Kevin. "Do you know what this is about?"

He shook his head. "I was waitin' for Wendy after class when Ruby stormed by, sayin' something about makin' sure a couple of girls—she called them somethin' else—with big mouths stopped spreadin' rumors about Mary Anne. Wendy followed Ruby and I followed Wendy."

"Rumors? What kind of rumors?" James turned to Mary Anne. "Do you know why anyone would want to do that?"

In spite of what she'd told Ruby, someone must have found out about Sunday night's episode. Mary Anne felt ill. What should she say? If, by some slim chance, this whole thing *wasn't* about Sunday night, she certainly didn't want to spill the beans.

"I'm not exactly the most popular girl in school."

Mary Anne managed to shrug, although her shoulders felt as though cement blocks were sitting on them. "Maybe Ruby misunderstood what was actually said."

James looked back to Wendy, who was still crying, although not quite as loudly. "Do you know what was said?"

"I…" Wendy glanced at Mary Anne and then shook her head. "I can't say."

James lowered his voice. "The librarian just put down the phone and is coming over here. Someone, think of something to say."

The librarian didn't give any of them a chance to say anything. Instead, she adjusted her glasses and gave Mary Anne a stern look.

"Mr. Hund wants to see you in office. Right now."

Chapter Fifteen

Mary Anne wished she didn't have an entourage following her to Mr. Hund's office, but Wendy insisted on following her, and Kevin trailed after Wendy. Mary Anne had taken one look at the hard set of James' jaw and knew she wouldn't be able to persuade him not to come along either. Oddly, he seemed to have grown larger as he marched beside her, a determined look on his face.

Mrs. Todd, the secretary, looked up from her desk as all four of them entered the outer office—or purgatory, as most kids who got sent to The Hound called it.

"Mr. Hund only wants to speak to Mary Anne. The rest of you need to wait out here."

A muscle twitched in James' jaw and for a moment Mary Anne wondered if he were actually going to argue with Mrs. Todd.

"It's all right," Mary Anne said quickly, not wanting any of them going in with her and hearing the gritty details. "I don't think assistant principals are allowed to murder students."

Mrs. Todd frowned at her. "You might want to curb the sarcasm."

"Sorry." Geez. Mrs. Todd had no sense of humor. She wasn't even that old, but maybe working for The Hound made her all uptight.

The door to the assistant principal's office opened. To Mary Anne's surprise, two girls from her history class, Laura Hanson and Judy Gustafson, walked out. Since one of them had a red bruise under one eye and the other scratches on her cheek, they must have been the ones Ruby had fought with. Neither of them looked at her as they hurried off.

"That's them," Wendy whispered.

"I wonder where Ruby is."

"She has been sent home," Mrs. Todd said. "Go in. Mr. Hund is waiting."

Mary Anne felt James squeeze her shoulder. The gesture was strangely comforting. She took a deep breath and walked toward the inner office—or hell, as the students referred to it—where the assistant principal meted out what he called correctional measures but that students called devious cruelty.

"You wanted to see me, sir?" Mary Anne asked.

"Yes, Miss Wade. Shut the door and have a seat."

She sat down while Mr. Hund cleared his throat. That usually meant a lecture was coming. It couldn't be any worse than the one her mother had already given her.

"I received a phone call this morning—"

"From whom?" Mary Anne asked.

"That isn't important, and please do not interrupt me again," Mr. Hund said. "Some serious allegations were made that you were seen being taken home by a police officer on Sunday night and that you appeared intoxicated, as well."

Mary Anne did a quick revisit of the Rendezvous restaurant. She knew no students had been there, but someone who knew her must have seen her. Who was it?

"Have you nothing to say about that?" Mr. Hund

asked when she remained quiet.

Mary Anne shook her head. The guys on *Hogan's Heroes* never talked under pressure. She wasn't going to either.

Mr. Hund sighed. "Very well. I can't do anything about that, since it didn't happen at an event here at school. I suspect your mother has already decided on appropriate punishment. *But*, I will *not* have fights taking place at this school."

"I wasn't fighting," Mary Anne replied. "Sir."

"Your friend, Ruby Jones, defended you. Your sister nearly got involved, and so did the foreign exchange student. A *guest* from another country. Do you have any idea of how poorly that reflects on us?"

"With all due respect, *sir*, I didn't start this," Mary Anne said. "Laura and Judy decided to spread rumors."

"Don't get defiant with me."

Mary Anne lifted her chin and looked past him to stare at the wall. Apparently anything she said was not the right thing. She felt herself getting mad. It wasn't fair for him to accuse her of anything. She wouldn't even be in here except for those gossips.

Mr. Hund frowned. "Don't give me attitude, either."

Her temper snapped. "I'm not giving you attitude! You have no right to accuse me of something that isn't even your business!" The Hound's eyebrows arched nearly to the top of his hairline, and she knew she'd overstepped. "I just need—"

"—to have some time to think about your insubordination," Mr. Hund finished for her. "You are suspended until Monday. Go home." He reached for his phone. "I will call your mother and explain your impertinence."

Mary Anne opened her mouth, then snapped it closed. She rose and walked out the door with as much dignity as she could muster. She vaguely recalled James asking if she was all right, and Wendy's face being nearly as white as bleached laundry, with Kevin looking anxious, but Mary Anne moved past all of them in a numb state.

By the time she got home, her mother would already have heard The Hound's version and no doubt believed it.

Mary Anne felt like she was falling deeper and deeper into a hole she hadn't dug.

****

"I can't believe your mom is actually letting us visit," Ruby said on Friday afternoon as they sat in Mary Anne's bedroom, listening to "Paint It Black" on the phonograph.

"I was surprised too," Mary Anne replied. When she'd gotten home Wednesday, her mother had been waiting for her, just as expected. Oddly enough, she had been willing to listen to Mary Anne's side. Maybe because Wendy had nearly been involved in a fight. The Hound would have made sure he gave their mother that information as well. Vivian's lips had tightened into a thin line afterwards, a sure sign she was angry, but she hadn't ladled out any punishments. Instead, she seemed to be more upset about the rumors or who had started them.

"Well, I'm enjoying my vacation from school," Ruby said. "Four days off in a row isn't bad."

Mary Anne shook her head. "I don't know if I'd call it a vacation. James dropped off a ton of homework yesterday."

"Did you talk to him? What are the kids saying?"

"I was at work when he came by," Mary Anne answered, "but Jo said Laura and Judy aren't looking real pretty right now."

Ruby grinned. "Too bad I got pulled off them before I could finish."

Mary Anne studied her friend. "I still can't believe you actually hit them."

"I gave them a chance to take back what they said and apologize to you. They laughed." Ruby shrugged. "You didn't do that in the city neighborhood I grew up in. You don't get any respect if you back down."

"I hadn't thought about that. Everyone in Middletown knows everyone else."

Ruby frowned. "That brings up the question of who do you think rat-finked on you if you didn't recognize anyone at the Rendezvous?"

"I don't know. I've been going over it and over it in my mind. The door hostess was real flirty with Bob, but she had no idea of who we were. I know there weren't any kids in the main restaurant. Bob went into the bar to get the drinks. He'd have said something if he'd seen other kids. There was a private dining room opposite the bar, but it looked like a bunch of old people."

"Someone's parents maybe?"

Mary Anne thought about it. "Probably not. I couldn't see much, but I think they all had gray or white hair."

"What about those two old ladies who have their noses in everything?" Ruby asked.

"You mean Minnie and Millicent Gustafson?" Mary Anne laughed. "I can't see them going to a place where liquor is served, let alone a place like the Rendezvous, which is practically a nightclub. They think that kind of thing is a sin or something."

"Still, isn't Judy's last name Gustafson? Is she related?"

Mary Anne sobered. "Oh, my gosh. I think those old biddies are great-aunts or something like that. Do you really think they could have been there?"

"It makes sense. How else would Judy and Laura have found out?"

"I don't know." Mary Anne crawled off the bed to turn the record on its flip side and then flopped back down on the bed. "But why would Minnie and Millicent call the school and make trouble for me? I've never done anything to them."

"It may not be you, especially," Ruby answered. "You said they didn't approve of drinking, so they'd probably consider it their moral obligation to squeal on you. Some people think everyone needs to play by their rules."

Mary Anne frowned. "They should mind their own business!"

"Are you forgetting where you live?" Ruby asked.

"I guess you're right," Mary Anne said. "In a small town, your business is everyone's business."

"Right on."

Mary Anne sighed. Just one more reason she couldn't wait to move after graduation. Of course *where* would be up to Bob.

****

James could hardly wait for Saturday afternoon to arrive, but finally, it was here. Classes on Thursday and Friday had dragged and English class, which he looked forward to because he shared it with Mary Anne, had seemed dull and dreary too. Even the classroom debate on violence, which was Dante's seventh circle of Hell, had not interested him. It should have, since the project he was working on related to civil rights issues and Vietnam, both of which fitted into that particular circle's description. Without Mary Anne or even Ruby taking a stance, the discussion had seemed mild.

Since he knew Mary Anne would be working this morning—her mother hadn't completely grounded her—he let Kevin use his horse for the riding club. Kevin had returned with the good news that Mrs. Wade had said James could come over.

Mary Anne appeared to be in a good mood when he arrived, although maybe she was just glad to have company after being suspended from school. He wasn't really sure what to say about that or whether to mention it at all.

"Did you get the homework done?" he asked as they walked toward the barn.

"Yeah, thanks for bringing it. Who knows if the teachers will accept it, though," she answered.

"Why wouldn't they?"

"I was suspended." She shrugged. "Some of them just give zeros for those days."

James frowned. "That hardly seems fair."

Mary Anne made a huffing sound. "Like they care."

"You don't think the teachers care?"

"I don't know. Maybe. They have so many rules, it's hard to tell. They won't even let you *talk* in class. Look where that got us in English."

James was pretty sure Mary Anne wouldn't be thrilled to hear that *he* liked where their talking had gotten them…working on a project together. Better to keep that to himself. "The 'no talking' has turned out to be kind of a good rule, for once," he said instead. "None of the teachers is letting anyone talk about what happened."

Mary Anne glanced at him. "You haven't heard anything?"

He hesitated. "Not directly. There was gossip at lunch."

She stopped. "Like what?"

"It's really not important."

"It is to me. What was said?"

James really wished he hadn't said anything. "Just stuff." When Mary Anne folded her arms across her chest, he sighed. They obviously weren't going to have a riding lesson until she got the information. "Judy and Laura told some kids Ruby beat them up for telling the truth. Not," he added quickly, "that anyone believed them, necessarily. I mean, Ruby wasn't there to defend herself."

Mary Anne eyed him. "And what is their version of truth?"

He really, really wished he had not brought this whole thing up. James took a deep breath. "Okay, I'll tell you, but don't get mad. They said you were seen with a police officer taking you away from the Rendezvous and that it looked like you had been drinking. Like I said, it's just gossip." When she didn't answer, he reached out to put his hand on her shoulder, then dropped it. She definitely didn't look like she wanted to be touched. Or maybe just not from him since he was the bearer of bad news. "Are you mad at me now?"

Mary Anne looked away and shook her head.

"I don't know why Judy and Laura would make

something like that up, but I didn't believe it," James said.

Mary Anne turned back to him. "Believe it."

"What?" He wasn't sure he'd heard right.

"Believe it," Mary Anne said again. "It's true. Bob took me there for dinner the night before he had to leave. He had a fake ID and we had drinks. When we went to leave, the police officer was waiting." She paused. "The slinky door hostess probably called him."

James hoped he didn't look as stunned as he felt. He knew Mary Anne had some kind of crush on Bob Colby—it was the reason she'd agreed to take riding lessons, after all—but for him to use a fake ID and get Mary Anne drunk? What had the guy been planning to do afterwards? Maybe it was a blessing the cop had shown up, although James knew Mary Anne wouldn't think so. But if Colby had meant to take advantage of her… James felt his jaw clench. He was glad the guy was gone or there might be another fight looming if that had happened. The thought was followed by an even worse one. One that made his stomach feel as though he'd just swallowed hot coal. What if Mary Anne had wanted Colby to take advantage? James had always thought the guy was a real jerk.

"So now you know," Mary Anne said. "It's okay if you don't want to be friends anymore. You can go home."

James frowned. He didn't like the conflicting emotions that were swirling around in his mind, but giving up on Mary Anne wasn't one of those feelings.

"I'm not going anywhere," he said.

Chapter Sixteen

"You still want to do the riding lesson?" Mary Anne asked. She had just told James the truth about what had happened Sunday night.

"Why wouldn't I?"

"It doesn't bother you that I kind of got into trouble with the law?"

James shook his head. "That officer did you a favor bringing you home."

"That's what my mother said,"

James grimaced. "I didn't mean to sound like your mother."

"Just don't give me a lecture on drinking and driving, like she did," Mary Anne said. "Bob wasn't drunk."

"I didn't think he was."

"Well, I'll admit I'm lucky I didn't get hauled off to jail for being underage. I guess the cop did do me a favor."

"He did you two favors, then."

Mary Anne tilted her head. "What's the other one?"

James hesitated. "Never mind. Just forget I said anything." He walked to the barn and went inside.

Mary Anne followed him. "Don't start to say something and then stop. I want to know what you meant."

"You're going to get mad if I say. It's really not any

of my business."

"Is this about Bob?" She frowned. "You don't like him, do you?"

The tips of James' ears turned pink. "I just think maybe he was planning to take advantage of the situation by getting you tipsy."

Mary Anne stared at him. "How dare—"

"There you are!" Wendy strode into the barn. "I saw James' horse outside. I thought I'd come say hi."

Relief flooded James' face only to be followed by a quick look of concern toward Mary Anne before he turned back to Wendy. "Hi. How did the ride go this morning?"

"Okay. We missed you," Wendy said.

"Kevin really wanted to ride. I haven't found a horse for him to use yet," James answered.

Mary Anne only half-listened to them. She really wanted to tell James off, but the subject they'd been discussing wasn't something she wanted Wendy ever finding out about. It really wasn't James' business if she made out with Bob. It might have even been *her* plan too. After all, she was Bob's girl, wasn't she? What was wrong with kissing and necking?

Another thought struck her like one of Flame's powerful hooves. Maybe James thought she was just a tramp…like someone who would go all the way in a back seat. The notion hurt. The relationship wasn't like that. Bob cared about her.

"Maybe we should do this riding lesson another time," Mary Anne said.

James nodded slowly, not looking directly at her. "If that's what you want."

Mary Anne nodded too and turned to leave, but

Wendy's voice stopped her.

"Aren't you forgetting something?"

Mary Anne stopped. Drat it. Trust Wendy to remind her what their mother had said. Since Bob wasn't available to date, Mary Anne had decided she no longer needed to continue with lessons, but that idea had been squashed flat before she'd even gotten the words out of her mouth. Her mother had told her in no uncertain terms that their agreement had no ending time. If Mary Anne wanted to even think about being allowed to see Bob when he got back from boot camp, she would exercise Flame, which meant learning to ride.

She turned back. "I haven't forgotten. I'll saddle Flame."

James looked from Wendy to her. Mary Anne could almost hear the questions forming that he wanted to ask, but he snapped his mouth closed instead. "I'll saddle her."

"I'll help you," Wendy said.

"I'll wait outside," Mary Anne said and walked rapidly to the door, picking up a large feeding pail as she left. It would do nicely for a mounting block since she wasn't about to have James help her up.

He glanced at the overturned pail a few minutes later when he led the mare out. He didn't say anything, but he looked resigned as he led the horse over.

"I'll mount by myself," Mary Anne said.

A muscle twitched in his jaw. "I figured that was the intention."

The pail wobbled as Mary Anne stepped onto it, but she managed to grab the saddle horn and get a foot in the stirrup, although in her side vision she saw James start to put an arm out to catch her. Luckily, she managed to get her leg across and settle in the saddle, although not very gracefully.

Wendy climbed onto the fence, hooked her boots behind one of the boards, and grinned at her. "I think I'll watch."

Probably so she could make snide comments. Any other time, Mary Anne would have glared at her sister, but instead she smiled. "Maybe you can help James by making some suggestions."

Wendy gaped at her, nearly losing her balance on the top rail. "You want advice?"

"Why not?" Mary Anne asked and gave James a quick glance. "Everyone seems ready to give it."

The muscle in James' jaw twitched again, harder this time, but he said nothing.

She probably shouldn't have said that, but *geez*. Why did he have to put down Bob? Mary Anne tapped her heels to Flame's flank and rode through the open gate into the paddock. Wendy would create a buffer zone, whether she realized it or not.

And Mary Anne needed one.

****

"How were your morning classes?" Mary Anne asked Ruby when they met for lunch on Monday in the school courtyard.

Ruby shrugged. "No worse than usual, I guess. You?"

"Nobody said anything, but there were plenty of looks." Mary Anne had dreaded her first period Fine Arts class. It was an easy elective and nearly everyone in it was part of the In crowd…athletes, cheerleaders, pom-pom girls and band or choir members. Second period Physical Science wasn't much better, filled with brainy kids who actually liked science and math. Although she knew all the students, none of them were personal friends. Neither Ruby nor James had any morning classes with her, although in James' case that was probably a good thing, since Saturday had not gone well.

"Yeah, I got the same thing. A few people even moved their chairs away," Ruby said and grinned. "I guess they thought I might punch them or something."

Mary Anne busied herself unwrapping her sandwich so Ruby wouldn't see the blush she could feel on her cheeks. Some of the boys in her classes had actually moved closer and the looks they gave her had been raunchy. She didn't need any words said to interpret *that*. One of them had actually made a snide remark, not that she wanted to talk about it. "Some of the girls wouldn't look at me at all."

"Snobs," Ruby said, with more than a little scorn in her voice. "Do they think they're better than us?"

"Some do, I suppose." Mary Anne took a bite of tuna salad and chewed. "We don't have many kids get suspended, though. It's kind of embarrassing."

Ruby glanced at her. "You shouldn't have gotten suspended. You weren't involved in the fight."

"The Hound said I was insubordinate to him."

Rudy snorted. "He thinks he can bark orders at all of us and we're supposed to just keep quiet and not say anything. Nazi."

"Well, he is the assistant principal."

"The only reason he suspended you for that was because he couldn't do anything about what took place at the Rendezvous," Ruby replied. "I wonder what *his* vices are."

Mary Anne started to smile and then stopped. "My

mother says I have to apologize to him."

Ruby nearly dropped her hot dog. "Apologize? What for? You only stuck up for yourself."

"That's what I was trying to do," Mary Anne said, "but then I sort of lost my temper."

"So what?" Ruby asked. "From what you told me, The Hound egged you on. He deserved it."

"Not according to my mother."

"Shoot. That'll be tough, having to go in and face him."

Mary Anne shook her head. "I don't plan to talk to him."

Ruby raised a brow. "You're going to defy you mother?"

"Not exactly." Mary Anne dug in her purse and pulled out a folded piece of paper. "I *wrote* an apology about not meaning to lose my temper. I'll leave it with Mrs. Todd when I know The Hound is out patrolling."

Ruby nodded. "Good thinking. That'll be much easier."

"Yep. My mother can't accuse me of not doing what she said." Mary Anne put the paper back in her purse. Maybe she should write an apology to James too.

She'd lost her temper with him and she felt much guiltier about that, especially since she'd walked into the house after the riding lesson Saturday without saying another word to him. After the smutty looks—and comment—she'd gotten this morning, she knew he'd only voiced what others were thinking. Unlike Mr. Hund, she owed James an apology

Mary Anne sighed. Passing James a note in English this afternoon wouldn't do it She'd have to apologize in person and in private.

It wasn't going to be easy.

****

James wasn't in English class. Mary Anne wasn't sure if she'd been given a divine reprieve or if God was punishing her by making her wait instead of getting the apology over with. Probably the latter, since her luck had not been good lately.

"Do you suppose James is skipping class?" Mary Anne asked Ruby before the bell rang.

Ruby laughed. "James? Skip a class? You've got to be kidding."

"Well, he's never tardy."

"Maybe he's been absent all day," Ruby replied. "We don't have any other classes with him."

"I don't think he's ever been absent either."

Ruby gave her a sideways glance as the bell rang. "Why do you care? Are you developing a crush on him now that Bob's gone?"

"No. Of course not."

"That's good, because if Wendy found out, she might start a fight right here. The Hound would have a complete meltdown." Ruby paused. "On second thought—"

"Girls. Didn't you hear the bell?" Mrs. Howell asked. "You know the rules."

"Yes, ma'am," Mary Anne said and hurriedly took out her binder. The last thing she needed was to be sent to the assistant principal's office on the first day she got back.

Another English teacher appeared in the doorway and Mrs. Howell went to talk to her. Ruby made a face at her retreating back. "I wonder if she allows her husband to talk at home. Probably not."

"Shhh! Don't say stuff like that," Mary Anne whispered back. "Let's not get suspended again."

"I'm probably right," Ruby replied as other students' conversations began to buzz around them. "Anyway, why are you concerned about James not being in class?"

"It's… I…" Mary Anne tried to think of what to say. "He might be mad at me."

"I didn't think James ever got mad." Ruby's eyebrows rose. "What did you do?"

Mary Anne bit her lip. "We kinda had an argument when he came over Saturday for my riding lesson."

"About what?"

"Bob." Mary Anne looked toward the door. Mrs. Howell still had her back to them. Mary Anne moved her desk closer to Ruby so no one else would hear. "James said maybe Bob bought me drinks to take advantage of me later. It wasn't like that. Bob didn't force me to drink. I wanted to."

Ruby frowned. "So why is this James' business?"

"That's what I thought. I kinda told him off."

"Good for you, I say."

Mary Anne shook her head. "This morning in first period, a couple of the football players sat down next to me and gave me smirks. One of them asked if I was lonely. The other one winked." She felt her face grow warm with embarrassment. "They weren't flirting. They think I'm easy now."

"Geez." Ruby lowered her voice too. "Don't those idiots know girls these days are making their own choices? Look what's happening in 'Frisco. Girls are flocking there because they want to be free to do their thing."

"Yes, but—"

"Enough talking." Mrs. Howell was back at her lecture stand. "Today's lesson is an exploration of treachery, which is Dante's last circle of Hell."

How fitting, Mary Anne thought as she opened her literature book. In a way, she felt betrayed because the boys thought she was something she was not. Even worse, though, was those same boys implying she might be willing to cheat on Bob. That she would never do. She was his girl.

****

James sneezed, using another tissue from the bunch he'd stashed into his binder, then threw it into a trash container as he continued down the hall toward English class on Wednesday afternoon. He'd come down with a virus over the weekend, much to his irritation. He seldom got sick, but shortly after he got back from the Wades on Saturday afternoon, his throat had started feeling scratchy. By suppertime, he was running a fever, and by Sunday morning his head felt as thick and heavy as a cement block and twice its normal size. Three days in bed had made him feel only marginally better.

He doubted he looked much better than he felt. His eyes itched and watered, his nose probably looked like Rudolph's, and his voice sounded as though he smoked a pack of cigarettes a day. But that hardly mattered. He'd already missed two and a half days of school, and this was Wednesday, the afternoon they met in the library for their project.

Wendy had called Monday night after Kevin had told her after school that James was sick. His mother talked to her.

Mary Anne didn't call.

That left James with misgivings. If he could take back what he had said, he would, but travelling backwards in time was impossible unless the transponder on that new TV show, *Star Trek*, was real. James had only meant to express concern about the drinking, but Mary Anne had taken it for an insult instead.

He entered the classroom just as the tardy bell rang. Mary Anne sat in her usual place near the back of the room. Their eyes met briefly and her face turned pink before she busied herself with her book. Was she still angry with him? He wanted to go sit beside her, but Mrs. Howell was already frowning, so he took an empty seat in the front row. Now he would have to wait nearly an hour until the class was over. James coughed and hoped he wouldn't succumb to a sneezing fit.

Mrs. Howell was concluding *Inferno*, explaining that after seeing the depths of Hell, and justice meted out, Dante had earned the right to climb out of Lucifer's grasp back to the surface of Earth and see Heaven's stars as his reward. James felt like he'd taken the trip too, having bumbled his way into criticizing Mary Anne and incurring her wrath, For the past three days, he'd wandered in the dark forest of his own mind. Although no mythical beasts had confronted him, his worry and anxiety over Mary Anne's reaction Saturday and his not being able to see her until today had created his own unique circle of Hell. Would he be able to climb out of it?

The class dragged slowly as though some unseen force was pushing the minute hands of the wall clock backwards. Too bad he didn't have a warp-speed button that he could press and have the final bell of the day ring.

When it finally did ring, James started sneezing

again, to his chagrin. He closed his eyes. *Lord, not now.* He heard his classmates moving away. One pair of footsteps halted near him. He took off his glasses to dab at his watering eyes.

Mary Anne stood there frowning. "You've been really sick?"

He nodded, noting the rest of the students had gone. "Didn't Wendy tell you? She called the house Monday night."

Mary Anne shook her head. "I had to work until ten o'clock Monday night. Last night, she had a sleepover at Tommy's girlfriend's house. I haven't talked to Wendy."

So Mary Anne didn't know he'd been sick. Had she thought he was avoiding her? This whole thing needed to be fixed. Now.

James stood. "I owe you an apology."

She looked surprised. "For what?"

He frowned, wondering if his congested head had left his brain confused. Mary Anne had been so angry Saturday she hadn't spoken to him. Now, she wanted to know what he was apologizing for? Females were certainly confusing.

"For what I said Saturday. I was out of line."

"You weren't. Not really. I just didn't want to hear it," Mary Anne said.

"I know. I'm sorry."

Her eyes widened. "I'm the one who owes you an apology."

Maybe he'd taken too much cough syrup and his thinking really was affected. "Why are you apologizing?"

She blushed and looked away. "I practically threw a temper tantrum like a little child Saturday."

James smiled. "I've never thought of you as a child."

Mary Anne looked back at him, her eyes flashing briefly. "Neither do the rest of the guys around here."

James stopped smiling. "What do you mean?"

"Nothing." Her face turned red. "Forget I said it."

James hesitated. If he questioned her, was he going to make her angry again? He'd already poked his nose into her business when he shouldn't have. If she didn't want to tell him what she meant, maybe he should respect that. But she looked miserable. Had someone insulted her? "I would really like to know what you meant."

She shrugged, looking down at the floor. "I got a few smutty looks. A couple of remarks were made. That's all."

"That's all?" James set his jaw. "What kind of remarks?"

Mary Anne shook her head, causing her long hair to fall forward, covering most of her face. "Some of the guys think I'm easy and cheap after what happened. Just like you warned me about."

James clenched his fists, then forced himself to unclench them. "Would you please look at me, Mary Anne?"

Slowly, she brought her head up to meet his gaze.

"I would never, ever think that of you. Never. Ever."

Mary Anne studied him for so long, he thought she wouldn't answer. Finally she did. "Thank you for saying that."

"I mean it."

She studied him again and then she smiled. "I believe you."

Dante had seen the stars of Heaven as his reward,

and James felt like he was receiving his right now. Mary Anne's smile lit up his world.

****

Two days later, James dumped his books on the small table in the entryway of his house and headed for the kitchen. Kevin gave him an inquiring look as he followed.

"It's Friday! Why are ye so glum? We've got the whole weekend ahead of us."

"With not much to do," James answered as he opened the fridge and took out the container of chocolate milk and glanced at the note his mother had left saying she'd be helping decorate the school cafeteria for the Autumn Harvest festival. She'd left a casserole for dinner.

"Are ye upset ye'll miss the ridin' lesson because the football game this week is tomorrow afternoon and not tonight?" Kevin took two glasses from the cupboard and set them down, then opened the cookie jar. "I doubt Mrs. Wade will mind if ye reschedule it for Sunday afternoon."

"You haven't heard?" James asked as he poured their milk. "Luke Roundtree is getting some kind of award at college."

"Jo's boyfriend?" Kevin furrowed his brow. "So?"

"The Wades were invited to the event." James carried the plate of cookies to the table and sat down. "They left for St. Cloud right after school."

Kevin flopped onto his chair. "They're gone for the whole weekend?"

"Yep. No riding with Wendy for you and no riding lesson with Mary Anne for me," James said. "Bummer."

Kevin sighed. "Then they won't be at the football

game tomorrow either."

Mary Anne wouldn't have been at the game anyway, since she was still grounded. James wasn't at all sure Mrs. Wade would have let Wendy attend either since she didn't approve of Wendy nearly getting into the fight, but he didn't point that out to Kevin. No use in bringing them both down further. It was going to be a long, boring weekend.

"I was hopin' to sit with Wendy," Kevin said. "I've been tryin' to get up the courage to ask her to the Homecomin' dance in three weeks. The more I talk to her the better chance I think I have that she'll say yes…not that I really understand the reason for this homecomin'."

James smiled. "It's an American thing. The alumni are invited back to the school as kind of a reunion one weekend a year. There's lots of hullabaloo about it. Coronation of a Homecoming Queen and her court on Thursday night, parade and bonfire with a pep rally on Friday night, and then the big game Saturday afternoon followed by the dance Saturday night."

A hopeful expression crossed Kevin's face. "So if Wendy says yes, she'll be my date for all of those things?"

"I don't know how they do it in Minnesota," James replied, "but in Georgia the date is only for the dance."

Kevin looked crestfallen, then he brightened. "Still. It doesn't hurt to try. The most important thing is the dance, though. Are ye goin' to ask Mary Anne?"

James hesitated. More than anything in the world, he wanted to escort her to the dance. Since their mutual apology Wednesday, Mary Anne had acted much friendlier in class, even volunteering the information that they would be gone this weekend, but he didn't think she would say yes. He didn't have his head stuck so far into the sand that he didn't realize she was really hung up on Bob Colby. James could only bide his time on that.

He shook his head. "Her mother grounded her. Remember?"

"Ye don't think Mrs. Wade would make an exception?"

"I doubt it." Even if her mother did, he was pretty sure Mary Anne would say no. He didn't want to push it. At the present, what mattered most was becoming friends.

"It wouldn't hurt to ask her mother," Kevin continued, warming up to his argument. "Maybe Mrs. Wade would even insist on Mary Anne goin', just to get that other loser out of her head."

James shuddered. The last thing he wanted was for Mary Anne to be forced to go on a date with him. She would be miserable and, worse, probably compare him to Bob Colby all night. Right now, Bob would probably win. James could do without that humiliation. "I don't think that's a good idea. I'll just go stag if I go at all." When Kevin looked like he wanted to contradict him, James added, "This is just my first year here. It's not like I know anyone who would be returning."

'Ye should think about it anyway." Kevin became contemplative. "I hope Wendy will do me the honor and say yes."

"I hope so too," James said and got up to carry the empty glasses and plate to the sink as the doorbell rang. "Would you get that?"

"Aye." Kevin hopped up and went to the door.

James rinsed out the glasses and wiped the plate

before putting it away. He was deciding whether to take the casserole out and let it warm to room temperature before putting it in the oven when Kevin reappeared in the doorway. He was pale and holding a yellow piece of paper in his hand.

James frowned. "Is that Western Union?"

Kevin nodded mutely.

"Who's sending us a telegram? What does it say?"

Kevin looked at the paper as though it were a foreign object he'd never seen before. "My father's been killed in an accident," he whispered. "I have to go home."

Chapter Seventeen

"So Kevin has already gone back to Ireland?" Mary Anne asked when James gave her the news Monday out in the hall before English class.

James nodded. "As soon as my mom got home Friday night, she called the airlines for a reservation. He left yesterday."

Mary Anne drew her sweater closer as someone opened the outside door down the hall and a cold draft swept through. "Will he be coming back?"

"I don't know," James answered. "He's got a brother a year younger than himself and two little sisters. I suspect Kevin's going to feel he needs to stay home and help out."

"When our dad died, my uncle—the twins' father— pretty much took over. Of course, he couldn't stay at the house, since he had his own family," Mary Anne said. "It would have been nice to have had an older brother."

"How old were you when it happened?"

"Ten."

James gave her a sympathetic look. "That must have been hard, being so young."

"Yeah," Mary Anne said, thinking back to those first few days afterwards. Her uncle, being career military, hadn't been inclined to hugs like her father had been. He'd concentrated on getting the finances in order. Her mother had moved around the house like a wooden puppet on loose strings, hardly talking, and Wendy hadn't stopped asking where their father was. Mary Anne had felt pulled between the two of them. It hadn't been so bad during the daytime, when her aunt would be there, but the nights were long and scary. She didn't like thinking about it. "It happened a long time ago."

"Still. You had to be brave," James said.

"I guess." She really didn't want to talk about it, either. "You mentioned Kevin wanted to go to Notre Dame. I hope he still can."

Thankfully, James took the hint and changed the subject. "He can reapply for the student exchange program. My dad's already written a letter saying we'd be glad to sponsor him next year."

"But you'll be away at college."

James nodded. "I think that's one reason my parents, Mom especially, wants Kevin to come back. She doesn't like an empty house."

"I know my mother would have liked to have said goodbye. It's too bad we weren't home," Mary Anne replied.

"That reminds me," James said and pulled a sealed envelope from his binder. "Kevin asked if you'd give this to Wendy."

"Sure." Mary Anne took the envelope, which simply had Wendy's name written on the front of it. "I'll do it."

"I think Kevin was almost as upset not to say goodbye to Wendy as he was to leave." James paused. "He was hoping to ask your sister to the Homecoming Dance."

"Ah," Mary Anne replied, trying to sound neutral. She doubted very much that Wendy would have accepted a date, given her big crush on James. A crush that James must be oblivious to, hard as that was to believe. At least, Kevin had been spared rejection.

Mary Anne slipped the envelope into her notebook. "I'll give this to Wendy as soon as I see her."

****

Mary Anne wasn't as worried about Wendy's reaction to the news of what had happened to Kevin as she was Jo's, since her cousin had lost her own parents in a car accident less than two years ago. No one at school knew yet since James' father had not called the principal until this afternoon, and no announcement had been made.

She found Jo in the kitchen making hot chocolate. The day had certainly grown cold enough for it, but the rich aroma didn't entice her today.

"Want some?" Jo asked.

"I don't think so."

Her mother paused from removing an apple pie from the oven. "You love hot chocolate. What's the matter?"

Mary Anne shook her head, ignoring the spicy smell of cinnamon apple, too. She set her books on the table and sat down, not sure how to break the news. Her mother joined her. For once, Mary Anne was glad she was there.

"What's wrong?" she asked.

Jo brought her mug over and sat down too. "Did something happen after school? Did someone say something to you? I thought everyone had gotten over the gossip."

"It's not that. Kevin—"

"Mom!" Wendy burst into the kitchen. "Did you hear Kevin went back to Ireland?"

"No," her mother answered and gave Mary Anne an

inquisitive glance. "Is that what you wanted to tell us?"

'Sort of." Trust Wendy to fly in at the worst moment. Mary Anne looked at her sister. "Do you know why he left?"

Wendy shook her head. "Tommy got into trouble in math class and was serving detention in the office. He heard The Hound tell Mrs. Todd to withdraw Kevin from school. Do you know why?"

"Yes." Mary Anne took a deep breath. "His father passed away Friday. James told me earlier."

"Oh, sweet Lord," their mother said. "What a horrible thing to have happen with Kevin so far away from home."

"Kevin didn't say anything about his father being sick." Wendy sounded much more subdued as she took a chair. "His dad couldn't have been that old."

"Did James know what happened?" Jo asked.

Mary Anne took another deep breath, then slowly nodded. "He was killed in a car wreck."

Jo's face paled and Mary Anne heard her mother gasp. Even Wendy looked stricken. "I didn't want to be the one to tell you."

Jo's eyes brightened with unshed tears as she put her mug down and shoved her chair back to stand. She swiped her cheek with the back of her hand and ran from the room.

Vivian rose too and rushed after her.

"I was afraid Jo would take this hard," Mary Anne said.

"Mom will take care of her." Wendy's voice sounded shaky. "I can't believe this happened."

"I can't either." Mary Anne pulled her binder toward her and pulled out the letter. "James said Kevin wanted you to have this."

"What is it?"

Mary Anne was tempted to roll her eyes. "It's a letter."

"I can see that." Wendy grabbed it from her.

"Then don't ask a stupid question," Mary Anne replied and then softened her tone. Wendy was as shocked as she had been. "James said Kevin wanted to ask you to the Homecoming Dance."

Wendy's eyes widened. "Really?"

Mary Anne could have sworn her sister blushed just a little. Did that mean she would have said yes? "Aren't you going to open it?"

Wendy studied the letter as though transfixed. Then she shook her head and stood. "I think I'll read this in my room."

Mary Anne stared after her as she left. Was Wendy's one-sided crush on James finally fading? Had Kevin's constant attention made an impression?

She took Jo's mug to the sink and poured the now-cold chocolate out and went to get her coat, since she was already late for work.

She'd have to find out later what Kevin said in his letter. He really was a sweet guy and Wendy should have appreciated him more. Now it was too late. He was gone.

****

"Aren't you going to open it?" Ruby asked Mary Anne the next day at lunch after she'd given her the letter from Bob.

Mary Anne ran her fingers over the closed envelope with its air-mail red-and-blue-striped border, feeling the thin, slick paper. How odd that she had just asked Wendy that question yesterday. And, like Wendy, she would have preferred privacy in reading this first letter. But that meant she'd have to wait until she got home. Reading a personal letter in class would be considered like reading a note passed. If the teacher confiscated it and read it… Mary Anne would die of embarrassment. She'd never be able to face the class again. And she definitely did not want to wait several hours for school to end. She started to edge her nail along the seam carefully.

"It's not a Christmas present," Ruby said. "Just open it."

"I might tear the letter." Mary Anne wanted to savor every single second. It seemed Bob had been gone months. She pulled out the single sheet of note paper.

Ruby eyed it. "It's not very long."

"He probably didn't have time to write much," Mary Anne said. The twins' father had told her recruits were kept really busy the first couple of weeks of boot camp. "Wow," she said as she began reading. "Uncle Martin was right!"

"About what?"

"Bob being kept busy. Just listen to this." Mary Anne smoothed the letter over her binder cover. "They have an hour of running before breakfast and then five and a half hours of field training, a thirty-minute break for lunch, and then four and a half *more* hours of training."

"Yikes, that *is* a long day," Ruby said.

"It doesn't end there," Mary Anne continued. "After supper—only thirty minutes—their drill sergeant lectures them for another two and a half hours. They don't even get their mail until eight o'clock, and lights are out at nine."

"What time do they get up?" Ruby asked.

Mary Anne looked back at the letter. "Four thirty."

"Geez. It sounds like prison."

"It does, doesn't it?"

"No wonder guys go to Canada to dodge the draft," Ruby said. "Who'd want to go to boot camp, only to be sent to Vietnam afterwards?"

Mary Anne chewed her lip. "I'd never really thought about it like that." Her uncle had never mentioned how hard boot camp was. "There are college kids who think President Johnson is doing the right thing."

Ruby rolled her eyes. "Yeah, they would. They won't be getting drafted."

"I guess that's true."

"True? It's a fact. Luke's in college, right? Tim and Tommy will be going after they graduate, right? The draft isn't going to touch them. It's the guys who can't afford school who have to worry about getting killed overseas."

Mary Anne felt the blood drain from her face. "What if that happens to Bob?"

"Oh, geez. I'm sorry," Ruby said. "Me and my big mouth. I didn't mean—"

"I know," Mary Anne replied. "It's just... I mean..." She swallowed hard. "What if something happens to Bob?"

"Don't think about it like that." Ruby put an arm around Mary Anne's shoulders and squeezed. "Not everyone gets sent to Vietnam."

Mary Anne shook her head. "Mom watches the news every night. There are over 350,000 soldiers there right now and more are needed."

"But not everyone is out in the trenches fighting," Ruby said. "I mean, there have to be guys doing other jobs."

Mary Anne felt her eyes begin to sting with unshed tears. "Like what?"

"I don't know. Stuff like mechanics or electronics. They take tests to see what they qualify for, don't they?"

"I think so," Mary Anne answered. "Bob might be good at those. He likes to fix things."

"There, you see?" Ruby gave Mary Anne's arm another squeeze before dropping her hand. "He might even get office work somewhere."

"I hope you're right," Mary Anne said as the bell rang for class and she put the letter back in the envelope and slipped it into her purse.

"I hope I am too," Ruby replied as they both started back. "Just be glad we're girls and we don't have to go too."

Mary Anne hadn't given that much thought either. Girls didn't get drafted. She frowned, not quite sure if that was really fair.

****

The question was still on Mary Anne's mind Wednesday afternoon when the group met in the library. She'd spent the last two days thinking about what girls really did, besides getting married and having children. Mostly they were secretaries or nurses or teachers. Even the elective courses at school steered girls in that direction: Typing, Shorthand I and II, Home Economics and Early Childhood Development. The trade classes, like wood shop, were closed to girls as though they wouldn't know how to hold a hammer or drive in a screw.

A group of women headed by Betty Friedan had just established the National Organization for Women to fight for equal rights, but what did that really mean? That girls could be doctors instead of nurses? Bosses instead of secretaries? Airline pilots instead of stewardesses?

James set a stack of papers on the table as they took their seats. "This is research that Kevin did the past couple of weeks. He intended to bring it today, but..." James let the sentence trail off.

It felt strange not having Kevin there and hearing his lilting brogue. Mary Anne hadn't realized how he kept the conversation going. She never did find out what Kevin had written in his letter to Wendy, but whatever it was, her sister had been more subdued than usual. And, wonder of wonders, not looking completely starry-eyed at James.

"What kind of research?" Wendy asked.

"Do you remember Kevin said there was a lot of unrest in Northern Ireland?" James asked as he began to separate the paperwork into piles. "He wanted to compare that and the problems in Vietnam to trouble elsewhere in the world for the paper he had due in history class next month. He started taking notes on the nightly news. My dad brought home copies of the *New York Times* and the *Washington Post* too."

"So how is that going to affect us?" Ruby asked. "Our project is supposed to focus on what's happening here."

"Comparing our counterculture to what's taking place worldwide will make the presentation better," James said.

"Well, we don't have to write a book."

James gave her an incredulous look. "Don't you want an 'A'?"

Ruby shrugged. "I don't really care. It's extra-credit

punishment."

"But it's—"

"What did Kevin find out?" Wendy interrupted.

Mary Anne refrained from smiling since Ruby would probably misunderstand the expression, but since when was Wendy interested in actual information?

"There's more stuff out there than we think. This is just a recap," James replied as he picked up a sheet of paper. "A massacre on Braybrook Street in London killed several police officers in August. People are being shot every week trying to cross the Wall in Berlin. Mao Tse-tung's Red Guards are invading private homes in China to destroy 'western' items. Egypt is threatening to invade Saudi Arabia. Muslims and Kurds are fighting in Iraq, and tension is building between Israel and the United Arab Republic." James laid the paper down. "Where do you want to start?"

Mary Anne tapped a sheaf of papers with her pencil. "Israel."

"Okay," James said and picked up the stack. "Any particular reason?"

"Yes," she replied. "Don't Israeli girls have to serve in their army?"

"I think so." James shuffled the sheets until he found what he wanted. "Everyone over eighteen has to serve, the women two years and the men three."

"Do the women fight?" Mary Anne asked.

James scanned the paper. "Not combat. They can be clerks, welfare workers, nurses—"

"Hmph. Just like us," Mary Anne muttered.

Ruby stared at her. "Do you think women should fight in war?"

Wendy's eyes widened as she waited for a reply.

James looked puzzled. Mary Anne sighed. "I don't know. I don't want to shoot anybody, but I just don't think girls should be told we can't be what we want to be."

James looked back at the paper he was holding. "Well, in the Israeli army women can also do other stuff like be truck drivers, radio operators, and flight controllers. Does that sound better?"

"Yes, it does," Mary Anne said, her mind flitting to thoughts of Bob. Maybe Ruby was right and Bob would get one of these jobs that didn't involve actual fighting. She would pray for that.

Wendy still had owl-eyes. "Why would you want a guy-job?"

"I didn't say I did. I just think girls should have a choice."

James looked thoughtful. "You mean choose any career you want?"

Ruby started laughing. "Oh, yeah, I can see it now. We'll all be hot-shot lawyers, stockbrokers or astronauts."

Wendy giggled. "Move over, Captain Kirk. Mary Anne wants to be captain of the *Enterprise*."

"Why not President of the United States?" Ruby said between laughter-induced hiccups.

"Why not?" Mary Anne frowned at both of them. "India has its first woman Prime Minister. Why not a woman president?"

"There's about as much hope for that as getting Mr. Spock to smile," Wendy said and dissolved into giggling fits again.

"Yeah." Ruby wiped tears of laughter from her eyes. "Imagine that. A woman President of the United States."

Chapter Eighteen

"Isn't it great that Mom relented and is letting you go to the crowning of the Homecoming Queen tonight? Wendy asked Mary Anne the Thursday evening of Homecoming weekend as they were getting dressed.

"I suppose." Mary Anne really didn't see what all the fuss was about. It wasn't like the Queen actually did anything except sit on the back of a convertible for the parade the next night and then again during halftime at the game.

"Too bad Jo isn't feeling well." Wendy prattled on, oblivious to Mary Anne's disinterest. "I wonder who will get Queen?"

"Janie Nelsen, of course," Mary Anne answered. "Is there any real competition?"

Wendy drew her brows together. "Sure there is. Three other cheerleaders got nominated and so did a couple of pom-pom girls."

"Cheerleaders get nominated for everything," Mary Anne said. "It's like the whole school puts them on pedestals and practically worships them."

Wendy swabbed her lips with her nearly colorless lipstick and then waited for it to turn color before blotting it. "Well, they are popular and pretty."

Popular and pretty, Mary Anne thought. Those kinds of girls always had things easy. They smiled at boys who practically slobbered like puppies at the attention.

Teachers always seemed to make allowances too. She would bet that none of the Queen candidates would have been assigned an extra project for talking in class. "Like that makes them special?"

"Sort of, I guess." Wendy dabbed cologne behind each ear and fluffed her hair.

"Well, they're not. Neither are the football players, although from the way the whole town goes wild when they win, you'd think they'd accomplished something really important."

"Winning is important." Wendy reached for her jacket. "It's who we—who Middletown—*is*. Our team has taken the district trophy three years in a row. Aren't you proud of that?"

Mary Anne shrugged. "I'd be more proud of them if they could bring our soldiers home."

Wendy stopped, one arm in a coat sleeve. "So that's what's bugging you. Bob."

"So what if it is? He's not playing some stupid *game*. He's in the Army. That's *real*. It's dangerous."

"I know." Wendy finished pulling on her coat. "There's nothing we can do about it, though."

"I don't even know why we're in Vietnam," Mary Anne said as she put on her own jacket and pulled her long hair out from under the collar. "From everything I've been reading for our stupid project, the United States has no business being over there."

"You sound like one of those anti-war protesters on TV," Wendy said.

"Maybe I am." Mary Anne tossed the lengthy strands of her hair behind her shoulders and walked toward the door. "Maybe I am."

****

Mary Anne hung her jacket on the coat rack by the door when they came home later that evening. Janie had been crowned Homecoming Queen, to no one's real surprise. She was one of those students who was good at everything, made the honor roll, and never got into trouble. Plus she was friendly to everyone. Even Mary Anne had to admit that Janie didn't fake it like so many of her clique did. Her tears seemed genuine too, although Mary Anne suspected they weren't so much from being crowned as it was the fact that the Homecoming King wasn't Billy Hoffman.

Mary Anne could relate to that. She didn't want to think about losing the guy you loved. She wasn't sure she could go on like Janie had.

She hardly listened to Wendy's running commentary as they climbed the stairs to their rooms. She said good night quickly before Wendy decided to come into her room and keep talking. "See you in the morning."

Wendy stopped in midsentence. "You don't want to talk about how great everyone looked? The formals and tuxes and everything?"

Mary Anne shook her head. "Go tell Jo. I'm sure she'll want to hear about it since she caught that cold and couldn't go."

Wendy pouted. "Okay, then."

Mary Anne watched her sister go down the hall before she went inside her room and closed her door. She changed quickly into her pajamas and turned out the main light, lest Wendy should decide to return. Instead she flipped on the small lamp beside her bed, took Bob's letters out of the drawer in the bedside table, and crawled into bed to re-read them like she did every night.

There had been only three letters from Bob since he left, but she knew from what he wrote that he was exhausted at the end of each day.

He'd successfully completed Phase I, which included procedures for marching, standing at attention and at ease, although it didn't sound to Mary Anne that "at ease" was at all relaxing. The classroom instruction in map and compass reading and land navigation didn't sound too bad, but the hand-to-hand combat training sounded horrible. Bob had sustained a bunch of bruises, according to one letter. Then there were the obstacle courses, which included climbing to heights using rope ladders and makeshift bridges and then rappelling down stone walls.

But it was Bob's last letter that had Mary Anne cringing in fear. The recruits had been sent to a gas chamber with masks that they had to take off and actually be exposed to the effects of CS gas. Her hands shook as she re-read that letter. The drill sergeants made them recite the Pledge of Allegiance or answer questions so they'd actually have to breath in that stuff.

In addition, two recruits from the platoon had to be awake at all times, patrolling their barracks and watching for recruits trying to leave. For what Bob called the Change of Quarters, recruits' shifts rotated throughout the entire company, but still two had to stay awake continuously, which cut into badly needed sleep time.

And that was only Phase I. Bob had two more phases to go before he'd complete basic training and come home.

Folding the letters carefully, Mary Anne put them back into their envelopes, then reached into the drawer again and pulled out a small diary. She'd seen them at the grocery store. They were classier than the journal she'd been using. One of the older cashiers, whose husband was overseas, had told her it helped to write out some of the fears she was feeling.

Mary Anne took the small key she hid inside her pillowcase and inserted it into the keyhole of the fold-over pad to open the diary and then picked up a pencil.

Thursday, November 3

Dear Diary,

It doesn't seem fair that we are celebrating past students returning to their old school by crowning Queens and holding parades and playing football when the true meaning of 'home-coming' should be about bringing our soldiers back.

These college kids have no idea of the hardships that Bob is going through. And he hasn't even left the U.S. yet!

What am I going to do when he does?

Mary Anne blinked back tears and closed the diary. She couldn't write any more tonight. She locked the book and tucked it into the back of the drawer and then turned out the light. Pulling the covers to her chin, she stared into the darkness.

How was she going to cope when Bob went overseas?

*****

Jo was feeling better by the next evening and accompanied them to the parade. Mary Anne would rather not have gone at all, but when she said so, her mother had given her an exasperated look and mentioned something about Mary Anne not appreciating leniency and if she wanted to be obstinate, she could stay grounded. Mary Anne had acquiesced, feeling like no one understood her.

The parade route was not long, just down the few blocks of Main Street, around the town square, and then to the football field at the edge of town. A mile at the most. Mary Anne stamped her feet to keep them warm and tucked her hands inside the sleeves of her sweater. Autumn had lingered this year, with many of the maples still in full foliage of orange, red and yellow, yet the air was crisp and cool, carrying a hint of winter snow not too far away.

"You should have worn a coat," Wendy said smugly as she pulled on her gloves.

"It wasn't that cold earlier," Mary Anne snapped. "Besides, it'll be plenty warm at the bonfire."

"I'm probably going to melt then," Jo said, her eyes barely visible over the muffler she had wrapped around her throat and lower face. She patted her coat with mitten hands. "I feel ready for Alaska and the Yukon in all this garb."

"You've been sick," Wendy said. "Mom didn't want you getting worse."

"That's true," Jo replied. "Luke will be coming home for Thanksgiving and I want to be well then."

Mary Anne wished Bob were coming home too, but that wouldn't happen until January. The holidays stretched out in front of her like a straight country road disappearing over a flat horizon. There would be nothing for her to do. She pushed the thought away and looked impatiently down the street. "When is this stupid parade supposed to start anyhow?"

Wendy pushed back her glove to look at her watch. "In about five minutes."

"Well, I wish they'd hurry up."

"I think I hear the drums," Jo said.

Wendy nodded. "Me too."

It didn't take long after that before the leading line of pom-pom girls rounded the corner from the school to turn onto Main Street. Behind them, four John Deere tractors towed floats from each high school grade level.

"The class committees really did a good job decorating," Jo said. "You'd never know those floats were actually hay wagons."

Wendy giggled. "They don't smell like hay either."

The band followed, the majorettes strutting in front, wearing red tights under their white, short-skirted outfits, along with red jackets. In the gathering twilight, they looked like swirling peppermint sticks, the silver of the batons flashing under the street lights.

"There's James," Jo said to Wendy. "Doesn't he look good in his uniform?"

"Yeah," Wendy said, but her voice was subdued. She slanted a look at Mary Anne. "What do you think?"

"About what?"

Wendy gave an exasperated sigh. "About James. Don't you think he looks good in his band uniform?"

"I guess." *Uniforms*. Mary Anne's thoughts turned to Bob. She could hardly wait to see him in uniform. Would he be wearing it when he came home? Her thoughts were interrupted as the football players jogged by, followed by screaming cheerleaders.

Wendy hopped up and down. "Here comes the royalty!"

"They're not royalty," Mary Anne said, but her comments were drowned as everyone around them started clapping and yelling. She might as well just keep quiet.

The local car dealership had supplied three new convertibles for the parade. The nominees who hadn't won sat huddled together on the trunks of the first two cars, wearing borrowed lettermen's jackets over their formals for warmth. On the last car, Janie Nelsen sat alone on the back, wearing Billy Hoffman's jacket.

"She looks like Miss America!" Wendy exclaimed as Janie turned her head to the right and left, a bright smile fixed on her face, alternating arms in waving to the crowd.

Mary Anne had read somewhere that Miss America contestants actually used Vaseline on their teeth to keep their smiles in place, but what use would it be to tell that to Wendy? Mary Anne sensed Janie didn't seem happy in spite of the smile. Maybe it was because at first glance her formal looked black in contrast to the pastel shades of the other candidates, but as the car came closer, Mary Anne could see it was dark blue velvet, which made her think of the popular song sung by Bobby Vinton… Had Janie been thinking of the lyrics when she chose the dress? That in her heart there would always be a warm and precious memory of Billy?

How sad that someone still in high school had to lose her true love, Mary Anne thought as she followed the rest of the crowd closing in behind the motorcade heading for the football field. She didn't think she'd be able to handle it.

A sudden chill came over her that had nothing to do with the temperature of the air. She wished again that Bob were here.

****

Mary Anne coughed and then grabbed a tissue as she felt another sneeze coming on. Pulling the quilt tighter around her shoulders, she tucked up her feet and huddled deeper into a corner of the sofa. Miserable as she felt for having caught whatever Jo had—getting chilled at last night's parade probably hadn't helped—she was just glad she didn't have to attend the Homecoming Dance tonight. Best of all, her mother couldn't accuse her of being obstinate about not going.

"I feel really guilty about your catching my cold," Jo said as she came into the parlor carrying a mug of hot tea with honey and lemon. "Aunt Viv said you should drink this."

Mary Anne wrinkled her nose. "I hate tea."

"So do I," Jo said as she set down the cup, "but it really does help with the sore throat."

"Don't feel guilty," Mary Anne said as she took a reluctant sip. "You should have gone to the dance with Wendy."

"It's no big deal for me," Jo replied. "I wouldn't have anyone to dance with anyhow since Luke's at college."

"I feel the same way with Bob gone," Mary Anne said.

Jo tilted her head slightly. "How serious is it with you and Bob?"

"I'm his girl." Mary Anne set the tea mug down. "We talked."

"He asked you to wait for him?"

"He didn't have to. I told him I would." Mary Anne coughed. "We're practically engaged."

Jo looked a bit taken back. "Does your mom know?"

Mary Anne shook her head. "It's not official. I'm hoping it will be when Bob gets home from basic training."

"You think Aunt Viv will agree to your getting engaged? You're still in high school."

"I didn't say we'd get married right away. We can wait. But when Mom sees Bob in uniform, she'll see how mature and responsible he is."

"I hope you're right," Jo replied, although she sounded uncertain.

Mary Anne frowned. "I know my mother doesn't like Bob, but she doesn't really know him. Or understand him. She thinks he has a wild streak. Maybe he just wants adventure. So do I. Middletown, Minnesota is hardly exciting."

"I like it here," Jo said.

"I don't know how you can say that. You were raised in Brooklyn. Don't you miss New York? I know Ruby misses Minneapolis."

Jo shrugged. "Some people like the hustle and bustle. Living in a big city is kind of lonely, which sounds odd since Brooklyn is really crowded. When my parents were killed, though, most of our neighbors didn't even know about it. If I hadn't had my best friend's parents take me in, I don't know what I would have done. Here, everyone knows everyone."

"Way too well," Mary Anne replied. "If it hadn't been for nosy Minnie and Millicent, I never—"

"I'm home!" Wendy called. The door slammed behind her and a moment later she hurried into the living room.

"Did you have fun?" Jo asked.

"Yeah. The gym was decorated real nice and we had pizza."

"Did you dance with James?" Mary Anne asked.

"Once. He stayed with Janie the rest of the time and

kept her company."

"That was nice of him," Jo said. "I don't suppose Janie felt much like dancing."

"I wouldn't," Mary Anne said and looked at Wendy. "At least, James asked you to dance."

"Yeah." Wendy hesitated. "He asked how you were feeling."

Mary Anne sneezed again and grabbed another tissue. "Did you tell him I feel like I've been hit by an eighteen-wheeler?"

"I told him you were probably going to live."

"That was optimistic of you." Mary Anne tossed the tissue onto a growing heap on the coffee table and then frowned when Wendy stood there watching her. "What? Don't you think I'm going to make it?" She started to laugh only it turned to hacking.

Wendy didn't smile back. "You'll make it."

"What is it, then?" Mary Anne asked when she finished coughing. "I'd think you'd be delirious that James asked you to dance when he didn't ask anyone else."

"The only reason he danced with me was to ask about you."

"I'm sure that's not true," Jo said. "Mary Anne and James are friends. He's naturally concerned, that's all."

Wendy didn't answer.

Mary Anne grimaced. "For gosh sake, Wendy. I'm not trying to get James' attention. I know what a crush you have on him."

"It doesn't matter how I feel about him," Wendy finally said. "What matters is how he feels about you."

"Huh? My ears are plugged. I don't think I heard you right."

Wendy's expression turned mulish. "You heard me."

"What in the world are you talking about?"

"Don't pretend not to know James likes you. *Really* likes you."

"Really likes me?" Maybe her fever was higher than she thought. Mary Anne shook her head, although that did nothing to clear it. "And how did you leap to that silly conclusion?"

Wendy lifted her chin. "Kevin."

"Kevin?"

"He put it in his letter."

"In his letter?" Mary Anne asked thinking she was beginning to sound like a parrot repeating things.

Jo intervened. "What exactly did Kevin say?"

Wendy's voice began to tremble. "He said that James knew I liked him but didn't want to embarrass me so he didn't say anything. Then he said he hoped my sister would come to her senses and realize what a great guy James is because he really likes Mary Anne." Tears spilled down Wendy's cheeks. "Do you know how stupid I feel?"

"But…" Mary Anne started to say and then stopped. Wendy had already run from the room. Mary Anne turned to Jo. "Why would Kevin say that?"

Jo studied her. 'Because it's probably true."

Chapter Nineteen

Mary Anne put her half-eaten sandwich down on the cafeteria table Monday and then pushed it away. "I can't taste a thing."

"You should have stayed home," Ruby said.

"I have to work tonight. If I didn't come to school today and someone saw me at the store, The Hound would think I skipped school and then I'd get detention."

"Well, you look awful."

Any other time, Mary Anne might have resented that remark, even if it did come from her friend. She knew she looked horrible with her blotchy face and swollen eyes. She hadn't bothered with makeup, either. "Maybe James will take one look at me in English class and decide Wendy is much cuter after all."

"I doubt it," Ruby said wryly. "Not from what you told me."

Mary Anne dabbed at her wet nose. Another reason she wanted to come to school today was to talk to Ruby about James. Wendy had spent most of yesterday listening to sad songs, lifting the needle off the LPs to skip anything that sounded upbeat and putting it down again on the next melancholy tune. Mary Anne thought she'd run out of the house screaming if she had to listen to "Baby, Don't Go," "Losing You" or "World Without Love" once more. The lyrics to "Eleanor Rigby" had been the finishing touch. Even their mother had said enough was enough after Wendy played the song a dozen times.

Ironically, Wendy was the one who claimed to be sick today and stayed home.

"I really wish James hadn't told Kevin that he knew Wendy liked him. And I really, really wish Kevin hadn't mentioned it either," Mary Anne said. "Why would he be so mean?"

"Probably because Kevin had a crush on Wendy like James does on you."

"James does not have a crush on me!" Mary Anne started hacking again and reached for her water. "He knows how I feel about Bob."

Ruby raised an eyebrow. "When has that ever stopped someone?"

Mary Anne shook her head. "James has never said one thing about wanting to date me. Not one word."

"He's not stupid," Ruby said. "No one wants to get refused, let alone jilted."

"I'm telling you, this whole thing has been blown out of proportion. We're friends, that's all."

"Because that's all you want it to be." Ruby looked pensive. "James really is a nice guy."

"I never said he wasn't." Mary Anne frowned. "Do you think I should say something to him about Wendy?"

"Good grief, no!" Ruby stared at her. "Has your cold numbed your brain? She's already feeling bad enough. She'd be devastated if you interfere."

"I don't want to interfere. I just want to set things straight," Mary Anne said as the bell rang and they got up.

"Don't even try." Ruby gathered their books. "You'll just make it worse."

Mary Anne picked up the trash and threw it away as they walked to class. She didn't want to make anything worse. She wanted to fix things.

She just didn't know how.

****

"I knew you should have stayed home Monday," Ruby told Mary Anne late Wednesday afternoon when she came to the house. "Now you're really sick."

Mary Anne sat propped up in bed, a fleecy bathrobe wrapped over flannel pajamas and two quilts pulled up to her shoulders. She didn't want to argue the point. In any case, it was true. By the time she'd gotten home from work Monday evening, she had a high fever. Yesterday her mother had taken her to the doctor, who'd given her a shot and antibiotics to ward off pneumonia. Her head felt as heavy as a bowling ball, her throat as raw as uncooked sausage, and her chest hurt when she took a deep breath like Flame had kicked her. "I don't think you need to remind me."

"Sorry," Ruby said and plopped down in the one armchair in the room.

Mary Anne eyed the books Ruby had set down on the dresser. "Did you guys meet after school to work on the project?"

"No. James wanted to wait until you came back and Wendy didn't show up," Ruby replied. "Not that I blame her. I'd avoid him too if I were her."

"We really don't know exactly what James said, on the basis of what *Wendy* said Kevin wrote."

Ruby gave her a puzzled look. "What do you mean?"

"Wendy overreacts. Maybe she just took something the wrong way. I can't believe Kevin would be so rude as to actually tell her that."

"Well, we won't know unless Wendy lets us read the letter."

Mary Anne started to laugh and quickly coughed. "Fat chance. She's probably burned it anyway."

"Oh, I almost forgot." Ruby dug into her jacket pocket. "A letter came for you from Bob."

Finally. It had been over a week since she'd heard from him. "Thanks." Mary Anne tucked the letter under the blanket. "I'll read it later."

Ruby smirked at her. "You want privacy? Bob must be saying some hot stuff."

Mary Anne thought she blushed, although she wasn't sure since her face felt hot from the fever. "Mostly, he talks about what training camp is like. It sounds like that tenth circle of *Inferno* that Mrs. Howell has been preaching about."

"Thank goodness we're through with that," Ruby said and then wrinkled her nose. "Now we're going to be doing Chaucer."

Mary Anne looked at the books again. "Don't tell me you brought me that to read. I could use something a little more exciting. Like maybe *Valley of the Dolls*."

"Sorry. Although…" Ruby paused and then grinned. "Maybe we could incorporate some of those 'dolls' into the road trip in *Canterbury Tales*—have everyone all spaced out—and add it to our project's presentation."

"You're terrible," Mary Anne said. "We'd all get suspended for sure."

"Maybe." Ruby shrugged. "You gotta admit, it'd add some zing to boring English if those pilgrims were all trippin' out on medieval acid."

Mary Anne managed a smile. "Mrs. Howell would

faint."

"And The Hound's face would turn purple," Ruby added. "It might be worth it."

"James would never agree."

Ruby sighed. "You're right. He wants to get a good grade."

"Well, his mom works for the school district," Mary Anne said.

"That reminds me. James said to tell you hi and he hopes you'll feel better soon." Ruby gave her a sideways glance. "I think he does really like you."

"He only said what anyone else would say," Mary Anne protested. "Telling someone you hope they feel better isn't exactly flirting."

"No, but it's better than blaming you."

Mary Anne frowned. "Blaming me for what? Are the kids still talking about my drinking? Doesn't anyone have anything else to gossip about?"

"I haven't heard anything about that," Ruby said. "It's old news anyhow."

"Then what am I being blamed for?"

"Everyone getting sick. Half the kids, anyway. Someone called you Typhoid Mary, whoever that is. Anyway, the classes were really empty today," Ruby said as she pointed to the books. "I brought your books because the teachers weren't happy. They want you to stay home until you are totally well."

Mary Anne grimaced. "At least no one will ever accuse me of being a teacher's pet."

"I think The Hound even called your mother. Something about you being highly contagious. He'd gotten calls from parents. At least that's what Tommy said since he'd been hauled to the office again and overheard part of the conversation."

"Tim and Tommy have second homes in the office, I think," Mary Anne said and then drew her brows together. "But if I'm contagious, you shouldn't be here."

"As if I care. Those people can all go spaz out," Ruby said as she got up to leave. "I'm your friend."

Tears welled up unexpectedly in Mary Anne's eyes. "Thank you. It seems I can use one."

Ruby's eyes got suspiciously bright too. "I'll keep you posted on what's happening," she said, and then she was gone.

****

After Ruby left, Mary Anne contemplated saving Bob's letter to read when she felt a little better. She quickly rejected the idea and tore the flap open. This was the longest letter he'd written…nearly three pages. He'd entered the second phase of training, which he called "Gunfighters." Mary Anne conjured up images from *Gunsmoke*, or maybe *The Virginian*, until she read that Bob was talking about assault rifles and grenade launchers.

Mary Anne sneezed and reached for yet another tissue. Even though she lived in the country, where pheasant and deer hunting was popular and boys learned to use shotguns and rifles while in elementary school, Mary Anne had never liked guns. The more she read and heard about casualties in Vietnam—on both sides—the less she liked the idea of Bob handling guns. She looked back at the letter. How could he sound so enthusiastic about learning to be a sharpshooter? Or a sniper, as he called it. News on TV had recently reported that just this year over six thousand Americans had been killed and thirty-thousand wounded. The White House had compared that to over sixty thousand Vietcong that had been killed. Like that was a good thing?

Mary Anne dabbed her eyes, not sure if they were watery because of her sinus infection or because of the casualties. Bob was being trained to go fight. What were they actually fighting about anyway? No wonder young people were protesting. She sighed, knowing she couldn't change anything.

The sigh turned to jubilance as she flipped to the third page of Bob's letter and she quickly forgot her despondent feelings. This last page was personal. He told her he missed her. He was looking forward to seeing her in January and he would try to call over Thanksgiving. He should be in the third phase of training then and given "liberty" and allowed to use the payphone, although his conversation time would be limited. That kind of sounded more like a prison release to Mary Anne, but she wasn't going to argue, if only she could talk to him.

Rolling over, she opened the nightstand drawer and reached for her diary.

Dear Diary,

Thanksgiving is only two weeks away! Bob is going to try and call. I can't believe I will actually be able to hear his voice again. How am I going to survive until then? I really, really, really wish he could get out of the Army.

She paused, chewing on the edge of the pencil, and then continued.

More and more, I agree with the hippie slogan "Make love, not war."

****

"I am so far behind, I don't know if I'll ever catch up," Mary Anne said as she joined James and Ruby a week later after school in the library. "Being sick for ten days is a real downer."

"It's your first day back," Ruby said. "Don't worry about it."

"I'm just glad you're better," James added. "Your mom sounded really worried."

Mary Anne nodded. After Ruby's visit, Mary Anne had gotten worse. Even though the antibiotics had warded off serious bacterial pneumonia, a viral infection had settled in her lungs. James had called several times, but her mother had talked to him. He'd sent a get-well card home with Wendy, which strangely enough she hadn't seemed too upset over. She'd actually smiled at the cartoon James had drawn of The Hound sniffing for contagious caricature germs in the hallways, even though no epidemic had taken place.

"I still feel a little shaky," Mary Anne said.

James stopped shuffling papers. "We don't have to meet if you aren't feeling well. Do you want to go home?"

Mary Anne shook her head. "The project is due next Tuesday, before we break for Thanksgiving. This is probably the last chance we'll have to get everything in order."

"Can we just put the finishing touches on it and go?" Ruby asked.

"Yes." James separated the papers into three piles and tapped the first one. "This deals with current Civil Rights, mainly what impact the new Black Panther party will have on Martin Luther King's nonviolent approach to equality. Who wants to present it?"

"I will, " Ruby said. "I want to talk about the riots breaking out across the country."

"Okay. It's all yours." James slid the papers to her and looked at Mary Anne. "The other two stacks deal with anti-war protests and how the hippie peace movement is growing in San Francisco. Which do you want?"

"Anti-war. According to TV, college kids are demonstrating everywhere," Mary Anne said and pulled the stack toward herself. "Besides, I've got a personal interest."

James didn't respond, although a muscle twitched in his jaw. "I'll take the hippie thing, then. The more I read about it, the more I kind of like the idea."

Ruby laughed. "You? A hippie? Come on."

"I didn't say I was going to run off to join them," James replied, his tone unruffled. "Hippies are protesting the war too, but in a different way. Instead of rioting and causing damage or yelling insults at soldiers, they're passing out flowers at their rallies and using music and mimes to get their point across in a peaceful way."

"Probably because they're spaced out of their minds and can't think straight," Ruby said. "Or aren't you going to mention how getting stoned is part of the culture?"

"I don't think everyone gets high," Mary Anne said. "Groups like the Diggers get donated food and clothing to share with the kids out there. Everyone is expected to help out. You can't do that if you're blowing your mind on drugs."

"Yeah, well. Just mention Haight-Ashbury and watch Mrs. Howell swoon, or worse, call for The Hound to come and get us," Ruby said, rubbing her palms together like a villain in a horror movie and darting her eyes from side to side before beginning to sing, "They're coming to take me away, ha-haaa! They're—"

"Shhh!" Mary Anne poked her. "The librarian is already watching us."

James shook his head. "I can't very well talk about the hippie movement without mentioning the Haight. Or drugs."

"Well, Mrs. Howell did want a comprehensive report on the counterculture taking place," Ruby said. "So that's what she's going to get. And, if anyone asks questions, we can quote the Stones and tell her to get off our cloud."

"That'll go over big," Mary Anne said. "She'd probably have The Hound suspend us for insubordination again."

"Perhaps a better song would be 'Blowin' in the Wind,' " James said, "because that's really where the answer is."

Chapter Twenty

Mary Anne parked the car in the garage the following Tuesday afternoon and walked the short distance to the house, glad that school was finally over for the Thanksgiving holiday. Although she was recovered from her illness, she still got tired easily and having this break would give her time to recuperate.

Their presentation had gone surprisingly well, although Mrs. Howell had raised her eyebrows when James began talking about drug use, but she hadn't sent any of them to the office. It probably helped that James' mother was a counselor and some of the statistics he quoted on the increased use of marijuana and hallucinatory drugs came from her office. Still, as Ruby said, the project was finally over and they'd all breathed a sigh of relief. Well, she and Ruby had anyway. James had no comment.

Mary Anne let herself in the back door near the kitchen. As soon as she entered she heard voices coming from the parlor down the hall. Wendy was giggling and Jo sounded excited and Mary Anne saw why as soon as she entered the room. Luke Roundtree was back.

She'd known he was coming home from college since Jo had mentioned it about a god-zillion times. She was almost as glad to see him as Jo was, albeit for a different reason. Mary Anne wanted to enlist his help in convincing her mother that Bob was one of the good guys, since Luke had befriended him in the past. That conversation was obviously going to have to wait since Jo was snuggled against his side and Luke had his arm around her shoulders. Mary Anne could practically feel electricity sparking between them.

"Welcome back," Mary Anne said. "I didn't see your car in the drive."

"Engine trouble on the way home," Luke said. "I had Dad drop me off on the way to town." He smiled at Jo. "I couldn't wait to see my girl."

Mary Anne's heart pinged. It was exactly the kind of thing she imagined Bob saying when he returned from boot camp. She felt a twinge of envy at the look Jo and Luke exchanged. Words weren't need to know how they felt about each other. Suddenly, mid-January and Bob's homecoming seemed a long, long time away.

"Luke and his dad are going to come to our house for Thanksgiving dinner," Wendy said. "Won't that be great?"

"Yeah. We always have tons of food."

Luke grinned. "I remember."

"Mom will probably make you eat seconds of everything. She's always telling Tim and Tommy they need to put some meat on their bones," Wendy said and then added, "Not that you need to. You look great."

"I'll *second* that," Jo said and squeezed Luke's hand.

Mary Anne noticed how Luke's thumb gently stroked Jo's palm almost absently in response. Luke was one of those guys who probably looked good even when he was a kid. His blue-black hair, a legacy of his dad's half-Ojibwa roots, and light hazel eyes were a striking contrast. Luke had a quick, easy smile with a dimple in one cheek that Mary Anne would bet had also gotten him out of childhood escapades. She gave her sister a tentative look. A couple of years ago, before Jo had come to live with them, Wendy had had a crush on Luke. She wondered if Wendy was going to rebound the same way since the rejection thing with James. Luke hadn't noticed her before either, as far as Mary Anne could tell, and he sure wouldn't notice now, as in love with Jo as he was.

If that were the case, though, perhaps Mary Anne could thwart any bad feelings over this weekend. She just didn't want Wendy to get hurt again by letting her crush grow for the wrong guy.

****

Thanksgiving Day dawned cold and breezy, with a definite threat of snow in the air. The low, gray clouds contrasted sharply with the vivid color of the handfuls of autumn leaves still on the trees, although Mary Anne suspected if the wind kept increasing the limbs would be bare within twenty-four hours. Perhaps the reds, oranges, and yellows seemed even brighter today because it was their swan song.

Luke and his father Zeke followed them home from church services, Jo having opted to ride home in their truck instead of the family car. Mary Anne watched Wendy's reaction, but her sister had developed a poker face suddenly and kept her expression neutral.

"We knew we couldn't compete with Mrs. Wade's cooking," Luke said once they were all inside the house. He held up a bag. "So we brought yeast rolls from the bakery."

"Perfect," Jo said. "I'll go put them in the oven to warm."

"I'll help," Luke said and followed her into the

kitchen.

Wendy looked as though she wanted to follow. "Let's set the table, kid," Mary Anne said, to divert her, and then breathed a sigh of relief when her sister didn't argue.

"Please make yourself comfortable in the parlor," their mother said to Zeke. "I need to check on the turkey and get the potatoes boiling."

"No need to treat me like a guest, Vivian," Luke's dad answered. "Since my wife died a while back, I've learned my way around a kitchen. At least," he added as an afterthought, "I haven't burned anything lately or set off the smoke alarm."

Vivian raised an eyebrow. "Do you think you can handle a salad, then?"

He gave her a solemn look as though he were seriously considering whether the task was doable. "I reckon I can try, ma'am."

Mary Anne stared at him, wondering if the man really couldn't make a salad. Then she noticed just a touch of a smile as a corner of his mouth slowly lifted.

"I'll make sure you don't have a sharp knife so you won't cut off any fingers," her mother said in an equally serious tone.

Mary Anne looked at her mother in surprise for using sarcasm. How often had they been told not to use it? Then Mary Anne caught the same weird half-smile on her mother's face before she turned and walked off.

Mary Anne watched both of them leave. If she didn't know better, she'd think her mother was actually flirting. Her *mother*.

"Are you going to stand there all day or help me set the table?" Wendy asked.

"Yeah. Okay," Mary Anne replied and then busied herself with getting her mother's linen tablecloth out, along with the bone china, fine crystal and sterling silver. It took practically as long to set the table as it did to cook the entire feast, since her mother insisted that formal settings be used. Mary Anne didn't really see the need for three forks and two spoons by each plate or why a salad plate had to be placed on top of the dinner plate. She didn't think Mr. Roundtree's salad-making skills would warrant it.

"It does look nice, doesn't it?" Wendy asked when they were finished and she lit the candles on both of the silver candelabras.

Mary Anne had to admit that it did. She wondered what Bob would say. The one time he'd been to dinner had been casual and her mother hadn't been particularly impressed by his manners. Mary Anne didn't think being so proper was all that important. Bob would probably not like all the extra silverware and plates either. They were so much alike.

She glanced at her wristwatch. Nearly noon, which meant it was already one o'clock on the east coast. Had Bob had a turkey dinner? Did the Army even make an exception for a holiday or had Bob spent the whole morning shooting guns and crawling through those horrible obstacle courses he said they referred to as "confidence" courses. She wished she knew. Would he be able to call her today? She hoped so.

Her thoughts were broken by the sound of everyone coming into the dining room from the kitchen. Luke's father carried the turkey with Mary Anne's mother following him with a bowl of mashed potatoes and the gravy boat. Jo brought in the rolls and salad. Mary Anne noticed it had sliced radishes, cucumbers, and tomatoes along with the lettuce, so her mother must have let Mr. Roundtree use a sharp knife after all. Luke came last, balancing a huge tray—it looked like the heavy plastic lid from one of her mother's storage containers—that had the rest of the serving dishes on it. He handled it as though it weighed no more than a pizza pan, but Luke had a job in St. Cloud as a waiter in a fancy restaurant, so he must be used to this kind of thing.

"Everything smells so good!" Wendy said. "I can't wait to get started."

Her mother gave her a firm look. "We'll say grace first."

"Allow me," Luke said as they took their seats. He picked up Jo's hand and extended his other to Wendy. In turn, Wendy reached out for Mary Anne's hand. She noticed Mr. Roundtree had taken Jo's free hand, but had also taken hold of her mother's. Her mother's face was pink, although that might have been from the warmth and bustle in the kitchen. Mary Anne took her mother's open hand, making the circle complete.

Luke gave thanks and Mary Anne had a déjà vu moment in which she could imagine James doing the very same thing. Somehow, she couldn't picture Bob doing so. The thought was unsettling.

After grace was said, no one seemed to be in any hurry to release hands. Wendy sat still as a statue, still keeping contact with Luke although he was smiling at Jo. Mary Anne was beginning to wonder if the food would be cold before they got to eat. Perhaps her mother read her thoughts, because she abruptly dropped her hands.

"Let's get to the bird, shall we?" she asked.

"Would you like me to carve?" Luke's father asked

and a twinkle lit his dark eyes. "I survived the salad-making."

Mary Anne's mother smiled. "You did manage to keep all your fingers."

"They come in handy," he replied as he picked up the sharp carving knife, along with the serving fork. He slid the fork across the knife with a clicking sound and then, in a motion so quick Mary Anne wasn't sure she actually saw it, he flipped the knife into the air, caught it by its handle, pierced the bird with the fork and made a perfect slice into the turkey.

Her mother blinked. "That was impressive."

Luke's father grinned. "Just something I learned growing up."

Wendy passed the salad. Their mother seemed almost mesmerized by the quick movements as Mr. Roundtree deftly carved the rest of the turkey. Mary Anne didn't think she'd ever seen a blade flash so quickly, either. In no time, the bird was sliced and arranged neatly on the carving plate.

Luke's father turned to their mother, holding a long, plump piece of turkey breast skewered to the fork. "May I serve you?"

Her mother blinked again and held up her plate. Mary Anne felt a little bit guilty. Always before, their mother had made sure everyone else had gotten served before she filled her own plate. Even when her dad was still alive, her mother had always served him first.

Mary Anne wondered if Bob would be so gallant. James probably would. She frowned. That was the second time today that she'd compared James to Bob. What was wrong with her? She was Bob's girl. She was just making comparisons because Luke was treating Jo like royalty. Bob would too, if he were home.

She glanced at her wristwatch as the serving bowls were passed around.

Would Bob call?

****

Mary Anne offered to clean off the table and do the dishes after the huge feast, partly because she didn't want to watch whatever football teams were playing on the television and partly because she was trying very hard not to be jealous of Jo. It wasn't her cousin's fault that her boyfriend was home and Bob was not.

Besides that, she was going to drive herself nuts if she sat still and waited for the phone to ring.

Oddly enough, Wendy joined her in the kitchen, carrying a stack of dirty plates.

"Don't you want to go watch TV?" Mary Anne asked as she filled the sink with hot water.

Wendy wrinkled her nose. "If they're not Middletown players, I don't really care. Besides, Jo and Luke are acting all lovey-dovey."

Mary Anne lifted a brow. "Even with Mom and Luke's dad in the room?"

"Mom's acting kind of weird too, if you ask me," Wendy said.

"Yeah, I noticed." Mary Anne gave Wendy a sideways glance. "I'm sorry about James."

"There's nothing to be sorry about," Wendy said and bent over to dump scraps into the wastebasket.

"I know you really liked him," Mary Anne said.

Wendy straightened, trying to look nonchalant. "Yeah, well. James likes you."

"We're just friends," Mary Anne replied as she rinsed several crystal glasses and put them on the drying mat. "Have you considered Kevin might have said that because *he* felt like *you* rejected him?"

"What do you mean?"

"Think about it." Mary Anne picked up the roasting pan and poured water into it to soak. "It was obvious to everyone that Kevin thought you were it."

Wendy frowned. "It wasn't obvious to me."

Mary Anne smiled. "Because you were taken with James."

Her sister's face turned pink. "Yeah, well. I'm through making a fool of myself. I used to have a crush on Luke too."

Mary Anne gave her a thoughtful look. "Not anymore, though?"

Wendy stared at her. "How stupid do you think I am? Luke is in love with Jo. Any nincompoop can see that."

Mary Anne felt a sense of relief at hearing Wendy say that. "That's true. They've been going steady for almost two years."

"Let me ask you a question," Wendy said as she scooped leftover vegetables into plastic containers.

"Sure. What?"

"How serious are you and Bob anyhow?"

"We're serious. I want to marry him."

Wendy's eyes widened. "Mom is going to have a fit."

Mary Anne grimaced. "Just because she doesn't know Bob that well. Once he comes home from boot camp I intend to have him over here a bunch. She'll change her mind once she sees how nice he is."

Wendy looked doubtful. "Has he asked you?"

"Not yet. Right now, he's got the Army to worry

about."

"Well…" Wendy started to say when the kitchen's wallphone rang.

Mary Anne quickly wiped her wet hands on a towel and grabbed the receiver. "Hello?"

"Hi, Mary Anne."

Bob! She felt her knees nearly give out and leaned against the wall for support. "Hi, yourself! How are you? Tell me what you've been doing."

As he explained about training and challenges that sounded more like punishment to Mary Anne, her sympathy for his plight grew stronger and stronger. "I can't believe you're having to go through all that. When you get home, I'll give you a back massage every day, just to make up for it. Would you like that?"

"Who wouldn't?" Bob said. "But really, all this work is about making soldiers of us. Besides, I'm packing on muscle."

"I can't wait to see you!"

"I've still got another six weeks," Bob replied.

"That sounds like forever," Mary Anne said. "When can you call again?"

"Um…probably not soon. They don't give us much liberty during boot camp," Bob answered. "In fact, you might not see too many letters, either. Phase three is going to be really difficult and busy."

"I understand," Mary Anne said. "I'll keep writing so you'll have letters to read."

The long-distance operator interrupted. "Time's up."

"Okay," Bob said. "Gotta go. Don't have any more dimes."

"Okay," Mary Anne repeated. "Goodbye. Write—"

"Time's up," the operator said again. Then the line went dead.

Mary Anne hung up the phone, feeling elated that Bob had called. Yet something niggled at her. Bob had sounded a little like he actually enjoyed the training. That maybe he liked the Army. And he hadn't said he missed her.

Mary Anne quickly put that thought aside. Bob had called. That's all that mattered.

Chapter Twenty-One

Mary Anne rose the first Saturday in December to find a fresh blanket of snow covering their yard, its silvery whiteness blinding to the eyes. A cold rain had been falling when she went to bed and the bare limbs of the trees were now coated in thin sheets of ice with a bluish sheen that gave an otherworldly look to them. Icicles sparkled like thousands of diamonds in the early morning sun. As pristine and untouched as everything was, she almost felt as though she were gazing out the window at a movie set for *Dr. Zhivago.*

She turned away and wrapped a thick, fleecy robe over her flannel pajamas and slipped her feet into oversized fuzzy slippers. She wasn't scheduled to work today, and there would be no riding lesson, given the weather conditions. There hadn't been one last week either because winter had blown in right after Thanksgiving with a fast-moving, frigid Alberta Clipper, icing roads and leaving piled banks of snow several feet deep where the ploughs had pushed the white stuff from the roads. School had even been cancelled one day due to white-out conditions, and Luke had been delayed going back to college by a day—not that either he or Jo minded.

Mary Anne padded out into the hallway and down the stairs to the kitchen. Once again, she wished Bob were home. This would be a perfect day to stay inside, curled up together on the sofa with a big, warm blanket and mugs of hot, steaming chocolate, listening to groovy songs like "How Sweet It Is" or "Back in My Arms Again." Her mother had better not say anything about sharing a blanket either, since that was exactly what Jo and Luke had done the day before he drove back to St. Cloud. The sight of them holding hands with Jo's head on Luke's shoulder was as clear in Mary Anne's mind as a picture on the wall. They hadn't even noticed when she walked in or out of the parlor.

She and Bob would do that when he came home. Maybe she could get the LP with "I Got You Babe" on it. Bob liked to call her "babe."

The scent of cinnamon filled the downstairs hall and Mary Anne entered the kitchen to the tune of Christmas carols coming from the radio perched on top of the refrigerator. Her mother looked up from the stove where she was scrambling eggs. Wendy and Jo were already seated at the table, devouring hot oatmeal liberally laced with spice. They were both dressed in heavy sweaters, sweat pants and boots.

"You aren't going out in this, are you?" Mary Anne asked.

"Someone's got to check on the horses," Wendy said.

Her mother glanced over. Mary Anne felt a twinge of guilt. Even though she'd gotten somewhat comfortable riding Flame, she'd just been glad she didn't have another riding lesson this morning. She hadn't thought about feeding the mare. "I'll go get dressed."

"Don't bother," Jo said. "I'll take care of Flame when I feed Silver."

"You sure?"

Jo nodded. "It's your Saturday off. Enjoy it."

"I guess the club won't be riding today," Wendy said, sounding disappointed.

Mary Anne wasn't sure if the tone was due to not being able to ride or not seeing James. Since their talk at Thanksgiving, Wendy had acted only friendly toward James at school. She didn't gush over him like she had before, but Mary Anne doubted her sister would turn down a date if James asked.

Their mother brought over a bowl of scrambled eggs and a plate of buttered toast and set them on the table. "If the snow packs down a little, maybe Tim and Tommy will bring over the sleigh tomorrow."

"Yeah!" Wendy exclaimed. "That'd be really cool. Maybe some of the kids from the club can come along too."

Mary Anne hid a smile. She was pretty sure which kid specifically that Wendy was referring to.

"The sled only holds six, plus the driver's seat," their mother said.

"We can sit close and share blankets," Wendy replied. "It'll keep us warmer, too."

Mary Anne felt her lips twitch. Obviously she wasn't the only one thinking of cuddling under blankets. "I can stay home to make more room for your friends."

Her mother gave her a sharp look. "If there's a sleigh ride this weekend, you should go. It doesn't do you any good to sit here brooding about Bob."

Her good mood left her. "I don't brood."

"You don't participate in things. This is your senior year. You should be more active. Be with your classmates instead of waiting for the phone to ring."

Mary Anne frowned. She didn't think she'd been

that obvious, but maybe she had by trying to be the first one to answer it. "I miss Bob. There's no law against that, is there?"

"If he cares about you," her mother answered as she ladled out eggs onto plates, "he would want you to enjoy yourself."

"He hasn't told me I can't do things."

"And he had better not," her mother replied. "But my expectation is that you take part in school activities. You're only a senior once. You should have good memories."

Mary Anne picked up the subtle warning. Do what her mother wanted her to do or not be allowed to see Bob when he came home. She felt the old, familiar resentment rising. She knew what she wanted to do and not do. When was her mother going to let her make her own decisions? But she bit back a retort, like she always did. She didn't want to risk being grounded when Bob was home on leave.

"*Fine*, then." Mary Anne picked up a piece of toast. "I'll just eat this in my room."

She half-expected her mother to call her back, but there was nothing but the sound of "Blue Christmas" on the radio.

****

Mary Anne zipped her parka the next afternoon, pulled the hood over her head, and put on mittens. Her breath came out frosty white in the cold air as she waited with Wendy and Jo on the porch for Tim and Tommy to arrive. She was not at all looking forward to the blasted sleigh ride. If only it had thawed enough overnight for ice to form on the road, it would have been too dangerous for the horses and they wouldn't have been going.

211

Instead, it had snowed again, leaving a couple of inches of light powder over the hardened snow, making good traction. Just her luck.

She stomped her feet in the heavy, fur-lined boots. With the woolen socks she'd put on, the boots felt clunky, but at least her feet would be warm. She didn't mind looking at snow as long as she didn't have to get out in it. She hated wearing layers of clothes. The flower children in San Francisco were probably running around in tie-dye shirts, granny skirts, and sandals.

What she really wanted to do was go into town to see Ruby. Had a letter from Bob come? Mary Anne had gotten only one letter since Thanksgiving. That one had been postmarked November 23, the day *before* Thanksgiving, which meant she hadn't had any news since the telephone call.

"Here they come!" Wendy said as the jingling of sleigh bells preceded the soft clopping of hooves as the horses turned onto the yard road.

As they got closer, Mary Anne saw that Tim was driving and Tommy was sitting between their girlfriends, Carla and Susan. Neither of them had ever been overly friendly to her. James sat on the opposite seat. Mary Anne quickly did the math. The sleigh held six people, plus the driver, and there were eight of them. Maybe she would get a reprieve after all.

"We can't all fit," she said quickly. "I'll stay back. I need to go into town anyhow."

"You know Mom wants you to come with us," Wendy said.

"I can ride up on the driver's seat," Jo said. "It's big enough for two."

Carla glared at her. "Then I will ride up there."

Jo shrugged. "If that's what you want. It'll be cold."

Tim wrapped the reins around the brake and jumped down to help Carla. "I'll keep her warm."

Carla giggled. "I was counting on that."

Mary Anne tried not to be envious over how Carla tucked her hand into the crook of Tim's arm and huddled close to him or how Susan cuddled against Tommy with a blanket covering most of them.

Jo had climbed up to take Carla's place beside Tommy. Mary Anne suddenly realized James had gotten out and was holding out a hand to assist her. Wendy was already seated inside.

Mary Anne put her mittened hand in his leather-encased one. She lifted one foot to step up, miscalculating the height of the small sideboard that kept snow from flying onto the floor of the sleigh. The toe of her boot thumped against it, unbalancing her. She lurched forward, saved from sprawling flat on her stomach by James' quick action. His arm went around her, pulling her back and placing her back on her feet.

"Sorry I'm such a klutz," Mary Anne said.

"Don't worry about it," James replied as he looked at the sideboard and then back to her boots. "Allow me."

Before she had time to ask what he meant, he'd put his hands on her waist and lifted her inside. As with the time he'd helped her onto the horse, he had picked her up as effortlessly as though she weighed no more than a doll.

Wendy gave her a suspicious look and Mary Anne gathered her wits enough to sit down quickly against the side of the sleigh, leaving room between her and Wendy for James to sit. As he slipped past her and settled into that spot, Wendy's expression smoothed, although she only gave James a slight smile.

Tim loosed the reins and clicked his tongue. As the sleigh started to move, James shook out the heavy throw and Mary Anne felt it settle over her legs with instant warmth as though it had been wrapped around a hot brick. Then she remembered James had been using it when they arrived just a few minutes ago. The slight scent of his cologne wafted from the wool. Mary Anne wondered if Wendy would notice it too.

It had become a familiar smell, and strangely comforting, as well. With a start, Mary Anne realized that what she'd told Wendy was true. James truly had become a friend.

****

"You're *sure* there hasn't been any letter from Bob?" Mary Anne asked Ruby as they took seats at the soda bar in the corner drugstore after school a week later.

Ruby removed her cap and shook the snow off it. "I'd have given it to you as soon as I got it."

"Yeah. Sorry." Mary Anne knew Ruby wouldn't hold back a letter, but as the calendar edged closer to Christmas, she became more and more anxious. It had been three weeks without a letter from Bob. School would be closing for the holidays tomorrow, and Ruby's dad was taking her and her mother to Florida on Monday. Mary Anne probably wouldn't see her until school began again. How could she wait that long without knowing if there was a letter? She didn't expect a present, since he said he didn't get to leave base, but she had hoped for a letter before Christmas.

"Maybe it got lost in the mail," Ruby offered after they'd ordered cherry cokes.

"I hope not."

"Or it could just be late," Ruby added. "There's a ton of stuff being delivered for Christmas."

Christmas. How could she handle the holiday all alone if she didn't hear from Bob? Well, she wouldn't actually be *alone*, since her mother always invited a bunch of people to the midafternoon Christmas buffet. Neighbors always looked forward to that feast. Mary Anne took a sip of her drink and grimaced at the thought of how crowded the house would be.

"You don't like your coke?" Ruby asked.

"It's fine." Mary Anne took another sip and set the glass back on the counter. Since the snow had started to fall again, the place was empty, so at least she wouldn't be overheard. "I guess I shouldn't worry about Bob's not writing. He did say phase three of his training was going to be really intense."

"That's probably it," Ruby agreed.

"I'll be glad when this boot camp is over." Mary Anne said. She'd sent Bob a Christmas card nearly two weeks ago. She hoped it hadn't gotten lost.

"When's it going to be finished?"

"January 13th," Mary Anne said. "If he can get a flight out the next day, he'll be here Saturday, the 14th."

"Perfect," Ruby said. "Saturday is date night. You can take him to dinner to celebrate."

"Neat idea!" Mary Anne smiled suddenly. "Even my mother can't get upset over my welcoming a soldier home."

Ruby grinned too. "Of course, she won't have to know that you plan on steaming up the car windows afterwards."

Mary Anne felt her face warm. "Yeah, that too." A shiver of anticipation slid down her spine. To feel Bob's arms around her again, to cuddle against him like Jo did with Luke… "That would be so fine."

"Less than a month away," Ruby said.

"That sounds like ages, but Bob has already been gone over six weeks, so I guess it's not so bad," Mary Anne said and finished her drink. "I'd better get home before the snowdrifts close the country roads."

"Yeah, I gotta go too. Mom's not real good with packing. I don't want to get to Florida without a swimsuit."

"You'll probably come back all tan," Mary Anne said.

"I hope so," Ruby replied as they both stood and walked outside. "Maybe I'll find some funky guy to hang with."

Mary Anne laughed. "Well, I have *my* funky guy all picked out."

"Lucky you," Ruby answered. "And only four more weekends before you see him!"

"I'm counting." Mary Anne waved as she walked toward her car, thinking about Bob coming home. She did some quick calculations in her head. January 13th was only twenty-eight days away. Mary Anne paused as she reached the car. January 13th was a Friday. She hoped Bob wouldn't run into bad luck that day.

****

Mary Anne supposed she should be grateful that Christmas Day at her house was always a whirlwind of activity. It would keep her mind off the phone that hadn't rung. She'd hoped Bob would have the opportunity to call, but so far nothing. Of course, the day wasn't done.

Her family attended a midnight Christmas Eve service and on Christmas morning had opened their gifts.

The wrapping paper had hardly been trashed when cooking aromas wafted from the kitchen throughout the house. A dozen pies, baked the day before, sat on warming trays. There would be platters of sliced roast beef, ham, and pork loin with sandwich fixings, along with scalloped potatoes, wild rice, and the usual green-bean and broccoli-cheese casseroles. Two gallons of fresh eggnog were in the refrigerator as well.

Her mother had started the buffet tradition the year after Mary Anne's father had died and she'd never understood, until now, why her mother wanted to go through so much work. For the first time, Mary Anne thought she might know why…it kept them busy and their thoughts from remembering who was not there.

Neighbors started arriving around two o'clock, and an hour later the house was packed. Mary Anne surveyed the chaotic scene from the small foyer where she'd volunteered to greet guests and take coats. It was better than serving food in the kitchen, listening to her mother and Luke's dad exchanging cutesy remarks, and way better than being in the living room where Jo and Luke were sharing an oversized armchair and looking at each other with puppy eyes. Tim and Tommy were schmoozing with their girlfriends on the sofa, pretty much oblivious to the disapproving looks some adults were giving them. At least they weren't totally making out. Even James and Wendy were having an animated conversation near the punch bowl.

Mary Anne watched them a moment, thinking about with the way the last three weeks had turned out at school. She doubted anything was going to develop between her sister and James, even though he'd brought her a small ceramic horse for a Christmas present, but it

217

looked as though they were becoming friends. Maybe what surprised Mary Anne even more was that she and James were becoming friends too.

He was more studious and serious about grades than most of the students, but he also had a sense of humor. His Christmas present to her had been a new LP album he knew she'd wanted. He said he'd remembered her telling Mrs. Howell about the cover that first day in English class when they'd gotten into trouble. James was solid and dependable too, traits that Mary Anne found increasingly desirable, given her anxiety about what was going on with Bob at boot camp.

She and James had gotten to know each other during those afternoons spent on the English project. He asked questions and listened to her answers as though they were actually important. She knew she wasn't any kind of honor student. Teachers didn't call on her and usually passed her up even when she raised her hand to respond, not that she did it often. But James asked "why" and made her think. She realized she had actually liked learning about the ideals the kids flocking to San Francisco believed in. Like Elsa the lioness in *Born Free*, the hippies were looking for freedom too. The theme resonated with her, even though the lifestyle was foreign and she knew she was only dreaming of a California that so many popular songs were about.

Although the project was over and the riding lessons had stopped due to the snow, she had begun to look forward to seeing James in English class. Ruby had teased her once about James flirting. Mary Anne had laughed at her and said she didn't think James knew how to flirt. He was always courteous, sometimes to the point that Mary Anne wondered if his mother had read too many King Arthur books to him as a child.

"I think everyone who's coming is here," her mother said, coming down the small hallway from the kitchen along with Luke's dad. "Why don't you join the others in the living room?"

Mary Anne would rather have gone to her own room and listened to the new *Flowers* album—or better yet, retreated to the kitchen now that it was empty, to wait for the phone to ring—but she had fat chance of getting away with either of those things.

The twins were still on the couch with their girlfriends when she entered the parlor. Jo and Luke had gone to stand by the window, looking out at the falling snow. He had his arm draped over her shoulder and she had her arm around his waist. Mary Anne spotted a slim gold link bracelet on Jo's wrist. That must have been Luke's gift to her. Mary Anne knew Jo had given him a hand-knit muffler from cashmere wool that she'd had to special order. Mary Anne tried not to feel envious. Maybe next year she and Bob could exchange presents too.

"You must be missing your boyfriend," a voice from behind her said.

Mary Anne turned to see Janie Nelsen watching Jo and Luke. This was the first year Janie's family had come to the house. Mary Anne had been surprised to see her since they didn't hang out with the same crowd. She nodded. "I wish he could have made it home from boot camp. I can't wait for him to get back."

Janie nodded a wistful look on her face. "It's hard being alone at this time, isn't it?"

Mary Anne felt her face heat as shame flooded over her. Bob would be here in three weeks. Billy Hoffman wouldn't be coming home. "I'm sorry. I shouldn't have said that."

"It's okay." Janie fingered his class ring that she wore around her neck on a chain. "Billy gave this to me the night before he…the night before he got hurt at the game. I hid it because we were going to wait for Homecoming to announce going steady, but…" Her voice trailed off and she blinked several times, then forced a smile. "It's comforting to know I have it."

Mary Anne understood exactly how Janie felt, but she was at a loss for words. Nothing that had been said when her father died had made her feel any better. If she lost Bob—she pushed the thought away—no words would ease the pain.

Suddenly, James was at their side. "My mom says the first year after losing someone is always the hardest."

Mary Anne hadn't heard or seen him come up, but it was obvious he'd heard at least part of the conversation. She thought back to her sixth-grade year and all the important rites of passage from elementary school to middle school that her father had missed, not to mention birthdays and other holidays.

"James is right," she said. "The first year is the worst."

Janie nodded. "That's what the psychologist said, when I saw him. Still, I think I'll be glad to go away to college next year."

Mary Anne understood that too. She didn't know about college, but she definitely wanted to experience city life.

"My parents might even let me start in June," Janie added and then looked over to where her parents were gathering their coats. "It looks like we're leaving." She gave Mary Anne a quick hug. "Thanks for listening."

Mary Anne was so surprised she didn't respond. Janie Nelsen had not only hugged her, but thanked her as well? That was a first. Ruby wouldn't believe it. She finally found her tongue. "Thanks for coming over."

Wendy joined them as Janie left. "What do you guys say we listen to the new album?"

"I guess we could," Mary Anne answered and then wondered if that sounded only lukewarm. "I mean, yeah. That'd be great."

"Cool. I'll go and get my portable phonograph and meet you in the study," Wendy said.

Mary Anne retrieved the album from behind the Christmas tree. "The study is down the hall past the kitchen," she said to James. "It's really kind of an office and mini-library."

"That's a neat idea, having a room like that."

"It used to be my parents' bedroom because the downstairs bathroom also opens into it," Mary Anne explained as they walked out of the parlor and down the hall. She didn't add that her mother hadn't liked sleeping there alone and so had moved to a room upstairs.

When they reached the study, she pushed open the door to step inside, and realized James had stopped a couple of paces back. She turned. James had an odd look on his face and she wondered if he was hesitating because he didn't think it proper to be alone with her. Gosh, they were in a houseful of people. "Wendy will be here in a minute."

That seemed to spur him to move. She started to take another step, but his hand on her shoulder stopped her. "What?"

James smiled and pointed upward.

Mary Anne tilted her head. Mistletoe. One of the twins must have put it up. They were probably planning to bring their girlfriends back here as soon as they could. Well, too bad. Her group had gotten here first.

And then she realized James had cupped her chin. He bent down and brushed a featherlight kiss across her lips. He dropped his hand and straightened before her brain fully registered what he'd done, but her lips tingled from the contact. An odd sensation shimmied through her.

James studied her. "I shouldn't—"

"Here's the phonograph," Wendy said as she came down the hall toward them.

For once, Mary Anne was glad of the distraction.

Chapter Twenty-Two

School began again on January 2nd despite the fact that it had snowed four inches overnight, the skies were leaden gray, and no one needed to listen to the forecast to know more snow was on the way. The dreary weather matched Mary Anne's mood. She had called Ruby as soon as she got back from Florida on Saturday and no letter had come from Bob.

"Maybe they'll cancel classes this afternoon," James said as he joined Mary Anne, Wendy, and Ruby in the cafeteria at lunch.

"I wouldn't count on it," Wendy replied and took out the transistor radio she'd gotten for Christmas. "Minnesota schools don't close unless there's a blizzard and white-out conditions."

"Even then, they'll probably expect us to snowshoe in," Ruby said.

James shook his head. "In Georgia, we pretty much close down once the first snowflake falls."

"If we did that, we'd be going to school all summer." Ruby wrinkled her nose. "School's bad enough as it is."

Wendy, turning the radio up to the sound of "Surfin' Safari," said, "I'd sure like to be in sunny Cal-i-forn-ee-a right now."

James nodded. "That'd be nice."

Mary Anne wondered if the weather was warm

where Bob was.

"Speaking of California," Ruby said as she dug into the bottom of her purse. She looked around before she pulled out a thin copy of a newspaper. "A friend of mine in Minneapolis sent me this."

Mary Anne's attention turned to the paper and she widened her eyes at the sight of the purple cover with a bearded hippie who had a third eye painted on his forehead.. "Oh, my gosh! Is that one of those underground newspapers?"

"Yep. The San Francisco *Oracle*." Ruby half-slipped it under her binder to keep it hidden. "The editor was busted by the cops before Christmas for selling a book of love poems to the vice squad in a psychedelic shop."

James raised an eyebrow. "Love poems?"

"Well, not really," Ruby said. "Use your imagination and another word. Anyway, the guy's cool and so is the 'zine."

"What does the headline say?" Mary Anne asked.

Ruby lifted her binder. "A Gathering of the Tribes for a Human Be-In."

"What's that?" Wendy asked.

"It's going to be a really, really cool party at Golden Gate Park on January 14th. There are going to be *sooo* many neat bands there!" Ruby grimaced as "Surfin' USA" began playing on Wendy's transistor. "Nothing square like that."

"I like this kind of music," Wendy said.

Ruby rolled her eyes. "You would."

"Too bad our project is already done," James said. "We could have included this."

"Don't go giving Mrs. Howell any ideas," Ruby

warned.

"Just kidding," James said and then added, "But we did get an A, remember?"

"Yeah, well. The extra credit did keep me from failing the stupid class. I can't wait to graduate." Ruby folded the *Oracle* and put it back in her purse. "I sure would like be in San Francisco on January 14th for that party."

January 14th. Mary Anne couldn't wait for that date either. Bob would be home.

****

January 15: Dear Diary: Bob should be home. Is he? I don't know... Mary Anne laid the diary down on her dresser and paced in her room Sunday afternoon. She stopped to look out her bedroom window at the solid white blanket of snow extending across the yard, down the road, and across the fields as far as she could see. The snow had been continually falling since Friday. Had Bob made it home? The TV news hadn't mentioned any cancellations at the Minneapolis-St. Paul airport. Maybe he was stuck there? She hadn't heard any reports of roads being closed either, and she'd seen the snow ploughs out. But if Bob were home, why hadn't he called? She frowned. Why hadn't he called anyway? Maybe the Army hadn't released him on schedule?

She wished Jo were here to talk to about her worries. Since she had a steady boyfriend who was also gone, she would understand. But her cousin had decided to use her three allowed college visitation days to go back to St. Cloud with Luke and check out not only the university but also St. Benedict's. She probably wouldn't be back until next weekend. Mary Anne sighed and picked up her diary and flopped back on her bed. She was going to drive herself nuts. Better to write down her feelings.

I don't know what to think. I'm worried that something has happened to him, and he's not telling me. Maybe he's been hurt in training... Mary Anne stopped writing. When Bob didn't call at Christmas and there had been no letter waiting at Ruby's when they returned to school, she'd nearly panicked. Each day got worse. She couldn't concentrate in class. She'd slipped up at work, too, because she was tired due to lack of sleep. She wasn't hungry either and lost weight. James, who strangely enough acted like the mistletoe kiss hadn't happened, kept asking what was wrong. She couldn't tell him. She knew Wendy, Jo, and her mother were worried too, but what could she say unless she wanted to admit she'd been exchanging secret letters with Bob.

Ruby finally suggested she send Bob a certified letter asking if he was all right, simply for her own peace of mind. She'd done that and received the green signature card back, but it was signed by a sergeant. That had nearly thrown her into a complete tizzy. Probably the only thing that had saved her from a nervous breakdown was that two days after that, a postcard with the camp picture on the front had finally, *finally*, arrived from Bob. He said he was fine, busy, looking forward to graduation, and to coming home.

Mary Anne slipped the card from the back of the diary where she'd put it and reread it for the umpteenth time. There was nothing to indicate anything was wrong. He said he was glad to be coming home. That meant to her, didn't it? He wasn't that close to his uncle, after all. She'd sent an immediate reply, telling Bob she wanted to take him to dinner his first night back, but she didn't know if the letter would have reached him before he left camp.

Saturday night came and went and I didn't hear anything. I guess that's okay since Mom probably wouldn't have let me take the car out anyway. I just wish I knew… Mary Anne closed the diary and let out a frustrated sigh. Her brain was going in circles and so was her writing. This wasn't solving anything. She slipped the book into the back of the bedside table's drawer.

When Bob's letters stopped coming, the first thought in Mary Anne's mind was that he had met someone else. Ruby reminded her that he was in boot camp, which was basically prison. The soldiers' daily routine wouldn't have allowed time to meet anyone, even if they were allowed to leave base—which they weren't until the last two weeks of training.

At least one thing she didn't need to worry about was whether Bob had met a girl. But where was he? Why hadn't he called?

****

"Have you heard anything from Bob?" Ruby asked Monday when they met in the cafeteria for lunch.

Mary Anne shook her head, which didn't help the throbbing tight tension she'd waked up with. She'd barely been able to sit through the morning classes, her brain in a fog, and she didn't have a clue what any of the lessons had been. She felt exhausted from trying to figure out what was wrong. If she talked about it now, she'd probably start screaming. "The storm must have delayed him. How was your weekend?"

Ruby hesitated, scrutinizing her. She must have looked as bad as she felt, because her friend didn't push the subject.

"Okay. I put gas in the Bug so we can drive around

once the snow lets up. Maybe we can go to Mankato and shop this weekend."

"Maybe." Mary Anne couldn't commit. Would Bob be home by then? "I'm really tired of all this snow."

"Yeah. Well, it's a Minnesota winter," Ruby said. "Florida was sure a nice break."

Mary Anne was grateful for the diversion. "Does Florida really look like scenes from that movie *Where The Boys Are*?"

"I think that was shot on the east coast of Florida. We went to Fort Myers, on the west side, but yeah, there were cute, tanned guys in swim trunks on the beach in Clearwater."

"That just sounds weird when we're up here with freezing temperatures," Mary Anne said, "but then, I guess they're surfing in California too."

"Probably," Ruby replied as the bell rang for the next class and they picked up their lunch trash. "I've got a doctor's appointment this afternoon, so I won't be in English. I'll talk to you later."

Mary Anne nodded. "Okay." Hopefully, Bob would call this afternoon and she'd have some news to share this evening.

****

Mary Anne walked into her English class later that afternoon, determined to put her worries about Bob on the shelf until she got home. Talking about Florida at lunch had helped. She needed the distraction.

James was already seated, which didn't surprise her. He was always prompt and she was almost always late. As if to prove that point, the tardy bell rang just as Mary Anne slid into a seat across the aisle from him. He gave her a questioning glance. She pasted on a bright smile.

As intuitive as he seemed to be, the last thing she needed was for James to pick up on how upset she was.

"Are you okay?" he asked.

Blast it! How did he know she wasn't? Even though he never mentioned what had taken place in the doorway at Christmas, it seemed James had developed some kind of sixth sense regarding her feelings since then. Or maybe her emotions weren't that hard to figure out, since she knew she was moody. "I'm fine."

Mrs. Howell cleared her throat, peering over her glasses at them. For once, Mary Anne was glad the teacher was a stickler for rules. It meant she didn't have to answer any more questions from James. Mrs. Howell read a list of students who would be going on a field trip the next day because they had made the honor roll. James was on the list. Mary Anne wasn't. No surprise there.

As Mrs. Howell droned on about the Elizabethan world, Mary Anne felt James giving her side glances while he took notes. He looked like he wanted to ask a lot more questions, so as soon as class was over, Mary Anne grabbed her books and stood. "I gotta go. I have to get Ruby the homework."

James started to say something, but was interrupted by one of the other girls asking him if she could compare notes. Mary Anne took advantage of the situation to take her leave.

She was at the end of the hall, just about to go outside, when she heard her name being called. Turning, she saw Janie Nelsen hurrying toward her and plastered another smile on her face while she waited. Janie had been acting friendlier since Christmas too.

"Hi," Janie said as she caught up. "I just wanted to tell you I'm so glad for you."

"Uh, thanks." Mary Anne couldn't recall anything spectacular that she'd done. Had her decision to smile and act as though she didn't have a care in the world already been noticed? She'd only started acting like that at lunch. But then, Janie was perceptive.

"You look so happy."

Wow. She must be a better actress than she thought, not that Mary Anne had ever considered acting. But maybe putting on a fake mask did help.

"You must be absolutely thrilled," Janie continued. "I know I would be."

"You'd be thrilled about what?"

"About spending time with your boyfriend," Janie said.

Mary Anne frowned, totally confused. "You want to spend time with Bob?"

"No, silly." Janie smiled at her. "I meant, aren't you thrilled he's home?"

"*What*?"

"He's home. I saw him at the gas station yesterday."

Mary Anne stared at her. "Bob is…home?"

Janie's smile started to fade. 'Didn't you know?"

Mary Anne felt the blood drain from her face. Her stomach knotted and her body went numb. A faint buzzing sounded in her ears.

"Are you all right?" Janie grabbed her arm to steady her. "I'm so sorry. I thought… Oh, gosh, I would never have said anything."

Out of the corner of her eye, Mary Anne saw James coming down the hall. The worried expression on his face snapped her out of her near faint. Had he heard Janie? Or…or worse, had he too known that Bob was home? Was that why he kept giving her those odd looks in English class?

Mary Anne turned and stumbled through the door and down the steps, ignoring both Janie and James calling to her. She couldn't face James. She couldn't face Janie. She couldn't face anyone right now.

She started running.

Chapter Twenty-Three

James raced out the door after her. "Wait up! Mary Anne! Please! Stop!"

She didn't listen to him, of course. He hadn't expected that she would.

"Maybe we should let her go," Janie said, running to keep up with him. "Maybe she needs time to think."

"Maybe." James started to slow and then widened his eyes as he saw Mary Anne dash across a street without even looking for cars. "You stay here," he said to Janie and then sprinted after Mary Anne. The highway was only two blocks from the school. If she reached it and didn't look…

He saw the semi rounding the bend in the highway known as Deadman's Curve. It was a blind spot for anyone who didn't know that the edge of Middletown sat just a few hundred yards from the turn. Mary Anne wasn't slowing down and neither was the truck. James pumped his arms and legs harder as he raced towards her, grateful he'd run track.

The big rig's horn blared and smoke surged from the screeching brakes as the driver tried to slow down without jackknifing. James prayed there wasn't a patch of black ice on the road as he ran flat out.

The noise must have broken through to Mary Anne because she stopped suddenly, just feet from the edge of the road. James collided into her, knocking them both to the ground.

He managed to twist his body to take the brunt of the fall. "You could have been killed!"

Mary Anne looked dazed. "What—"

"You nearly got hit!" The cab was so close to where they were that James could feel the heat from the engine. "Didn't you see that thing coming?"

The driver of the truck came running over. "Is everyone all right?"

"I think so," James said as he helped Mary Anne to her feet. "She's just shaken up." Which was an understatement if he'd ever made one. He could feel Mary Anne trembling like a newborn foal trying to stand. Her face was nearly as white as the snow drifts on the sides of the highway. He put his arm around her waist, cupping her elbow to brace her in case her legs gave out.

"Are you sure?" The driver still look worried.

"I think I'd better get her home," James replied.

The man reached into his jacket pocket and pulled out a card which he handed to James. "That's the company address and phone. I'll have to file a report. Let them know if she's hurt. The boss doesn't want any trouble with the law."

"Okay." James took the card, then turned to Mary Anne. "Let me get you back to school."

She took a deep breath and some color reappeared in her cheeks as she stepped away. "I'm okay."

That was debatable, but James held his remark. His own adrenalin was having its effects now that the danger was passed, leaving him shaky too. A few laps around the school track would have worked it out, but he wasn't about to leave Mary Anne.

They were both quiet while walking the few blocks

back to school. They'd almost reached the school doors and James could see Janie waiting on the steps. He glanced down at Mary Anne. "Why did you run?"

She shrugged, looking down at the ground. "I just did."

"Why?" He had a pretty good inkling since he'd heard the last part of the conversation with Janie, but he wanted to hear the reason from Mary Anne. His mom always said getting someone to recognize why they acted out was a step toward fixing the problem. Mary Anne was quiet so long he didn't think she was going to answer.

"I…I didn't know Bob was home. The news shocked me." Mary Anne looked up suddenly, anger in her eyes. "You knew, didn't you?

James took a deep breath. "I saw him leaving the gas station yesterday."

"That's why you kept looking at me so oddly in class. You weren't going to tell me, were you?"

"I didn't know if he'd contacted you or not. I was going to ask you about it after class." He saw Janie coming toward them. "I'll be on the field trip tomorrow, but we can talk on Wednesday, okay?"

The stormy expression left Mary Anne's face. "I guess I should say thank you. You kind of saved my life."

James felt his face warm. "You stopped in time. All I did was knock you down. Are you sure you aren't hurt?"

"I'm not hurt."

James held back another retort. Mary Anne might not be hurt physically, but he didn't need to be a counselor like his mom to know Mary Anne was hurting inside. The Bob guy was a jerk and he didn't deserve someone like her.

James didn't say that, either. It was something she would have to find out for herself.

****

"Here's your homework." Mary Anne put the books down on the table in Ruby's kitchen an hour later. It had taken her that long to compose herself. She'd told Janie and James she was going home, but she'd driven out to the old bridge by the river instead. It was quiet there and she could cry without anyone hearing. Eventually she felt the turmoil inside herself recede. She still didn't understand why Bob hadn't called.

Mary Anne turned to her friend. "Did you know Bob was home too?"

Ruby's eyes widened and she started to shake her head, then nodded instead. "I saw him when I was getting gas for the Bug."

"Was the whole town at the gas station yesterday?" Mary Anne asked. "Everybody but me?"

"I don't think so." Ruby frowned. "He said he'd just gotten back."

Mary Anne stared at her. "You *talked* to him? And you didn't tell me?" Was everyone conspiring against her?

"I figured he'd call you," Ruby said.

"Was that why you asked at lunch if I'd heard from him?"

"Yeah."

"And you didn't say anything?" Mary Anne felt her eyes start to burn with more tears. "What kind of a friend are you?"

Ruby's mouth tightened. "I don't like being the

bearer of bad news."

"So you let me sound stupid? Saying I thought Bob got stuck in bad weather must have sounded really funny when you knew where he was."

"I didn't think it was funny."

Mary Anne didn't care. "What if I'd told other people that? I'd be the laughing stock of the town. Poor, silly Mary Anne. Thinking her boyfriend wasn't home yet when everyone else knew he was." She turned and walked to the door. "Thanks for being such a good friend!"

"Hey, don't be mad at me," Ruby called after her. "Go talk to your boyfriend."

Mary Anne didn't answer as she stomped toward her car. She intended to do just that.

****

Ten minutes later, Mary Anne knocked on Bob's uncle's farmhouse door. When there was no answer, she knocked again, louder this time. As she waited, she felt her temper rising. The hurt and humiliation she'd felt built into anger. She pounded the door again. "I know you're in there! Your car is here."

She was about to turn away in frustration when the door finally opened. Bob's uncle stood there.

"Bob's busy right now," he said. "It would be better if you went home."

Mary Anne lifted her chin. "Whatever he's doing, he can stop. He owes me an explanation."

His uncle studied her silently. She was tempted to stick a foot in the door so he wouldn't slam it on her. Finally, he nodded and stepped aside. "Maybe he does owe you an explanation. He's in the living room."

Mary Anne swept past him and then stopped

abruptly once she was inside the living room. Bob stood at the window, looking out. Her heart gave a little lurch in spite of her anger. He looked so good. And different. His hair had been shaved short, but that wasn't it. He wore khakis instead of jeans and an Army camouflage T-shirt. His arms and face were tanned from the sun. He looked taller, broader, bigger. She took several steps toward him, wanting to be in his arms in spite of being mad.

He turned and something in his eyes made her hesitate. There was no flicker of interest or glint of flirtation. His mouth was flat and unsmiling. "Hello, Mary Anne."

No "Hello, babe"? Mary Anne swallowed hard. "It's good to see you."

"Is it?"

Mary Anne started to nod, then stopped. "Why didn't you call me when you got home?"

"I needed some time."

"Time for what? You've been gone for ten weeks! I've been looking forward to the moment you'd be home." She paused, not wanting to ask, but needing to know. "You sound like you aren't glad to see me."

He hesitated. "The Army makes you look at things differently."

"I know it's like a prison."

"Not that," Bob said. "I didn't mind the tough training. I've been chosen to attend Aviation Logistics School in Virginia."

Mary Anne felt a sense of relief sweep over her. "You're not going to Vietnam?"

"At least not for a year." Bob shrugged. "Maybe the war will be over by then."

She wanted more than anything to take his hand and sit with him on the sofa, but he remained standing and so did she. "That's good news. What's wrong, then?"

"Nothing."

"Nothing?" Mary Anne practically gaped at him. "What do you mean, nothing? You didn't call at Christmas. I only had one letter and a postcard since Thanksgiving. Why didn't I hear from you?"

He sighed. "I was hoping you'd get the hint."

"Hint?" Mary Anne's stomach suddenly felt as though she'd swallowed a hot coal. "What do you mean?"

"It's over."

The coal turned into an acute, burning sensation that welled up into her chest, threatening to cut off her breath. Her tongue felt too thick for her mouth. She had trouble forming a word, but finally managed. The sound came out as a croak. "Over?"

"It's better this way," Bob said.

"Why?"

"It just is. I like the Army."

"So? Is that a big deal?"

Bob shook his head. "You don't understand. Two years ago I got into trouble in Chicago. A couple of buddies and I went joy-riding in a car after we stole some booze and cigarettes. Part of my probation was coming to stay with my uncle. I went back this summer to complete the community service hours I needed for deferred adjudication. I have a clean record now and can look forward to a real career."

"I would never hold you back," Mary Anne replied, her voice not much above a whisper. "Once I graduate, I can join you at whatever base you're at."

"Why don't you just tell her the truth?" Bob's uncle asked from the doorway.

Mary Anne nearly jumped. She hadn't heard him approach, but then, her mind wasn't functioning. "Truth?" she asked, looking at him and then back at Bob.

Bob glared at his uncle. "I don't want to make this worse."

"Something you should have thought of when you went back to Chicago," his uncle said.

Mary Anne frowned. "Did something else happen in Chicago?"

Bob hesitated. "I saw an old girlfriend."

The hot embers in Mary Anne's stomach reignited. "Old girlfriend?" She didn't know he'd had one. "Did she start writing you in boot camp? Was that why you stopped writing me?"

Bob didn't answer. His uncle crossed his arms. "Do you want me to tell her or are you going to be a man about this?"

Bob scowled at him and then turned to Mary Anne. "Okay. Tina wrote me at Thanksgiving that she's pregnant." He straightened his shoulders. "We're getting married."

Mary Anne stared at him as the blood in her veins turned to ice.

Chapter Twenty-Four

Mary Anne sat in the cafeteria the next day, her food growing cold on her plate, as she half-listened to the buzz of conversation around her. California news had finally made its way to rural Minnesota and everyone was talking about the Be-In. Ruby had been right. It had been one big party with 30,000 people.

Not that she cared whether Ruby was right or not. Mary Anne was still angry that her friend hadn't told her Bob was back. It was a good thing Ruby was out today, because Mary Anne sure didn't feel like talking to her.

She didn't feel like talking to anyone. Last night had passed in a blur. Somehow, she had managed to drive home from Bob's uncle's place, although she had no recollection of it. She vaguely remembered telling her mother she wasn't feeling well and going to her room. When Wendy had poked her head in later, Mary Anne had pretended to be asleep. This morning, when her mother had asked how she was feeling, she'd said she was fine.

She was anything but *fine*. She knew she'd lost her job at the grocery store for not showing up to work last night—that was one of the rules—although she hadn't told her mother yet. Her best friend had held out on her. That hurt. Worse though, Bob had betrayed her.

How could he? All this time when she had thought she was his girl, he had a girlfriend in Chicago. And he had gone all the way with that girl. He had led Mary Anne on. Would he have lied to her if his uncle hadn't been there last night? How could she have been so stupid?

Bob was getting married. Getting *married*. Married…and not to her.

Mary Anne's mind was still half-numb from shock. She'd stumbled to class, sat in a chair, stared into space, gotten up when the bell rang, and moved to another class. She let herself be swept along with the flow of students to the cafeteria where she would sit until another bell rang.

"Hey! How come you haven't touched your food?" Wendy asked as put her own tray down and stuffed a fry into her mouth.

The thought of eating made her nauseous, although she couldn't say that to Wendy. Her sister would want to know why. Mary Anne looked at the glob of noodles covered in tomato sauce and hamburger. "I really don't like the 'Hot Dish' here."

Wendy eyed the food. "I can't blame you. They need to put some seasoning into that stuff. Do you want to share my burger?"

"No. I'm fine." The lie again. Fine, fine, fine.

"Well, okay." Wendy popped more fries into her mouth. "That Be-In thing turned out to be pretty cool. My social studies teacher said it wasn't only hippies. Families went, and took their pets too. Kind of like when we have town picnics, only bigger."

For the first time since yesterday afternoon, Mary Anne almost smiled. "I don't think Middletown folks would get high on pot and acid."

"Not *that* part, silly. My teacher said the point was

that there were all kinds of people there—young, old, hippies and straight—and it was peaceful. That group Diggers gave out free food." Wendy giggled. "Hell's Angels even helped. They corralled children."

"Will wonders never cease," Mary Anne said wryly.

Wendy stopped chewing and looked at her. "You're right, you know. We have a horrible war going on and yet everyone could get along at the Be-In. It's almost like there's a season of war and a season of love. It didn't matter at the Be-In who the people were or where they were from—"

"To each his own," Mary Anne said as the bell rang and she picked up her untouched plate. "Maybe you can get your teacher to lead the class in singing "Turn, Turn, Turn" and shake a tambourine or something."

Wendy stuck out her tongue. "Funny."

Mary Anne didn't mean to be funny. The "season of love" had hit too close to her invisible but open wounds, but it did get her to thinking. Really thinking.

Much later that night, she crawled into bed and took her book out of the bedside table.

Dear Diary,
I know what I'm going to do…

****

James caught up with Wendy on the steps after school on Wednesday. "Is Mary Anne sick?"

Wendy looked surprised. "Not that I know of. Why?"

"She wasn't in English class."

"Mary Anne was in a real funk yesterday. I didn't see her at lunch, so maybe she and Ruby skipped out."

"I didn't see Mary Anne at lunch either," James said, "but Ruby was in class. She said she hadn't heard from

Mary Anne."

"That's weird. She seemed okay when she drove us to school this morning." Wendy pointed across the street to the parking lot. "The car's still there, so she must be around."

James felt a prickling at the back of his neck. "Let's check with Mr. Hund and see if any of her other teachers marked her absent."

"Okay," Wendy said. "We'll probably see either Tim or Tommy in there doing detention. Maybe they'll know."

Any other time, James would have laughed at her reference to her cousins, but the hair at his nape was practically crackling.

His unease turned to real concern when the secretary said Mary Anne had been absent all day. "Did you call her mother?"

Mrs. Todd shook her head. "Students usually bring a note the day they come back." She looked at Wendy. "Was you sister with you this morning?"

Wendy nodded, her face growing pale. "Yeah. We walked into school together."

The secretary reached for the phone. "Let me check with your mother. Maybe Mary Anne went home."

"The car is still here," Wendy said, starting to cry.

James pulled a tissue out of the box on the desk and handed it to her. "Let's see what your mother says."

But he didn't have to hear the words. The look on the secretary's face when she hung up the phone said it all.

"Mary Anne didn't go home."

Chapter Twenty-Five

Sheriff Danfield's car was pulling into the yard road as James drove Wendy home in her family's car. She had stopped crying, but she clenched the note they'd found in the car so tightly that James hoped it wouldn't be in shreds by the time they got to the house.

He could kick himself for not being in school yesterday instead of on the field trip. He'd known how upset Mary Anne was when she found out that jerk Bob was home and hadn't called her. She'd said she was going to take Ruby her homework. Had Mary Anne seen Bob after that? Had they had a fight? Wendy didn't know. He hadn't asked Ruby anything because he didn't want to talk about Mary Anne behind her back. Maybe he should have. He'd asked Mrs. Todd to call Ruby's house and ask her to come over. Hopefully, she would get there soon.

Mrs. Wade hugged Wendy as soon as she walked through the door to the parlor. "Thank God you're okay." She didn't let go of Wendy's hand as she led her over to the sofa. Once they were seated, she pulled her daughter close as if fearing Wendy would disappear as well.

The sheriff pulled a small notebook out of his shirt pocket. "When did you see your daughter last?" he asked, as tires could be heard crunching gravel out front.

"This morning," Mrs. Wade replied. "Mary Anne left with Wendy, for school."

The sheriff turned to her. "And when was the last time you saw her?"

Ruby rushed in as Wendy finished explaining. Out of breath, the newcomer gasped, "I got here as fast as I could."

"We heard." Sheriff Danfield looked as though he wanted to lecture her on speeding, but thought better of it.

James tugged the note from Wendy's hand and gave it to the sheriff. "We found this in the car."

"What's that? What does it say?" Mrs. Wade asked.

"Only that she says she had to leave and not to worry," James said.

"Not to worry?" Mary Anne's mother's voice rose to a near shriek. "Not to worry? My daughter just disappears and I'm not supposed to worry?"

"It sounds like she might have run away," the sheriff said. "Would there be any reason for that?"

"Nothing I can think of," Mrs. Wade said. "In fact, there's a young man in the Army that's due home from boot camp that she wanted to see."

"He's back," James said.

Mrs. Wade frowned. "He is? Mary Anne didn't mention it."

"I…she didn't find out until Monday," James replied.

"Who is he?" the sheriff asked and then scribbled the name in his notebook when James told him. "Any reason to think she might be with him?"

Mary Anne's mother wrinkled her brow. "I don't know. He called for a few minutes on Thanksgiving, but there hasn't been any other communication."

Ruby cleared her throat. "Yes, ma'am, there has."

Everyone turned to look at her. "They've been writing."

Mrs. Wade shook her head. "There haven't been any letters coming here."

Ruby took a deep breath. "Bob's been sending the letters to me and I give them to Mary Anne."

"You what?" Mrs. Wade stared at her and then tears welled up in her eyes. "My daughter didn't trust me."

"Did you know about this?" the sheriff asked Wendy.

Her eyes rounded. "No. Not a word." She looked at James. "Did you?"

"No." Something that felt like a sharp knife lodged in his stomach. He hadn't known they'd been writing, although it probably shouldn't come as that much of a surprise. It would account for Mary Anne's reaction. And it just proved that guy was a double jerk. "She was really upset on Monday when she found out Bob was home."

"Do you think they had a fight? Any reason to suspect he might have hurt her?"

Mrs. Wade gasped. "Oh, my God…"

"I don't think he'd hurt her," Ruby said.

James felt a muscle twitch in his jaw. Colby had better not have laid a hand on Mary Anne. "I hope you're right."

"Okay," the sheriff said. "We'll check out Colby's place first. If she isn't there, we can check out that old cabin in the woods and the cave nearby. Maybe she's just hiding, if they had a fight."

"Mary Anne didn't like either of those places," Wendy said. "She was held at the cave when she was kidnapped last year, remember? Why would she want to go there?"

"Just the same, we'll check it out," the sheriff replied.

James hoped the man wasn't thinking *in case there was a body.* He didn't want to consider the possibility.

Sheriff Danfield put his notebook away and stood. "If I can use your phone, I'll call my deputy and have him go out to Colby's place and put out an APB as well, just in case she's run away."

"The phone's in the kitchen," Wendy said. "I'll show you."

"This is all my fault," Mary Anne's mother said after the sheriff left. "If I talked with her more, maybe listened more—"

"Don't blame yourself, Mrs. Wade," James said. "You can talk to her as much as you want to once we find her."

"But we have to find her first."

"We will." James straightened his shoulders and set his jaw. "We'll find her. I promise you that."

And he said a silent prayer that it would be true.

****

Mary Anne stood at the corner of Haight and Ashbury and stared in wonderment at her surroundings. After three grueling days riding a bus and then getting lost and going the wrong way on Market Street, she was finally here!

Everywhere there was bustle. She felt like she'd been dropped into the middle of a gypsy camp—shaggy-haired, barefoot guys with torn jeans and leather vests over paisley shirts, leaning against the walls of the psychedelic poster shops on Haight Street, accompanied by long-haired girls in flowered headbands, street-length granny skirts and peasant blouses. Farther down the block, two mimes were acting as though they were locked in an invisible box while passersby tossed coins at their feet. In the other direction on Ashbury stood the rows of Victorian townhouses, the steps leading up to the entrances filled with more people lounging about. Not far past the first house, a guy sat cross-legged on the ground, picking chords on a guitar while his girlfriend tapped a tambourine with her hand. Across the street, a white-robed flutist stood, eyes closed, swaying to a drawn-out lonely melody. The sweet smell of incense hung heavy in the air. It was just like Mary Anne had imagined it.

"Did you just get off the bus?" a voice asked.

Mary Anne turned to see a girl with purple and green streaks in her blonde hair grinning at her. She smiled back. "Actually, yes I did. How did you know?"

"Your clothes." She pointed to Mary Anne's coat hung over her arm. "I'm guessing you're from cold country?"

"Minnesota."

"I'm from Seattle, not that it matters," the girl said. "My name is Bambi, like the deer."

Mary Anne felt her eyes widen. "For real?"

She shrugged. "Well, it's the name I go by here. What's yours?"

"Mary Anne Wade."

"First name is enough," Bambi said. "No one cares what your last name is. Nobody asks questions about where you came from, either. You know, just in case you don't want to be found."

Mary Anne nodded. She had decided when she left Middletown that she'd leave no tracks. She'd hitched a ride on a big rig—and had to admit it was both scary and exciting—to Mankato and then bought her Greyhound ticket from there. She hadn't thought to use a fake name, though.

Bambi lifted a brow as she looked over Mary Anne's cardigan sweater and slacks. "If you don't want to stick out like a sore thumb, you're going to need some different threads."

Mary Anne looked down at what she was wearing. She hadn't had much choice in what she wore, since the school had that stupid dress code. "You're right. Where can I buy something more casual?"

Bambi grinned again. "No need to buy anything. The Diggers have a free store over on Page Street where you can pick up something."

"Will you show me where it is?"

"I'll take you. Kinda show you around."

"Thanks. I appreciate that."

"Sure thing. Once we get you dressed right, we can go to the Panhandle at the park. Free food at four o'clock there."

"You really sound like you know your way around. Have you been here long?"

"Long enough," Bambi said, "but, like I said, we don't ask a lot of questions around here."

"Oh." Mary Anne felt her face warm. "I'm sorry. I didn't mean to pry."

"It's okay. Just a warning." Bambi tilted her head. "Do you know where you're staying?"

"I…I kinda thought I'd find someplace once I got here. I have some money."

"Well, don't broadcast that," Bambi said. "It isn't cool."

"Sorry," Mary Anne said again.

Bambi waved a hand. "Don't sweat it. You can crash at my pad for a while. I've only got three other roommates."

"They won't mind?" Mary Anne asked.

"Nah. Why should they? Come on, let's go get you some gear."

As they walked down Haight toward Page, Mary Anne thought how easy this had all been. She'd already made a friend and found a place to eat and stay.

She finally felt like she fit in.

****

Three long agonizing days had passed since Mary Anne's disappearance. As James sat in the Wades' parlor with the same collection of people who had been there on Wednesday plus a few more, he thought how it might have been a premonition that they'd read *Inferno* in English class. Dante's three-day journey through Hell hadn't been any worse than what James and Mary Anne's family had gone through so far. At least, Dante had the ghost of Virgil to guide him back to the light. Here in Minnesota, they were still milling about in the darkness of no clues.

"There must be something else we can do," Jo said. She and Luke had driven back from St. Cloud just that afternoon.

Sheriff Danfield looked down at his notes. "We interviewed Bob Colby and his uncle. They both said she had been upset when she left their house Monday night—"

"Because Bob told Mary Anne he was marrying some bimbo—"

"Wendy. That's enough," her mother said.

"Anyway," the sheriff continued, "they say that's

250

the last they saw of her. They weren't real eager to say anything else, but I don't have any reason to doubt their story, at this point."

"Did you check the cabin?" Luke asked. "That'd be a good place to go if Mary Anne wanted to be alone for a while."

The sheriff nodded. "First place we looked. We think she's run away, but just to cover all bases, we've had volunteers out scouring the countryside. No trace of her." He paused. "The river and lake are iced over, so that eliminates drowning."

Vivian gasped, her hand going to her mouth. "I hadn't—"

"She might have gone to Minneapolis. She talked about moving to the Twin Cities after graduation," Jo said and turned to Ruby. "You have friends there, right?"

"I don't think I ever gave her any last names, so she wouldn't know who to contact," Ruby replied, "but I did call them anyway. Just in case."

"And nothing?" Jo asked.

"Nothing."

"What about the bus stop? Did she buy a ticket, maybe?" Luke asked.

James knew what that answer would be. As soon as he left the Wades on Wednesday, he'd gone to the Dew Drop Inn and café that served as the bus stop. No ticket had been purchased and no one there had seen Mary Anne.

"Nope," the sheriff said. "Nothing there either."

"But she couldn't have just vanished into thin air," Jo said and looked at Wendy. "You left for school together. Was Mary Anne carrying anything extra?"

Wendy shook her head. "We were wearing coats

over our sweaters and slacks. I guess she could have been hiding some stuff under the clothes."

"Is anything missing from her room?" Jo asked.

"Just some makeup from the dresser," Mrs. Wade answered. "She usually carried that in her purse, though. I didn't notice any clothes missing from her closet."

Jo frowned. "Do you mind if I go up and look? I know what a couple of her favorite things are."

"Of course," Mrs. Wade said. "I could have missed something."

Jo stood. "I'll be back in a few minutes."

After she left, Luke continued to ask the sheriff questions, his facial expression alternating between anger and concern. James knew Luke had befriended Bob when the guy had first moved here from Chicago a couple of years ago.

"I think I'll go have a talk with Colby tomorrow," Luke said. "Maybe I can dig out some information that will give us a clue where Mary Anne went."

"I don't think you'll need to do that," Jo said as she came back into the room, carrying a small book. "I found this tucked in the back of her bedside table drawer, behind one of her favorite scarves."

"What is it?" Wendy asked.

"A diary," Jo replied and glanced at Mrs. Wade. "I probably shouldn't have opened it…"

"Never mind that," Mary Anne's mother answered. "What did she write?"

"Basically, that she wanted to go to where she would be accepted with no questions about her past." Jo handed the book to Mrs. Wade. "Mary Anne has gone to San Francisco."

James felt like one of the horses had kicked him.

Their project. All that talk about freedom from rules, freedom to be who a person wanted to be. Acceptance no matter what. A place with free food and communal living, where everyone shared everything. It all probably sounded like utopia for Mary Anne after Bob's rejection.

"I'll put in a call to SFPD," the sheriff said, "but with thousands of kids flocking there like pigeons gone to roost, they'll have a hard time finding her."

"Will they even look?" Ruby asked.

"They'll *look*," Sheriff Danfield replied, "but a lot of these kids don't want to be found." He gave Mrs. Wade a sympathetic look. "Especially if they get caught up with the wilder side."

James doubted Mary Anne had thought about the down side. *Make love, not war* meant more than just sharing a room…it meant sharing bodies. According to what his mom said, when people broke up in relationships, the losing party was vulnerable. Mary Anne might not be inclined to allow someone to do *that*, but drugs were everywhere and could influence her…if not knock her out cold and some guy could….

James leapt to his feet. "It may take me a few days to convince my folks, but I'm going to San Francisco."

****

"You're really uptight, you know?" Zander took a drag on his reefer and passed it to Candi, one of their roommates, and peered bleary-eyed at Mary Anne. "I got a 'lude that'll get you loose. You want it?"

Mary Anne shook her head and tried not to breathe in the thick marijuana smoke that hung in the air like fog over the bay. She looked around the cramped room that served as Bambi's apartment. Originally, it had been a bedroom on the third floor of one of the Ashbury

Victorians. Now it housed Bambi, her three roommates and Mary Anne, leaving hardly any room to move around. The only furniture was a small, wobbly end table and a wooden rocking chair that had one arm broken off. Not that anyone used it. They mostly sat on the bedrolls from the Diggers' store that lay scattered everywhere. A Styrofoam ice chest sat in one corner although it was usually empty since they ate their main meal at the Panhandle of Golden Gate Park. A portable phonograph occupied another corner, Grateful Dead music blaring from it.

"Oh, come on," Valentine, the other roommate, said as she attached a roach clip to the end of what was left of the joint and held it out to Mary Anne. "At least take a toke."

"You can have it," Mary Anne said. "I'm already high from the smoke." She would have liked to open the single window they had to get some fresh air, but the first time she'd done that, they'd all looked at her as though she'd gone bananas. Inhaling the smoke was part of the enjoyment, Bambi had explained.

All it did for Mary Anne was make her feel dizzy. And then hungry. Really hungry. She'd quickly learned to stash some food in her pockets from the free meal.

She pushed herself to her feet. "I'm going to take a walk."

"Suit yourself," Zander said, tapping out more weed from his baggie onto an unrolled paper. "But you're really missing out. This is good stuff from Mexico."

According to Zander, it was all good stuff. He stayed stoned most of the day. Mary Anne closed the door as she stepped into the narrow hallway, which only reeked slightly less of pot. When she reached the second floor landing, she looked toward the only bathroom, at the end of the hall. As usual, at least ten people were in line, waiting.

Mary Anne turned the other way and walked downstairs and outside. After the dimly lit room, the sunshine nearly blinded her. She was surprised it was still midafternoon. The smoky haze in the room distorted time.

Mary Anne walked toward the park to get away from the crowds wandering the street. She'd only been here a little over two weeks, but she'd already realized that most of the poster shops were really head shops, where everything from pot and acid to pills could be purchased under the counter. Bambi—the only one of the group who worked—had a job at one of those. She'd told Mary Anne they could always use help, especially with the "tourists" who wandered in, not quite sure what they wanted. The owner of the shop had told Mary Anne she still looked like a tourist, so they'd trust her. She was scared to take the job since those "tourists" could also be narcs.

Not that she couldn't use the money. When she'd offered to pay her share of the rent and been foolish enough to let the group see she had almost three hundred dollars, saved from her cashier job, Bambi had asked for half, just to "keep them going" until Valentine, Candi, and Zander could find jobs. It didn't take too many days to figure out those three weren't even looking for jobs. Mary Anne was pretty sure some of her rent money had gone to buy the stuff they were smoking.

She'd tried to find a real job in the retail area around Union Square, but when asked what her address was, she was told they weren't taking applications. The same thing had happened at the wharf and in the Castro district, where she'd also gotten a number of odd looks that she didn't understand at the time. To make matters worse, on one of her rides back on the crowded Market Street bus, someone had picked her pocket, taking most of the rest of her cash. She could almost hear her mother chastising her for carrying it in the first place, but Mary Anne didn't trust the roommates not to spend it.

She felt tears start to sting her eyes as she kept on walking. She'd quickly grown disillusioned with the hippie scene. Instead of kids interested in ending the war or cleaning up the environment, most of the ones she'd met spent their days lingering and loitering on the streets or allies, spaced-out and talking in slang she didn't always understand. She was tired of living with five people in a small room, sharing a bathroom with at least thirty more, and the constant foggy feeling in her brain from the never-ending smoke.

An expensive sports car rolled up beside her, but Mary Anne ignored it and kept on walking. The powerful engine began to idle, sounding like a kitten's purr as it slowed to keep pace with her. A middle-aged man dressed in a business suit rolled down the window.

"Want to make a twenty?"

Mary Anne shook her head and quickened her pace. Being mistaken for a prostitute or someone homeless would never happen in Middletown. More and more, Mary Anne found herself appreciating the small-town values she'd always thought so confining and rigid. The first time something like this had happened, she had simply gaped at the man, and he'd offered to double his price. Luckily for her, a police officer on a nearby corner started walking in their direction and the driver sped off.

The officer had looked concerned and asked if she needed a ride home. She'd refused, knowing that the rest of the commune would more than likely think her a narc if they saw fuzz bringing her back.

Giving her a ride home was something James would have done. Tears began to brim over in Mary Anne's eyes. Why hadn't she realized how wonderful he was? Kevin had been right. She wished she had come to her senses earlier.

She'd been such a fool to run away because of Bob. She'd had plenty of time to think, by now, and she'd come to realize that she had been the one pushing for a relationship and Bob had never really shown that he cared. His flip remarks hadn't been commitments. She had been a fool. Bob had never shared what had gone on in Chicago and, obviously, having an old girlfriend that he'd kept in touch with had not entered the picture either. Mary Anne had been living a fantasy that she'd invented.

And now she was living in another one of her fantasy inventions. Never would she have thought she'd be in such a predicament. What had seemed like a perfect nirvana when she'd arrived had quickly turned into hell. She didn't even have enough money for a bus ticket back to Minnesota. All she could do was swallow what was left of her pride and call her mother and ask for forgiveness.

By the time she reached the entrance to the park, tears were flowing down her cheeks and she stumbled over a crack in the sidewalk. As she lurched forward, a hand reached out and grasped her arm, steadying her.

Mary Anne swiped at her tears with her free hand. "Thank you."

"Any time."

She practically tripped again at the familiar voice. Mary Anne looked up through her blurred vision. "James?" Dear heavens! Was she having an hallucination? Had the marijuana been spiked with something?

Her hallucination smiled. "Yes."

Mary Anne felt a buzzing in her brain and prayed she wasn't tripping. "Is it really you?"

James nodded. "It's really me."

She stared at him. He wasn't wearing shining armor or carrying a sword and shield, nor was a white horse standing nearby, although with his short-cropped hair, glasses, and preppy khakis and polo, he stood out as much as if he had been decked in medieval mail. Not that it mattered. James had appeared like the gallant knight Wendy had always thought him to be, and Mary Anne didn't think she'd ever been so grateful to see anyone in her life.

"What…how did you find me?" she asked.

"I just got here this afternoon," he said. "I figured if I hung out at the free-meal place, I'd spot you sooner or later."

Mary Anne started crying again.

James turned her toward him. "I told your mother I'd find you. If you aren't glad to see me or you want to stay here—"

"No!"

He frowned. "You aren't glad to see me?"

"No! I mean, yes…" Mary Anne tried to stanch the flow of tears. "You have no idea how glad I am to see you. I just can't believe you're really here! That you came for me."

His expression softened. "I came because I had to

know if you were okay. I know how much you care for Bob, but—"

"That's over," Mary Anne said.

James studied her. "For sure?"

She nodded. "For sure."

He tilted her chin and leaned down to brush a kiss against her lips. The faint scent of his cologne and fresh soap wafted in the air. He tasted of mint, and Mary Anne put her arms around his neck as he drew her closer and let the kiss linger. So many sensations flooded her brain that she felt weightless, as though she were floating outside her body.

James broke the kiss and stepped back, his gaze intense. "Do you want to go home? Back to Minnesota?"

Mary Anne smiled for the first time in days and took his hand in hers. "Yes, James, I do. I want to go home with you."

That summer—1967—was known as the "Summer of Love" in San Francisco, but to Mary Anne Wade, it was a summer of love in Middletown, Minnesota, getting to know the man who would never betray her.

A word about the author…

Cynthia Breeding lives on the Gulf Coast of Texas with a very non-spoiled poodle-mix and enjoys walking and horseback-riding on the beach, as well as sailing.
www.cynthiabreeding.com